The Kneeling Woman

A Novel

G.A. Chamberlin

Titles by

G.A.Chamberlin

The Handmaiden Legacy
Cultural Attache
Rare Earth Element
Outbound
Somma
Unintended Consequence
The Particle
The Kneeling Woman
BLACKBIRD SECRET

~

Kathleen The War Years

The Kneeling Woman
Printed in the United States
- ISBN 13 978-0-99040278-7

Crown Eagle Publishing

Distribution by Ingram

Cover Image: *The National Museum of Art*

Rare Earth Element

...climate, culture, commerce...Too important to ignore, too well written to overlook. And too technically suspenseful not to wonder about...

* * *

The Handmaiden Legacy

The Handmaiden Legacy is a contemporary thriller full of corporate interests, beautiful seas and ancient legacies...
---*G.A. Chamberlin is an International Thriller Writer!*

"International Thriller Writers ...that will surprise "
--Agent, Thriller Fest, New York City

Cultural Attache

"...Amanda Wells is lecturing on the historical integrity of medieval works at the University when she is informed that the original manuscript of a major work...has been stolen from the vault.

The Particle

"…Amanda Wells, once at the top of her game as a reliable Researcher, discovers from an unsuspecting expedition the disruptive force about to unleash a catastrophic threat to national security –
…With only a team of economically displaced, unemployed joggers at her beach house, Amanda Wells must save her daughter from the murderous fate of an international malevolent…and solve the mystery of the cause

The Kneeling Woman

"Amanda Wells, in examining the provenance of a statue brought from Spain and donated to a city Museum as a fundraiser event, finds her husband's Firm suddenly under investigation as she discovers its story during WWII. ..Where it went, what it meant…And the traitor who underwrote an investment bank with his stolen assets…and a *murder –*

--the firm where he son is engaged as an Intern.."

Reviews & Interviews:

October 31, 2018 By ITW

"And suddenly, we're off and running, as THE KNEELING WOMAN seesaws back and forth between present time and the early days of World War II…"

Charles Salzberg, *International Thriller Writer*

November 25, 2018 by ITW

G.A. Chamberlin. ROUNDTABLE participant at International Thriller Writers Association

"Her latest, *The Kneeling Woman,* is her ninth in the series."

The Kneeling Woman

A Novel

G.A. Chamberlin

* * *

Chapter 1

In the shade of an awning, not far from *Puerta del Puenta*, Amanda stopped suddenly. The street was hot, thick with browsers and vendors selling everything from tourist souvenirs to prickly pears.

Trevor had drifted on. He stopped and returned to find his wife gazing at something that had caught her attention.

Not often did Amanda touch things. She leaned over the statuette and with her finger traced the dainty neckline of the saintly figure, its curvature smooth, its head bowed in merciful supplication with hair locks weaved about her head. Burnished by hand, the white granite carving gleamed in the light.

"San Raphael" said the storekeeper, coming forward. He grinned, his face darkly tanned by a Mediterranean sea, and he showed his collection. Surrounded by the bleached white stones of the ancient city of Cordoban, his shop sold many things.

"Si!" she replied, and Amanda reached into her bag for her purse.

"Allow me!" said a strong voice behind her, and Amanda turned to look up at Trevor McDonnell. "It's beautiful" he said, handing the storekeeper the money.

"Where was it made?" Amanda asked as the figure was being wrapped in large sheets of paper.

"Ahh..." waved the storekeeper, his hand intonating a long time ago "me padre!" he said. Then he handed over the parcel. "Per La Signora!"

They walked, pleased with their purchase. "Thank you" said Amanda. "It is lovely."

"Umm. Especially the neck..." he said, a facetious curl about his mouth, adding in a low voice "If not quite as beautiful as the neck I touched last night?"

She gave him an admonishing look for taking liberties, then averted her eyes at the memory.

"*Ahem!*" he cleared his throat.

Everywhere the soft scents of agave, aloe, euphorbia filled the air. It had been dusk when they approached the ancient Roman Bridge by the Tower of Calahorra, a fortress of the medieval world, and like adolescents they had descended to the Guadalquivir River.

Perhaps lured by the twilight reflected off the ramparts of the Barrio del la Catedral, they weaved down into the shadows of the bridge buttress fortifications, breathless, down to reach one of 16 massive stone arches, and they stood to watch the river flow through the Roman bastion of the twelfth century.

It could not have been sweeter. There, in the glow of night-burning torches and the soft sound of distant tourists, the night sky so still, Trevor leaned closer to his wife "You are as ravishing to me tonight as the first day I laid eyes on you..." His breath was warm across her face, and Amanda closed her eyes, her heart pounding at his very touch. It was not a moment to easily forget.

Now in the harsh sun of the market Amanda looked up, shading her eyes. Trevor was looking at her with a suppressed smile.
Trevor had greyed at the temples, his hair stubbornly curly and his eyes ever arctic blue. A retired member of the London establishment, he carried his age well, she thought.
She put the statue into her bag in a shy fidget, but it wouldn't fit. "Ok" she said, fixing her gaze primly forward. "Well it serves you right for dragging me to this Puento Romano *Spa!*"
"Oh!" he chortled "So you prefer the pub-infested streets of a freezing wet London to Marabella Spain?"
She handed him the bag to carry.
"Right...Only if we can get lost in the shadows of the 12th century, and especially if you are my masseuse for the night?"
It took them horribly by surprise. A vehicle swerved fast and gunshots tore into Trevor's body, his arms outstretched to protect his wife.

Nova Scotia, 1942

In the dark the sea heaved and fell in a glossy state of calm. At this latitude of the North Atlantic, the moon was low and reflected off the surface like an orchestrating conductor.

The Skipper of U-86 was sweating. In this visibility, his ship's profile could be easily discerned. Even as he felt confident that he was alone in these waters, he had maintained radio-silence. Neither had there been any message traffic.

Still, there might be lurking predators in these waters. So he took the U-Boat just beneath the surface, fresh air respite be-damned. Since Kiel they had remained submerged, passing Ireland in the North Sea, then full across the Atlantic to Boston Harbor where they released 5 mines from torpedo tubes. Now off Nova Scotia, they hovered, waiting for the intercept.

 "Periskope!" he barked.

A black stem emerged from the conning tower and it swiveled almost 360 degrees as he swept the horizon. He was about to shut it down. In the predawn light his trained eye detected a trailing thread of steam from a distant ship's stack.

 So far this month, he'd sunk over 2 million tons of cargo-supply destined for Europe from America.

"Ja!"

Just as anticipated, it was sailing out of Halifax. He re-trained his distance bearings, and the rush of adrenalin coursed through his body. The crew prepared. They knew the signs. This was a kill.

He would have to wait for the vessel to come out to deeper water to avoid detection by any surface combatant. He waited to shorten the distance from his position; fixed on his target, and calculated range. He relayed instructions to open his torpedo tubes.

He smirked. The ship approaching was without escort, easy prey.

He paused, anticipating a display of sunburst as the ship blew up, his crew waiting. He delayed just a tad, perhaps for theatrical timing...

Then he saw them. Two oncoming torpedoes cutting through the water at precisely the correct depth before impact with his hull.

The Skipper was thrust against the bulkhead as the submarine shuddered, then a hissing electrical whip tore open his Control and Command post, his face etched with rage and puzzlement.

Sitting quietly on the bottom of the sea at 800 ft depth, less than two thousand meters distant, a second submerged vessel was listening closely. It had heard the torpedo hatches open on the German U-boat.

The transmission seaman barely whispered to his commanding officer. Triangulating its position, the Royal Navy Captain released buoyancy from his Forward ballast to lift the bow for angle, and an offensive firing target was acquired.

Impact occurred just beneath the surface of the water, and the sea heaved in a giant swell. The German U Boat sank with an implosion so intense that they knew there would be no survivors.

The surface steamship that was advancing in the waters off Nova Scotia sailed by, unawares, chasing off dawn shadows from its bow waves. Only one man observed the surface through his binoculars. He guessed what had happened.

The British Royal Naval submarine vessel lifted gently off the bottom and rose to a depth of 50 feet beneath the surface. Observing no survivors, it quietly re-submerged to the deep, its mission accomplished.

The Allied assault submarine had been rewarded for its patience.

"You know.." said Trevor, applying hearty lumps of marmalade to his toast "your mother was never afraid of adventure!"

Amanda peered at him over her coffee cup, her eyes full of concern. They were having breakfast at the Savoy. That their son was entering his first year of University was sufficient to fill her with emotion. But added to their closing the house in London to retire in Scotland, coupled with a move to New York for business, and she was feeling apprehensive - especially as the moment of farewell approached.

Tray laughed. He looked so like his father, thought Amanda. Tray, as they sometimes called him was excited at his prospects and wolfed into his food.

Their breakfast together made light of a long three month ordeal in which Trevor recovered from his gunshot injuries. And this moment brought closure to the whole incident.

Tray was leaving the household, and clearly, he needed the assurance that all was back to normal. That's what his parents wanted to send him off with. Thus, the parting was to be a happy one, a new focus on his own adventure...

Amanda turned to Trevor and smiled. She could see that the lines of stress had left her husband's face. He too was content.

It was only later, on the train voyage north that Amanda had time to reflect. She watched him, the paper open before him, his arm still stiff and in a sling. He was at the center of her universe, she decided.

She would never forget the incident. At every opportunity in the ensuing years, she touched the

photograph of the statuette, noting the bore-hole that lodged the bullet that might have killed him had he not been carrying the bag...
Trevor had been the target of a failed assassination.

* * *

Amanda's finger hovered over the key on her laptop. In acknowledgement to an email she had received, she had written a few quick words.

"Ready to leave...?" called Trevor from the Lobby.

"Coming..." she called back, her eye reviewing the email.

Yes, she smiled. She attached an image, and pressed. Jacques would appreciate seeing the beautiful *Santa Raphael* statue that they had bought in Spain a couple of months ago. That is, before the incident that put Trevor in the hospital.

Certainly as a family friend, Jacques had communicated with them and expressed his best wishes for Trevor's recovery. It was for this reason that she was happy to be sending him images.

In all the investigation about the shooting, the matter of informing Jacques about the shopkeeper and the statue had gone by the wayside, and he had asked about it. Now it was time to tell him.

Jacques was one of Europe's most respected Antiquities dealer, and although Amanda was no expert, she sensed that this item had intrinsic value.

As a friend, she had meant to inform him about it.

Jacques and Trevor MacDonnald had a long history together, much of it because of Amanda. Not all of it easy. Over the years, they had reconciled whatever issues lay "on the margins of the law" as Trevor politely put it, and Jacques was reinstated as a reputable expert on medieval treasures.

This was just a beautiful item, and Amanda had wanted to share it with him. He might benefit from its sale if he had a buyer...

"*More importantly*" he had said in his reply to her email "*it is absolutely beautiful!*"

What she also sent him was the name and address of the shopkeeper who might tell him more. So it was with some surprise that she read Jacques' most recent reply.

"*Yes. Thank you!*

As the shopkeeper suspected, it is a genuine piece. So I paid him a handsome advance, and we have a signed Agreement for him to receive a percentage of the proceeds if it goes to Auction. I have received the item here with me in France. I've insured it, and with its Provenance. I shall be shipping it to New York. I've asked a friend of mine at the Metropolitan Museum to look at it before we decide how to proceed. I'm glad you're thinking of donating it. (I offered your name if he needs to speak...)

Again, with many, many thanks Amanda!

 As Always, my best to Trevor and to your son Tray.

Jacques de Toulaine..."

Amanda printed the email, tore it off the printer and grabbed a white cotton umbro-scarf to wrap around her neck. Trevor was holding open the elevators.

 "Jacques sends his best..." she said in her rush "And you'll never guess what he's doing..."

The doors closed on them.

* * *

Canada, 1942

The steam ship sailed another 50 miles out to sea then altered course. It did not cross the Atlantic. It changed its bearing to head South by Southwest, and steamed toward its port of destination.

That night, the docks unloaded the cargo from the vessel in New York City Harbor and reloaded the shipment onto the rail platform. In the dark, the docks of the city were under curfew for wartime blackout. In the shadows men working on rail heads moved like ghosts in the drizzle.

Slowly the train pulled out. Levers and signals at the main rail terminal opened up for the shipment to move south. Then as gradually as the locomotive approached, the rails shifted, and the train lumbered on, steel on steel, to align with girders that redirected track, its direction diverted.

From that night on, nobody could account for the whereabouts or content of its cargo. Sugar, some said. Wood and steel for ship-building yards in Europe others said.

Only the President was informed by his Treasury Secretary that the shipment had gone missing.

They agreed not to acknowledge its loss. Rather, to proceed as if the shipment had reached its intended destination in the mountains of Pennsylvania as planned. For safekeeping, they declared.

 No one would know of the disappearance of gold bullion - sent to Halifax by Russia as payment for American tanks to fight with the Allied Front against Germany...

* * *

The Assistant District Attorney of Manhattan wasn't accustomed to receiving requests from the Orphans Court. The matter had been shunted along from office to office until it reached her desk.
The official request entered by her clerk was neatly catalogued in a file folder, and it sat on her desk like a lead slate amongst a tall pile of urgent folders.
Karen McCullock ignored it. The request was related to a forensic matter, and the last thing she needed was some legacy issue pending someone's Last Will and Testament. She waited until all else had been cleared away from her desk, which took a week.
She stood up, her legs stiff. Glancing at the clock, she decided to wrap-up the workload on her desk. Most personnel on her floor had already left. She turned to the cabinets behind her to stow and secure her files. What happened to the day, she mused. It seemed like she just sat down with her morning coffee to start the day!
She glanced at the yellow jacket still on her desk. Well, what's ten minutes to look at it briefly?
"'Night Karen!" waved her secretary from outside the glass office hallway.
Karen waived, nodding. Yes, she'd be leaving too shortly...
She took a deep breath. Actually, she could leave any time she wanted. Considering the hours she put in, nobody would mind if she left early here and there - if only to catch up on sleep!
She picked up the file. Once opened, she read through the details. Not because she felt obliged but because she recognized the name on the signed Affidavit that disputed the alleged claim by the

estate. The Trustee who executed the Will had included it in the file.

The Orphans Court wanted the District Attorney to officially authorize their "sign off" on the matter since this testimony suggested foul play in a complete Deposition attached to a Last Will and Testament. The Orphans Court would need assistance to retire the file with a Department of Justice disposition.

Without having knowledge of any case, the Orphans Court deferred to the DA's office to decide: Given that there was no Statute of Limitations, this was a testament declaration of a possible homicide.

Karen turned the page and read the testimony. The diseased woman, a Mrs. Green, had previously filed a Last Will and Testament with a Deposition. In it, she recounted a matter relating to her husband's death. He had died, she claimed, after operating under instruction to divert a large shipment of material in his construction equipment. She knew he was murdered, she said, and could prove it.

He had a small construction business, he operated a cement mixer. It was during the war. At night, he would backup against a railhead at the New York docks. Crates lifted by crane released their contents systemically into his cement mixer to be camouflaged. The material was solid bars of metal – to be used for the fabrication of ship's bulkheads at the Naval shipbuilding yards, they told him: This process was to elude notice by enemy spies, they informed him.

This process would continue for several nights, and he was to deliver the cement-covered bars to wherever instructed by his client. Once he delivered them to a construction site, where steel girders lay exposed and awaiting for concrete sealing. Shortly after the last run, the statement alleged, he was killed, and his body was never recovered.

The wife suspected foul play since a tall building was erected over the site where he had delivered the material. She felt that the Shipyard never recovered the material for shipyard operations. She visited the site often over the years. She kept a list of instructions kept by her husband -a work-contract of sorts, signed by the construction project manager. Now, in her Last Will and Testament, she enclosed the list, and revealed the name of the client who had the bars...

She suspected something was wrong. He was killed because of something he knew. As long as he poured out the contents of his mixer down the funnel, he was free to drive off...

The statement was signed by Mrs. Green. Her Executor had no idea what she had included in the sealed envelope.

Karen examined the pages.

A Note was attached. Something added from a Navy office, a shipyard log account taken by a Chief Petty Officer in the Yard Master's Office.

The paper described an operation with which the contractor was associated. He cited a cargo that had been stolen from a ship.

Evidently, Mrs Green's husband had tried to report the activity to Navy personnel at the dockyards...

A hand-scribbled note above the transcription said: *This sounds familiar to another filing...*

It was on a yellow Post-it, written by someone in the Clerk of the Court's local state attorney's office. She read the document upon which the Post-it was attached.

"Upon review, the alleged 'site of a construction project waiting to pour cement' allowed him in the darkness of the night to upend trucks into its hollowed structural pillars, which he in-filled with cement. There, we should assume the metal bars were precious metals, like gold.

In such a state, the gold would wait - concealed, until after the war when he could reclaim it as a contractor. The question of how to break into finished structure to retrieve the bars is unknown.

However, one scenario consistent with the client's subsequent filing suggest that he could arrange for his return to the site for repairs.

The phone rang. Karen picked up.

"Bill Wickowsky?""

"Hey Karen! How *are* you? Haven't seen you since Law School! How've you been?..."

Karen was thrilled. She liked Bill very much and they chatted. Finally she added "how timely to receive a phone call from the very lawyer I was just reading about!" she giggled.

 "That's funny...and they say there's nothing to mental telepathy!"

"Coincidence?"

 "Ha! Now that's a possibility! I called you earlier today...."

"Oh, I'm sorry..."

"No. no.! Please... I just talked to Nancy again as she was leaving and she told me you might be working late."

"Thanks!"

"So, I have a question. I've been calling around for a week in that labyrinth they call the New York City Police Department trying to find out who was handling that stupid case on Green..."

"I got it!"

They both laughed. "Hope they appreciate *your* diligence, at least!" he said.

"If only they'd *pay* me enough..." she added.

"Chicken feed! You should try joining us on this side of private practice..."

"Right!" she said.

"Look, I know you've a hot date waiting, so I'll be brief. Please *don't* believe that drivel will you? Just sign off on it, and the Orphans Court can close the case..."

"I'm just reading it now. Fascinating..."

"So, I can assure my client its finished business then?"

"Who's that?"

"William Salaman ."

"Oh" she said, taken aback. "Well. It doesn't get more glamorous than that, does it...?"

"*Salaman & Salaman,* they   are a pretty big brokerage. But yeah! That's who it is. So you can understand my need to bring this to a conclusion?"

Her eyes narrowed slightly. The name of the Project Attorney on the document popped up.

"And the connection is...*what* exactly to this document?" she asked.

"Oh *Jesus* Karen! That was a name of a family that lived in New York during WWII, Salaman had a client whose father was implicated in some conspiracy claim, back in the day.... *He* was as dotty and clueless as the rest of the world at that time.

So...err, please end this thing. Sign off, and send me an email, will you?"

"Well... for an Old Dear like this claimant, the name was certainly well known to her. I mean who *doesn't* know that name? They're global players now, right?"

"Right."

Her office was quiet enough for her to hear background noise on his end, he was at a social event. She'd stayed on the line too long already.

"Ok then" she said "I'll keep you informed. Thanks for the call..."

He was gone.

She read the full report.

* * *

1944, New York.

The leaves of New England were just beginning to whisper of Fall when a breeze lifted from the Hudson River and curled up the embankment where the President sat quietly with his Treasurer.

It had been a long war, and already the daunting task of reparations loomed. It was one thing to end this war, another to rebuild.

The plan of which they spoke was one that had been discussed between the three Allies in secret meetings and missions across Europe. It was well known that Russia had fought relentlessly against the enemy with high mortality rates. Stalin, if not the man of their choice for his political views, was the leader of an Army as an Ally. Now it was time for reparations, and the aspirations of Russia were to be included in all discussions.

"That's what he favors..." said the Secretary of the Treasury.

"Come... Let's walk!" said the President. Roosevelt moved his wheelchair and they took the path along the waterfront.

 "Stalin wants Germany to be reduced to an agrarian society so that it can never again be the start of another war in Europe..." continued the Secretary.

The President nodded.

"I'll call it my plan, if you like..." added the Treasurer.

The President sighed heavily. They paused and looked out across the river. Without a word, they turned.

Roosevelt, now guided in his wheelchair by his old friend, was lost in thoughts of ferocious armies locked in combat. The dying, the dead and the destruction of war filled their hearts.

That so many American soldiers were dying in battle on foreign soil was unconscionable for the President, and the human cost of that awful reality weighted heavily: The Allies wanted nothing more than to end this war. By the same token, if not the battlefields abroad, then the shores of America were at risk...

Still, its cost was high. *How to encourage reconstruction?*

They would have to find a way to rebuild a destroyed Europe when the guns stopped. Reparations would have to be so orchestrated as to restore all that was expended by the allied armies, and then to ensure the peace...

They stopped suddenly. Situated at the edge of the lawn by the river they faced the kneeling woman. The statue rested on the green, her head bowed in graceful supplication, her arms sculpted from refined shoulders in gentle petition to a merciful God to heal a broken world, her very heart in her plea...

They gazed in silence.

Finally the President spoke. "I'm commissioning a new one." He looked up and smiled softly. "I've sent pictures and instructions to the sculptor..."

Emerging from the garden lawns of his estate, the President's private home came into view, and they paused before approaching, bracing themselves.

They entered a house full of noise. Personnel filled porches, hallways and every corner of the great rooms.

The President's home was Headquarters for all message traffic pouring in. Telephone calls, cables, coded and un-coded reports littered desks positioned everywhere, the place laced with wiring, telephone lines and lighting cables for staff.

In an effort to amass the full picture of intelligence, they focused on the processing, filtering, re-directing, advising and authorizing of operations – most of it dictated to typists perched along the hallways, doorways even stairways - amending, cross-talking, updating their data-points and signaling for action reports...

Had the world come to an end, thought the President. He glanced back briefly across the lawn where sat the kneeling woman, but he was quickly absorbed in the hub.

As time passed, the *Morgenthal Plan* that they had discussed would never be implemented. Yet it would have an impact on the affairs of state...

By 1951, the United States had grown wary of its Ally. All of the elder leadership with whom they had negotiated had been replaced by new Ministers, and robust statesmen now prevailed in Europe. A new era had dawned.

Germany was rebuilt as a strong nation.

They had entered the Cold War.

* * *

New York

The view from the 19th floor of the luxury apartment building in NYC was stunning.

The river glittered with diamonds as it bordered riverfront parks, greens and trees of the city as if man's footprint could never change its natural beauty. Tall buildings, flashing reflections off a setting sun on glass and chrome, promised lights of the night to come.

"Trevor!" a voice called out. A man raised his arm above the noisy crowd.

Trevor turned.

"Over here!" A champagne glass held high weaved its way through the crowd to reach him, and a short man wearing a black tie and dinner jacket emerged.

"How good to see you Derek!" grinned Trevor.

They shook hands heartily "The good life of New York city suits you well I see" chuckled the short man.

"What a wonderful place you have" added Trevor. "Thank you for inviting us to your party!"

The windows were open, if railed from the outside, and a soft breeze drove sounds of the night as excitement filled the air.

Derek Salaman turned to Amanda. He took in a long breath, saying nothing. Then he turned back to Trevor, raising his glass in a gesture of admiration. "Wow!"

Deep in conversation with another person, Amanda wore a black cocktail dress. Simply draped with a black satin bow and diamante broach, she looked stunning. Few wore long gowns, this was a private fundraiser. But there was little Amanda Wells could wear that did not command attention. Her features - dark green eyes and curling auburn hair that fell gently upon firm shoulders of a slender body were natural. Across her face, even with generous smile-lines, Amanda held her age with such grace that few in the room could compete. Many were standing in line to talk with her.

Only a few items from the Exhibit had been allowed up to the private quarters of Derek Salaman's apartment. There was ample space. Several grand rooms leading off from the central marble foyer were filled with guests. At the heart of the event was a baroque roundtable with a towering bouquet, and not far from the Quartet band of musicians, was a pedestal for the statue.

The statue was on display on a velvet platform. She was the reason for the fundraiser. She could have been a guest. Or she could have been an angel. With special lighting aimed at the crown of her head, the marble sculpture was remarkable. Everyone just stared, somehow moved. It was as if a spirit of translucence enveloped her and descended upon the party of guests to cast a spell.

 Amanda had made all the arrangements. But as host of the event, Derek Salaman was recognized by the Press who stood amongst the guests. They took notes, flashing images, video feeds, citing everything they knew about him.

Salaman's financial donation to the City museum was no secret. It was to feature in the New York Times with an article that gave his biography, including the list of charitable events that he chaired. Tonight was no exception. He started the bidding off with a few happy opening remarks. And the donations kept coming after that...

At the close of the evening, a record amount of money was raised by pledges for the City Museum. This, Salaman mentioned in his closing remarks, and he thanked both Trevor and Amanda for making it such a success. It was clear he was emotionally moved.

As they filed out Salaman gave them a hug. "What can I do to thank you both?...Of all the things that I do, tonight will stand out as a memory of the highest and brightest moments. I can't tell you..." he said.

"That's true!" added Steve Buckowski, his chief Counsel, happy to bring the evening to a close.

"How's your son doing?"

"Well as you know, he's knee-deep in his studies at Aberdeen University..."

"Can I have him as an Intern for one semester? Please? I'd like to show him the business!"

Amanda looked at Trevor a little anxiously, if smiling.

"Maybe not for the semester, but why not for his summer break? Will that do?" said Trevor.

"Absolutely! He'll be under the Supervision of my Senior Finance Advisor who will show him the ropes of an American brokerage firm. Miami?"

"I'll ask him!" said Trevor. And with that they shook hands.

It wasn't until they were in their car that Amanda let out a deep breath. *"Miami?"*

"It'll be a great experience for him..." insisted Trevor.

* * *

Breakfast was redolent with the scent of roses.

The delivery of flowers had arrived early in the morning. Concierge had handed the package to Trevor at the door with a Note. *'Thanks from the City Museum for the sums of money raised in donations.'*

They were thrilled, Amanda arranged the stunning bouquet of flowers in a tall crystal vase. She placed them in the front hallway.

"Are you sure you haven't a secret admirer?" said Trevor accusingly.

Amanda paused, then moved to lace her arms around his neck. "Only if he's standing in the room with me now!"

Later that morning she received a message from Jacques.

"...Umm. What you found in Spain... was the artist's original working model, prior to sculpting the main statue ....It is authentic. No question!"

"Well done!" Trevor grinned. "You had the eye to spot something significant!"

Amanda returned her gaze to her laptop, adding "...he goes on to say that he will not put it on the market but leave it as a loan to the Museum in New York where he feels it belongs!"

She nodded. "That's where I think it belongs. How good of Jacques to pass up on a fortune and allow the public to enjoy the statuette. He could have made an offer..."

Someone was at the door again.

* * *

The May event on the Delaware River, across from the city of Philadelphia was one of the most exciting college events of the season. Together with a city-wide Jazz festival that lasted a week, the place was packed with visitors.

Crew racing between University Sailing Clubs celebrated a boating tradition of a bygone era in Philadelphia, Pennsylvania.

Scheduled at the end of the academic semester to mark the beginning of summer-term, the event was traditionally participated by universities of the East Coast of America. But this year, two institutions from overseas joined. They were flown across the Atlantic for the challenge to compete for the Championship Title. One team was from the University that Tray attended. Moreover, Tray was a member of crew team.

Both parents appeared to cheer their son's event as spectators in the stands. They watched teams of rowers competing at top speeds in long shells, each vessel holding synchronized crews rowing like well discipline warriors.

Colorful college tents were pitched high along the waterfront, and the crowds cheered along embankments, the river a raceway of blue water and shinning sparkles in the sun with passing rowers.

By afternoon, eliminations had thinned out the teams to leave only the top contenders, Tray's college amongst them.

As the sun moved across the sky, it became a test of endurance and fitness. Now only teams of highly competitive athletes wearing the colors of their school stroked in tandem to achieve powerful pulling speeds to beat rivals for the Finish. And still Tray's crew remained in the competition.

Committee boats were refereed the racing from platforms, blaring announcements, firing guns and timing teams for the finish. Behind them the landscape of the city of Philadelphia gleamed in the sun, tall skyscrapers piercing the sky as icons of a financial world of corporate giants.

Tray was thrilled to see his family. Though attached to his team, he made arrangements to break free later for dinner, and they decided on a place in the historic district of Philadelphia, downtown.

They had to laugh at lot, catching up with their son's news and his university interests.

"With *this* championship posted on our dorm tower - we shall brag of beating the *Americans!*" declared Tray.

"Really?" said his mother, a gleam in her eye.

"Oh yes! They do train and build muscle for weeks on end to be the fittest..." Tray added, chewing on a mouthful of grilled steak.

"Well then..." said Trevor, hiding a smile "I hope you'll find the wits to win over Brown University tomorrow...They are amongst the best."

"Oh yes!" said his son, swallowing. "We aim to pull *devious* and deadly!"

They chortled. "Here's to our best wishes for the win!" said Trevor raising his glass.

"Cheers!"

"By the way, did I mention that we have one more Regatta on our schedule before summer break?"

"Oh? Where are you off to next?" asked his father.

The boy looked at them both, his face capricious. "Madrid"

"Yes!" he said. "Actually, it's just north-west of Madrid, an ancient university town that invited us to their annual festival and their first Challenge of the Carthaginians for the title of crew championship! . Our university accepted their invitation, and all our team is going. I can't wait!"

"Oh, you will find the girls lovely!" smiled Amanda, teasing her son.

Tray popped a large morsel of a buttered breadroll into his mouth, saying "They tell me, though, that they don't even have cell phones out there yet..."

"I for one, wouldn't mind that at all..." grinned Amanda. "But I'm sure they are as updated as any other European country!"

They chuckled.

"Indeed," said Trevor "it is an ancient city, the place where you are going. First conquered by the Cathaginians in the 3rd century B.C., it became a Roman settlement, then ruled over by the Moors until the 11th century..."

"Really?"

"Umm," mused Amanda. "The university is one of the oldest in Europe - first known during Salaman ca's golden age. Today, the city's historic center has important monuments. Romanesque, gothic, moorish, renaissance and baroque. It's Plaza Mayor has galleries and arcades famous for their finds and antiquities..."

 "I shall keep that in mind when I tour..."

The evening passed all too quickly.

Only as they parted did Amanda ask a question that she might have regretted. But later in the car Trevor assured her that it was alright. She had asked Tray to visit Cordoban again - the place of their vacation where she had found the statue.

She glanced ruefully at her husband, the incident of the shooting not entirely forgotten.

They stopped for coffee on the drive back home.

"You alright?" asked Trevor.

Amanda nodded. But her thoughts returned to Spain. It was clear she was hoping for some answers about the statue.

Tray had told them he wouldn't mind visiting their shop and asking the storekeeper a few questions...

"Then I fly directly to *Miami* where I begin my summer internship right? Err...at the Salaman Business offices, yes?"

"Right" chuckled his father. "Mr. Salaman has pressed me, if you'd like to go..."

"I would!" affirmed his son.

"Right then. It's settled!"

Before parting Tray turned to his mother "Can you send me a list of questions to ask the store keeper?"

"Sure! You'll find them in your Inbox in a day or two, if that's alright?"

"Happy to do it!" said her son, giving both his parents a final hug.

* * *

Chapter 2

London

He was in a class by himself. Thomas Legardier was a Level II Broker trading on the London Stock Exchange with a list of clients.

Little made him stand out. He was not a tall man, but he wore his age well, belying the fact that he was well into his sixties with a demeanor that resembled any other professional stockbroker. Except that he still wore a bowler hat and always carried his dark umbrella, a standard from a bygone era for financial bankers in London.

These days, everyone looked like any other professional in any other major trading city.
He crossed the Strand: Wearing a stylish suit, made of silky rayon that fitted trimly at the legs and brown stitched leather shoes that shone at every tread, he was yet distinctly British. Even his Bloomberg-styled skinny tie was fine, plus that requisite London Fog raincoat, but that Bowler hat was entirely his personal preference.
It was no longer worn. Neither did it belong in the high-end pubs celebrating high stakes trades and

victory drinks, nor favored by women frequenting the bars as affiliates or friends... It inhibited their *performance*, as they called it.

That suited Legardier fine. In fact, he wore it like a shield against promiscuous advances that followed him like bees to honey. That was the culture of the environment he worked in. See, he and his wife Jill did very well in the country. But he kept a place in the city.

His basement apartment suited him fine in Ewes. Alone and safe, his week-nights gave him privacy with all his trades on the stock exchange.

His quiet time.

Even Jill knew not to bother him. His routine was uneventful. A couple of tots of whiskey; a good news broadcast, and even a show or two. But that was it for him. An early night, then off the next day with tea and toast in his stomach for breakfast.

Mrs. Maluke came in daily, entering after he left. He might as well have been a hotel guest for the light footprint he left in his quarters. A towel or two from a shower...fresh razors...overnight bedding. He kept three drawers of neatly folded underwear in a closet styled *modern living*, and a dressing room hung with pressed suits, ties, shirts and polished shoes. That was his life.

Unexceptional. Lucrative.

He paid for his train ticket, and stood in line at the turnstile to place it into the electronic slit. It lit up, he passed onto his platform, and he kept his eyes down. The train would take him directly into the underground station of his building.

* * *

Amanda read the postcard.

"Won the Regatta, leaving now for Cordoban. Had a great time!. TA"
Tray must have bought a hotel postcard and dropped it into the mailbox of the lobby. He was in Salamanca. The boating Regatta sponsored by the University at Salamanca would be have been a rousing event attended by many of Europe's university teams.

Amanda looked up the Festival on the Internet. Just as before, the competition solicited spectators, colors, media and ceremonial flourish. She saw crews racing down through the ancient city, its river threading idyllic pastoral scenery and she had to smile at the cheering revelers caught up in the excitement...

She realized that Tray and his team would be entertained for a weekend of celebration tours and restaurant. His University had won the championship cup, and their hosts had proclaimed vows to repeat the challenge next year for all teams to attend...

* * *

Except for a sore arm, Tray was satisfied that he had done his best for the team.

He arrived at the car rental Depot about mid-morning, and drove a Fiat for the trip to Cordoban. It took him most of the day, driving from higher altitudes in Spain and descending to southern latitudes at the coast of the Mediterranean sea. For him, it was an experience. Motoring the open road, from scrubby barren hillside to terraced soils between sparsely populated villages bleached by unrelenting sun, was fun.

The heat was palpable but did little to deter tourists. They were found in towns set-up for visitors arriving for summer vacation from all over northern Europe.

More than once he was surrounded by stubborn goats, and on two occasions nearly ran out of gas. Twice, he gave a ride to hitchhikers, and once to a policeman who told him he was on his way to work.

His town came into view. Relieved to arrive at his destination, he checked into his accommodations at a small villa tourist spa.

Tray showered and relaxed for the evening in the cooler breezes of the veranda. He was stiff and sore, he had pulled a muscle in his shoulder from rowing. Added to the long drive, the place offered precisely the tranquility he needed.

Moreover, this was same local where his parents had stayed the year before. Tomorrow he would tour the town and find the shop his mother enquired about. After that, he aimed to drive down to Gibraltar and catch a flight back to Heathrow. He slept.

* * *

Legardier was pleased with himself today. Reaching for his seat by the window on the train, he liked the news he had recently. Except for a small item that shadowed his thinking, he was definitely gratified by the way things were going for him. Yet it persisted, that small item.

Never a full rainfall. Never the full story. Just an odd trend that had become a habit in the behavior of one of his clients. It occurred to Thomas Legardier that this client had a methodology of sorts. And while the results produced lucrative fees for him consistently, the matter puzzled him, this client.

That he was the thinker of numbers, trends and financial insights was always a source of pride. The LSE, where he held a desk, was a diversified international market infrastructure. It was the capital markets business of the world's financial community.

Still, this mystery bothered him. Every other client was busy with life. His investors were surgeons, lawyers and businessmen with hardly time to reveal motives. They just accepted his advice on where to place their money as investment placements...

But never *this* client. He was always regular and always ...meticulous. Anonymous!

Why?

Legardier took a big breath and watched the landscape rush by from verdant-green to city-living. The London Stock Exchange was his home. He was proud of what he did.

The LSE only yesterday announced the introduction of new enhancements to its hidden Mid-Price Pegged Order functionality - a function designed to facilitate Large-in-Scale, dark trading directly on the SETS orderbook.

Extraordinary! Who would have thought such a thing possible, he wondered. How fortunate he was to have worked his way up through the years! To most people, that was Greek.

The London Stock Exchange Group could trace its legacy back to 1698, since the beginning of the European Renaissance. The world of finance had evolved.

Today, they operated a broad range of international equity. Bond and derivatives exchange markets, including London Stock Exchange; Borsa Italiana; MTS, Europe's leading fixed income market; and Turquoise, a pan-European equities MTF. Home to one of the world's leading growth markets for SMEs, AIM, the Group offered international business for investors with unrivalled access to Europe's capital markets...

A global world of nations, once enemies. And now? He smiled. How far they had advanced! What was it Churchill had promised Roosevelt on the deck of the *HMS Prince of Wales* at that famous conference of the Allies? *A golden century of peace...* after the war was won.

And it was that, and more.

Even post-trade and risk management. Today's business operations included multi-asset global CCP operators like LCH, the Clearnet Group. Plus the LSEG operated others, like the CC&G, the Italian clearing house; Monte Titoli, the T2S-ready European settlement business; and even the globeSettle – a newly established CSD based in Luxembourgh...

Good God...It was hard to *imagine* such an array when he first started...

The train stopped. Approaching the center of London, more passengers were embarking, and he scootched over to make room for others to sit...

He had adapted well. A man without schooling or the profile of most others, he had done well with his head for figures...

Only recently new software was introduced, and he took the training. So now, in addition to their markets, his company provide over 35 other organizations and exchanges with use of their Millennium IT for trading, surveillance and post trade technology! His Firm was positioned *everywhere*, North America, Italy, France, Sri Lanka, with roughly 4,700 employees.

Could he have managed to enter the field today with the credentials of specialized schooling in financial instruments and tools? No. Of course not..

But he still had the trust of his clients.

He would make a post to his client today, he decided. He would inform them of new things such as Hidden Mid-Price Pegged Orders.

Still...

The train arrived at his destination and he walked out. It was raining, and he popped open his umbrella to cross the street to his building.

And there it was, the source of his concern...

The Order that he should want to solicit. This client was one step ahead of him! *Always one step*... Even those many years ago when he began his trades.

-A rich man, by now, for sure. But he was obdurate and obsessive...

On *what*, exactly? In fact, why was it that the word *dark liquidity* always associated with his client?

"Morning Thelma!" he said.

"Good Morning Mr. Legardier!" she replied, smiling brightly.

He sat at his desk which his Assistant had opened up for business. He had messages and announcements, in-house Memos about new regulation directives.

He would have to give this up soon, he knew. He was just getting too close to retirement. The business was changing. He had made sufficient money, that was for sure...

About noon, he got the telephone call from his client. "D" as he liked to call himself.

He was inviting him to meet for Lunch.

In twenty years, he had never met his client.

* * *

Chapter 3

New York

Mark Ruttenberg was the night's best looking 35 year old in the bar. His hair, still shiny and loosely fallen over dark features and glossy blue eyes, was saturated by perspiration from a night of dance on and off the floor.

The tie, if long gone, left an indentation through buttoned channels where it was fixed earlier in the day. He stood. Dark blue tailored pants, held up at the belt, remained creased with a sheen of high-grade fabric that constituted the brand of his man's wardrobe. But they were stained with spilled alcohol at the zipper and thighs. It was three in the morning. The *High Noon*, a former *Speakeasy* where it was said Earnest Hemming made out with women, was now officially closed. Nor was the place visible in these parts of the city for cabs.

For those able to afford the high life of playing downtown, it was the place to go on the last stop of a circuit where the sounds were mellow and intoxicants in command of the night. Later, if you were still standing and able to nurse your way back to reality, you aimed for the pre-dawn bakery of a New York city cafe bar.

Mark Ruttenberg had enjoyed the night. He could afford the tab which, depending on the number of people you had with you, could easily top a couple thousand dollars a night. There was no girl, or at least, none that he could remember... A sports game or another, they said.
Drinking, shouting, dancing, and swaying. Wait. Oh yes, there was a girl! Now he remembered. She was a blond, angular shoulders, hair loose now but clearly able to dress.
His head hurt. Yes he *remembered*. She was still in her dark skirt, her office-blouse loosely open and her shoes gone, along with her inhibitions, and he stayed.
She promised him sweet dreams as he stood and watched, his head swirling with dance, just as she promised. And the feelings did bend his mind - first with a kiss that passed the powder from her mouth to his, then another dose straight into his drink, and he could feel it go down like a shot of whiskey.
Careful now, he heard her say once. Oh yeah! Careful it was, alright. And now he was particularly thirsty.
Tonight, or rather, this morning, he couldn't remember where he had left his car. Oh, yes he could! Of course, what an idiot...
His car was never far from the place he would fetch up at the end of his night's journey. That is, long after his friends had left. The café bar. Around the Corner. But the underground parking garage was firmly locked for the night. So he'd have to wait a couple hours.
His mind was dreaming but he was wide awake - nothing like it: His surroundings were like fiction,

only in his head was there reality. It was a beautiful act of magic, being and seeing and feeling supremely empowered, while moving about as if normal.

He entered the café and took a seat, the waitress familiar with the task. Food, coffee and sobriety. That was what he wanted.

He needed to pull himself together. This place was for those who needed to firm up for the day's work ahead. Yet he felt somehow detached.

He smiled. Or he thought he did. The life of a stockbroker could be full and noisy, or calm and analytical. It could offer precisely the kind of screening that one could hide behind. He couldn't decide which, just now.

He looked about for the waitress. He had an urge to clean up and get his day under control. There was something important today. Earnings Reports from major accounts needing analysis, and he had a few phone appointments - some with major clients. This and that ... a meeting with his Supervising broker. A Lunch.

He ate, he drank and he cradled his head for forty winks until sunrise. It would come, sure enough. Then in less than an hour he would reach his Gym, open his locker, grab a sweat towel and take a short turn at the Elliptical exercise machine. Then take up a notch or two on the Weights training. That would be it, for today... With his membership he could enter the Sauna, take a swim or head for the shower. There was a change of clothes in his locker - a fresh suit, always! That should do it. Good as new! Nobody would know he'd been out all night...

But he felt thirsty. He left the café and went outside just as the dark of night began to dissipate. The waitress gave him directions to orient himself. He'd find his block, he told her. A bus came, just as she said, he climbed on, and paid. Then the driver told him it was his stop.

He walked a couple blocks. He drank from a water supply close by, and started to make his way to the Gymn. He found it, there was little traffic on the street. His pass opened the main door. He headed for a water fountain and thrust his mouth to drink.

The drink turned his stomach and he wanted to throw-up. He went to the Sauna, then fled the room for another quenching drink, a towel wrapped at his waist.

He headed for the bathrooms. In the toilet he thought he felt his heart pounding, his pulse racing...He sank, waiting, his head aching and his limbs heavy.

 What the hell had that girl put into his drink?
He filled his lungs with air. *My God!*
He would not be late, he decided. Yet he sat, the fog of disorientation slowly draining from his head. Finally he showered and changed his clothes.

His Ford Mustang came spinning out of the garage at a speed that seemed ludicrously slow, his foot a clumsy lead weight on the gas pedal. It was too early in the morning, the city was still half empty. His head was getting foggy.

There was a car waiting. What, what, *what* did it mean? It meant something, he knew. His head...

"May I see your Driver's License and car Registration please Sir?" said the NYCP Officer...

* * *

Trevor and Amanda were in the car to Newport. Their Lincoln kept a steady speed, blocking noise from traffic racing along US Interstate 95 to Boston.

"He did a great job" said Amanda "he sent me a couple of emails itemizing all that he discovered. The shopkeeper actually remembered his parents! He said the place was flooded with tourists..."

Trevor, his eyes on the road ahead, nodded "Yes. Spain is Europe's favorite spot for vacationing..." He glanced at his wife, his expression redolent with the memories of their romantic days spent there.

"But we caused quite a stir... The shooting incident was an unfortunate event the shopkeeper would like to forget, I'm sure."

"Oh for sure..." agreed Amanda. "Still, Tray seems to be enjoying the experience!"

They chatted about the regatta in Salamanca. Their son had given them ample details, and the subject livened the drive.

"So, tell me more about the Shopkeeper" asked Trevor.

"The shopkeeper is a local Spaniard whose father knew the artist who sculpted our statue. In fact they were related by marriage from centuries past when the family of the sculptor originally lived and worked in Spain."

"Oh? So there was a connection, like an Artisan family?"

"Yes. More like a trade. The shopkeeper told Tray that the statue was actually the work of a sculptor who was also a Jeweler, a diamond-dealer in Frankfurt. The artist's family had assets in Africa going back a century, since the European colonial era. They had mineral mines. The shopkeeper's father told of cargo loads arriving in Spain as boat packets from Casablanca. His father would then forward the raw material to Germany for the Jeweler. But that stopped, he said, shortly before the war, and then his father died."

Traffic was heavy, and Trevor was negotiating a full lane of heavy trucks. Amanda took in a breath as jammed haulers moved around them, deadweight behemoths on 18 wheels were full of shipped cargo moving north and south along the Atlantic seaboard from all major seaports of North America.

"Please go on..." said Trevor, finally.

"The shopkeeper showed Tray Ledgers that belonged to his father, accounts that his father had kept for the Jeweler. He looked for the statue but couldn't find any record. Evidently, they did quite a lot of business, his father and the Dealer in Frankfurt. His father was part of the supply chain, furnishing precious gemstones to the Dealer in Frankfurt.. Tray says the shopkeeper said they used to make cargo shipments of pure gold from South Africa. Diamonds, and other items, according to the accounts. Tray was allowed to take images on his iphone, which he forwarded... I have them!"

"Wow..." said Trevor "That kind of trust would need to be the bonds of family to purvey..."

"The shopkeeper knew the Dealer's work by heart, he knew of many sculptures of beautiful works of art. He showed Tray a sketch of a statue, a design for a commission from someone in the United States he said, during the war. His father said that he never heard from the Artist since the war, so he didn't know anything more..."

* * *

London

At an historic Pub in the district of Canary Square, the man sitting across the table from Tom Legardier was older than he had supposed.
For Lunch they had ordered Lamb in Mint sauce; pureed sweet potatoes, and string beans. A decanter of Australian Burgundy wine was at their serving, and they both faced a chocolate mousse for dessert.
But the client was not interested in the food. Nor the touches of seafaring décor within the colonial pub. His blue eyes, deeply shadowed by wavy grey hair and wiry eyebrows, inspected his plate abstractly, the years etched clearly on his face.
"Mr. Legardiere..." he said in a Scandinavian accent "I hope I have not surprised you...Please?"
Thomas lifted the table napkin to his lips, shaking his head with a big smile, and he swallowed his mouthful. He then sipped his wine, chiefly to organize his thoughts. Normally, he would have relished his meal. Finally to be meeting the man who had placed bets with him for over twenty years - was a surprise, yes.
But this conversation defied all semblance of being normal. For one thing, they were in London. These days, everything was possible in stock trading. The mark of an American-style business model in London was to accept whoever came through the door carrying money...
For another, this man was only now revealing himself.
This...this *revelation*, this nearly took away his composure, almost. Thomas Legardier was not often lost for words. Yet his face was grey and somber,

wine still rich in his throat, and his mind finding it hard to process what he had just heard. He looked away suddenly and gestured for the passing waitress. "Coffee... here! Please?" His guest nodded absently. "Yes. For both of us..."

There was no way to quantify what the man had been saying. At first, Legardier had been enumerating all the compliance regulations that he could muster to achieve satisfactory guidance, that is, to advise his client's investment strategy. He was even thinking of the equities and their valuations...But suddenly, he was here in the weeds with this *information*..

The legality of what had just been disclosed - let alone the implications and exposure that he himself might have had with this client was potentially a huge liability. He cleared his throat.

"Naturally, this would have to be verified..." he began.

Seeing the despair on the man's face, he leaned in and asked "Have you not consulted with an attorney Mr. Debien?"

"No!"

"Because...Why? Err, you fear retribution...?"

"No. Because *He* may find out...You have no idea about his reach!" said his client.

"And this err..."*secret disclosure*"...you have known all these years...Is there *proof*?"

"Yes!" Debien dug into his pocket and pulled out a wad of folded papers.

Thomas looked at the handful of papers distastefully. These days, when an investor came to you with his intentions, he was flanked by a senior financial adviser, if not legal council carrying a heavy briefcase of indemnification papers; insurance certificates and financial guarantees with bank warrants. If the party was a women, then that briefcase usually had wheels and was wheeled into the office with two Assistants waiting outside to support her meeting.

Not this man. He was holding a wad of half folded papers...

Thomas looked at him, preparing to recite the protocols of conventions when he stopped. Mainly, he observed something.

It was the gleam in the man's eye, a glow of sincerity that came only with those men who lived free of the artifices of life – those unimpressed people who knew the cost of freedom in battle.

"What I am about to tell you is something that may have legacy issues today! It is important. You see, let me tell it to you my way, then you can examine the documents?"

Legardier nodded.

"Alpha had informed the Germans of Klein's assets. It bought him his liberation. He showed all the papers, including names, places of business, parties who received the precious cargo and metals, including their workshop locations..." He paused.

"Itemized were all signatories; transportation itierary arrangements, inventories, documents and invoices of receivables..."

"Go on!" said Thomas.

"Business ledgers that were a veritable *network* of sculptors, goldsmiths, artists, painters, distributors, bankers, engravers and accountants. Europe was trading in markets for works of art, precious gems, jewelry creations and fine arts of the era.." he looked up, his face drawn "You have no idea..."

Thomas knew from own father, recruited to serve in North Africa, a young man from Wales who worked well with his hands. He served in the RAF, outfitting aircraft that landed on airstrips before lifting off again to give approaching ships cover from beach batteries of the enemy. His father, the Welshman, had told him all about the war years.

"Those round-ups..." began Debien, "they had all the information...The round-up of the elect, those most skilled in crafts of rare and original creations...their those others..."
"...their client? Oh my God, their *clients*?" interrupted Thomas "that list must have included their names - all those who could afford to commission such works of art, those who had wealthy...Europe's finest fortunes...All listed?"
Deben nodded, words eluding him. He cleared his throat. "Alpha knew that one cargo was being shipped across the Atlantic. The estimated time of sailing from Halifax to New York was discovered..."
Legardier sipped again.
"With that intelligence, the Germans only had to wait for its appearing on the sea, and they sent U85 to do the job of sinking the vessel. The idea was for that asset not to be converted to aid in the war effort..."
Thomas sat back.
"What the Germans could not know was that Alpha had also informed the Americans about his intelligence. He exposed to the Allies information

about how the Germans intended to sink the shipment. In that way, an Allied ship was in waiting off Nova Scotia, and sank the German U85-boat.

"With both the Germans and the Allies focused on the vessel that carried the shipment of gold from the Klein family, all Alpha had to do was wait for the ship to arrive in New York.

"When it did, he hijacked the cargo and diverted it to his own hiding place. Nobody knows for sure where he hid it. Some say he deposited in into the Federal Bank of Bond and Building Trusts, having Deposits in downtown New York where he was seen opening a Safety Deposit Box. Others say it was deposited in another bank. One man claims he saw Alpha hide the shipment in the dead of night in a construction heist of some kind...I don't know. That is where that trail ends.

"Anyway, Alpha had wealth suddenly. And while he may well have had to hide in for a while, he reappeared in London as a Stock Broker making extraordinary stock market bets with money he claimed was his from the days of selling Railroad bonds...(He never sold bonds)

"I watched him over the years. At every opportunity in which he bet on stock options to accredit himself with success, I counter-betted, and more than once I thwarted his intentions...

"Alpha even betted against new commodities as Europe was reconstructing itself after the war! He then started investing in currencies like the English pound in order to artificially inflate their value before selling... I beat him at it every time! I should tell you that I tipped off the British about his wild betting schemes...

"Once, he got into trouble with the law, and he was cited for misrepresenting the value of commodities on the Stock Exchange. They threatened to pull his trading license!"

Legardier looked away. His own father was that way, – that is, if anyone remembered the Welsh these days...

He reached out to the take the wad of papers.

One, a sketch, was stained and pen-inked and badly folded with a corner torn away. He unrumpled it. Not ink, it was smudged by the charcoal stick of an expert draftsman. It was the image of a statue, a woman whose body was roundly positioned, her head forward, and her posture kneeling.

"A sketch...of his work" said the man across from him.

"Whose?"

"Arran Klien!"

Thomas inspected the signature at the bottom of the page. Entirely illegible, of course. But he inspected it closely, as if vaguely familiar. It was not the name of the sculptor, it was the name of the buyer, the man who commissioned the statue, as if signing off on the sketch in Approval. He thought he should recognize it.

Whose? It was signed with a fountain pen, the nib parting from pressure boldly descending followed by a flourishing stroke and two posts. Was is a D? Then a open *R* and repeating loops that finished with a long tailed slash. It eluded him.

"Whose signature is this? The Assayer?" he asked, raising his eyebrow as if making interested conversation.

"No!"

Another sip of wine. Thomas looked again.

The signature of a lover no doubt, thought Thomas. Unfinished as a sketch, a nude perhaps… to be made by the artist. Only a patron who saw grace and love in this sketch would commission such a work… Thomas was about to speak when he realized his guest was standing to leave.

"Follow those leads, and you'll find the truth in what I said."

Thomas put cash in the Restaurant *Livre* proffered by the waiter. He left paper money well in excess of any charge, and he caught the eye of the Maitre'D who understood to come and collect the payment.

Thomas turned to his guest. "And you would trust me with this?" "Have I not trusted you with millions?" said the man, hefting on his coat at the entrance hallway.

"You have!" said Thomas, hardly needing reminder of the vast sums that had been placed in his hands from this man's account. He put the wad of papers in the vest pocket of his coat.

"Where can I find you…now that we are acquainted?.." began Thomas.

His query went unanswered as they stepped outside into the rain.

"Look" said Thomas "I meant no disrespect. It's just that there are… government agencies for enquiries and claims of this nature…"

"You mean related to the War?" interrupted to the man.

Thomas looked at him from under the umbrella labelled USB. "I'm hardly qualified…It's *old* property. I'm not sure how to deal with this asset, in all honesty."

The man looked at him. "You'll find a way to keep it private!" And with that he turned and walked into the rain, joined others in the street crowd. Thomas Legardier almost lost sight of him.

"...But your sketch. I mean, it's personal and it belongs to you!" Thomas called out, touching his padded vest pocket.

The man heard him. Turning slowly he said "It belongs to the owner and to his heirs...Find them! Give them back what is theirs!"

"But how...*Who*...?"

The man stared at him. "You mean *Why?*"

The distance between them widened, as if unspoken such a question should be the *only* question. Of course there always beneficiaries for assets of value, like endowments, memorials, hospitals, charities, schools, third-world nations, scholarships - the list was endless of where the wealthy could feel atoned for their modern amassed wealth.

But no. This was an old collection with spiritual needs of justice and redemption. It had been stolen during the war...The family betrayed.

The silence stretching between them said it all, even as the rain poured on them and the crowds moved around them.

Why? Thomas Legardier was left standing there.

Because the past had a way of imposing its moral will upon the present.

* * *

Thomas never returned to his office that afternoon. The luncheon with his client Debien changed his mood. He wandered about the park, walked down to the river. He stopped for coffee from a pavilion to stay out of the rain. Then it became windy, and finally the sun came out. Truth was, he doubted that Debien was even his client's real name.

Beneath the grand old clock-tower of GMT in the evening, with the sun pulsing through the clouds, he peeked into the papers for the first time. Not the sketch - lest the wind add to its frail folds and worn crumpling. But he read the papers, the names, dates, times and years...

Suddenly the lights that twinkled in the city-dusk gleamed not as they had; nor the new architectural buildings stand so bright and hopeful. They stood sullen and quiet as if removed from reality.

That night, in his apartment, when Legardier opened the wad of papers, he reviewed the documents and recalled the long table conversation that he had had with his client.

He sat down. He stood up. He looked at the picture of his father on the mantle-piece. A young man in his uniform.

One by one, the documents showed what Debien was telling him. The papers unfolded stiffly. Page by page, explanation by explanation.

He was still reading the wad of papers late into the night.

The stories of WWII had paled, he concluded. Relegated to sanitized classrooms a history class, how could these realities be grasped? But here was a real case, the incident of an event that brought feeling into his soul. Or was it the way his client told it perhaps?

"Alpha" had been the man's friend. They had known each other for years.

The man, Arran Klein was Jewish, a distributor and maker of jewels and gemstones to goldsmiths all over Europe and North America. When the round-ups occurred in Frankfurt, Klein gave Alpha his papers, all his accounts, his source of mines and the minted gold serial numbers of all supply lines. He also gave Alpha his sketches - designs, drawings, sketches of jewelry for clients, commissions for work and the names of goldsmiths in manufacture...

Alpha, in those difficult days, no doubt hugged him with a parting brotherly vow to care for his interests and family.

It was instead, the kiss of Judas.

Alpha not only betrayed his friend and told the Germans about all the assets and networks, but fled to the United States where the Government was already knowledgeable about Klein's assets. All mining-sources of raw materials for precious metals and rare minerals in the Middle East were to be shipped to the Allies for security...

The cargo was to travel through the Middle East by train, and then through Russia. Vessels sailing from the seaport *Archangel* in Russia would ship it across the Atlantic to America.

This shipment, as Alpha knew, was destined for Halifax, Canada and would be re-routed to New York to the Federal Bank Repositories where the cargo would be documented and stored for safekeeping...

Why? Because the cargo contained gold. Much of it was a supply from the source mines. Yes. But more was added by the Russians as payment for supplies and arms from America to fight the war.

Thomas Legardier put down the document, he raised his scotch and sipped. Outside, the night was clear, a low moon casting window grills across his apartment floor. He proceeded.

The papers had been typed in small type, without spaces, the words of a man wanting to record everything... These pages, coupled with the conversation that he had with Debien explained the situation.

"That's when he became suspicious that someone was trailing him.

Once, he might have identified me, I'm not sure...

He closed his London business and retreated to New York to set up his own offices. The NYSE welcomed him with open arms..."

Thomas put down the papers.

Clearly, to cultivate trust, Debien made multiple bona fide investments using Legardier.

Thomas got up and poured himself another Scotch.

No question...Debien himself was a wealthy man.

Debien told him he surveilled Alpha.

Legardier thought about what Debien said.

Alpha had never came forward as a man holding vast amounts of capital. In fact, he remained remarkably quiet. With one exception. He had received for himself a broker's license to trade on the Stock Exchange Boards of Europe.

Later, Alpha traded as a broker in New York declaring for surety his hidden assets that were unrecorded.

He listed bullion bars with Serial Numbers. But never sufficient to raise alarm. And never more than one or two, with combinations of stamped serial numbers...Such was the need for verification only as it entered in bank ledgers. Only occasionally he produced a real bullion bar as guarantee. But never more than one.

Thomas stood over coffee-table that contained the wad of papers. All those years of watching Alpha trade as a respectable brokerage must have consumed Debien. In fact, as Thomas thought about the trades that Debien as his client had placed with him, they all reflected a sort of counter-bet against all that which Alpha had been betting on over the years.

Yes, it consumed him

Thomas sipped. So...had he been played by his client?

Legardier took his seat and thought about it.

Alpha continued operating undetected, evidently.

But for one event. Debien anonymously lodged a complaint with the authorities citing Alpha as a fraudulent agent who solicited clients and gave false misinformation. He had even advocated betting *against* a standard sovereign currency.

Alpha was put before the Ethics Board, but it came to nothing. Still, the accusation was sufficient to tarnish Alpha, and he was shunned. Bets against a standard banking currency were considered unpatriotic, in those days...

Perhaps that was when Alpha decided to leave the for America. He never applied to renew his broker's license.

That was the early 'Fifties, noted Legardier.

After Alpha moved to New York, he started a new brokerage firm and never returned to London. His New York interests flourished into a large investment bank.

"Have you the *proof*?" was the question that Thomas had asked during their lunch meeting.

Legardier thought about their lunch meeting. Why the sketch? Debien produced the sketch from his wad of papers.

Debien believed it was done by Arran Klein, the artist as a commission for work.

"His sketch for a work commissioned by an American. What else could he do?" Debien had said. "The American would have correspondence to match the sketch, perhaps reveal the identify and outcome..."

Legardier realized what he was implying. Not only would it reveal the identity of the American, but reveal to whom the shipments were being sent by the Klein family...

But in exposing the Klein family, Alpha would be incriminating himself...So he had to find a way to distance himself and retrieve the supply himself independently.

Legardier picked up the sketch. He pursed his lips, perhaps smiling inwardly at his observation for the ages...

Thieves and forgers; fakes and fraudulence were everywhere sown as tares in the wheat. But true creative works of artistry were as indelible and unique as DNA. You were born with it.

Folios from a Ledger that had been kept up for decades prior to the war with active accounts. The ledger listed orders for diamonds in quantities from the Diamond Mine owned by the Klein family since the Boer war of the previous century.

The Kline entity had mined the diamonds there for almost eighty years, producing diamonds for jewelry made at the hands of Jewelers all over Europe. The diamonds were cut and shaped into finely designed works by Klein and his associates. Those pieces, some of them sketched, were ornaments for some of world's finest women who wore them as broaches, bracelets. Some pieces had been crafted for the collections of crown jewels...All had one distinction. They came from one diamond mine. Those diamonds were cut and shaped because of their blue coloration...

As Debien had explained, the diamond mines were shut down. Debien had pointed to an aerial paragraph.

Thomas examined this carefully. Just as Debien had said: "Here is the Manifest, with the full letter that explains the transport delivery" .

Thomas read the reports. He followed the Bill of Lading shipment of cargo that belonged to the Kleins. They were delayed in St. Petersburg during their battle against the Germans.

"The shipment *never* made it to *Archangel* in time to cross the Atlantic?" Thomas noted.

"No. It was *not* included with the gold that Alpha had arranged. But he did not *know* that..."

Debien explained. "That shipment was crated in sacks of straw but *never* delivered. They were diamonds from the mine. The entire mine's stock taken from its supply chain..."

* * *

Chapter 4

New York

Karen McCullock wasn't given many privileges these days, not that she much minded since it allowed her to operate simply, quickly, and with the kind of efficiency that you could effect at law school or in private practice but never on government time.

One young African-American worked in the Front Office of the DA. Shy and quietly dressed, he spoke only about his mother when pressed about his family, and clearly it was she who had directed his career path.

But his diligence irritated the young girls in his office, especially those of activist inclination.

Assailed by their relentless teasing, it was Karen's interference and tasking assignments that sheltered him. He earned a reputation as someone whom she could trust with good work. This case file was prepared by him. It was a case from the Juvenile Offender's Office.

The Hearing Room was small, one window, unadorned with yellow painted walls. There was barely enough room for one desk; one seat for the Hearing Adjudicator, and two chairs for the offender and his parent.

Still, it was the paperwork that mattered, she knew, and she took her place as the Hearing Judge for the day.

The door opened suddenly and it was with utter consternation that she saw who walked in.

"Bill..." she said spontaneously, thinking this to be a drop-in visit. "What a surprise!... I was going to get back to you on Mrs Green's Probate Case..."

She stopped, the query of why he was here more prescient.

"Hello Karen" said Bill Wickowsky, setting down his brief case and pushing back into his wooden chair. "Meet my client Mark Ruttenberg."

Clearly *not* a Juvenile Case.

Karen looked at them blankly, all cooped up in this cubicle of an office in a Hearing Room; one man an investment banker trading billions every day, and the other his attorney from the most reputable and influence law firm in New York City. Suddenly, she felt diminished.

 She opened the file, and was about to switch on the video taping of the interview...

"Excuse me" said Bill "Is that necessary, I have here a sworn affidavit as to the events that led up to the sorry situation in which my client finds himself, and we will have satisfied all your questions...As you can see!" He put down a statement before her.

"Thank you... Bill" she managed to say, looking at the beautifully typed document submitted by the Attorney's Firm with gold embossed letterhead at the top of each page...

She looked up, remembering her training. "He is a deponent...and I do have some questions considering the levels of toxicity that were found on him at the time of the arrest..."

"Of course!" said Bill "And I've taken the liberty to write up the kinds of questions that you'd ask in any kind of interrogatory. So, as you can see, we'd done it all for you...complete with a full explanation. No need for subpoenas or further discovery... "

She looked at him and said nothing.

"What we'd like to do is to find a settlement of any amount. And as you can see, my client is remorseful beyond reason, and he will do any kind of public service by way of probation that you ask...But we are looking for all this business to be expunged from his record when this is over..."

Karen took a breath, closed the file and sat back. "I see you'd done all the work Bill..."

Bill paused, eyeing Karen. The tactic of pressure to resolve the matter was clearly not lost on Karen.

 "Excuse me" he said without contrition. "I've over-reacted on behalf of my client – a *very* busy man with clients and investments waiting for his return to work. I didn't mean to bargain prematurely... "

Bill looked down. He waited.

Karen turned to Mark. "Would *you* mind - in your words - telling me what happened, and explain the level of toxicity at the time of your arrest, Mr. Ruttenbuerg?"

The story was long and Bill clearly shifted uncomfortably in his seat as he client showed lapses of memory.

"It says in the Arresting Officer's Police Report that - and I quote – 'the party seemed unable to process my instructions, and when asked to take the test, he lunged down and aimed his head to my chest before collapsing...'"

 Karen peered over her reading glasses to Mark "Is this correct?"

Bill spoke. "There were mitigating circumstances under which my client lost consciousness..."

"The officer, it says here... 'drew his gun' and 'thought him violent before he realized that the perpetrator had collapsed'" read Karen.

"He fell to the ground..." answered Bill.

"Lucky he wasn't shot on the spot!" admonished Karen

Bill, who was glowering, took a breath, then glanced at his client whose face was a total blank.

"How many investors do you represent, Mr. Ruttenberg?" she asked.

"The Firm has hundreds of clients..." jumped in Bill.

"And in all likelihood, hundreds of millions in assets, if I'm not mistaken?" said Karen

She turned to Mark. "Young man, I can certainly understand the police officer's reaction to your behavior and health. Thank God *you* were so swiftly sent to the hospital for treatment by that officer. He might just have saved your life!"

They waited.

"But if you wish to keep your license... you're going to rehab."

Bill looked down.

Mark also looked down, nodding barely. Bill was about to speak. She held up her hand.

"Off the record, if I were an investor I think I would have shot you myself for such irresponsible behavior! You have an Ethics Board to answer to... a fiduciary responsibility, a License that certifies you at the Securities and Exchange Commission...You are held to a higher personal responsibility in handling the affairs of others. Do you understand that?"

"He does indeed!" said Bill, his tone conciliatory.

Bill smiled at her, pleadingly. "My client is most remorseful, and will do anything he can to make amends, including a three month suspension from the Firm's trading activities, allowing him full time to consider his foolishness. He can submit to counselling, upgrade his license credentials with continuing education. But he is an upstanding citizen, without any prior record to his name, and he has worked hard all through school to achieve his goals..."

Karen jotted notes, listened carefully.

Finally she looked up at Bill. "Your client clearly is in trouble, and does pose a danger as things stand. Amongst my recommendations, I shall ask that he receive rehabilitative treatment. In the meantime Bill, I'll review his words and consult with some advisers, and let you know."

She paused, closing the file and folding her hands over it. "However, there is one condition that your client must meet above all others. He must disclose the name of the drug provider..."

If she weren't mistaken, being in such close quarters all of them, Karen thought she detected a flinching on Bill's face, if not a shortened breath at her last words.

She signed off the videotape recorder, and she looked down at her folder. Had she justly executed her responsibilities, she wondered.

She knew that there would be consequences...

Obviously this was more than defending a client charged with illegal substance abuse. Bill was more concerned about shielding the Firm from possible implication.

Karen knew that Mark Ruttenberg was at best, collateral damage. Nothing more.

She sighed.

Salaman Brothers was no small adversary.

It could have been worse.

* * *

"Hello?..."

Thomas Legardier pitched forward in his seat, gripping the phone to his ear as if he could alter the state of transmission between the telephone lines. He waited.

Everything was digital wireless or cable. He imagined a snake-like Cable laying deep across the Atlantic sea-floor from the continent of the United States to Great Britain. Or a satellite monitoring communications in the heavens. Or captured wireless data encoded, decrypted and recoded as intelligence data on the frequency wave-lengths, this he all knew. Yet here he was, frustrated. How difficult did it have to be to make a telephone call from England to Washington DC....

He jumped. "Hello... yes. Thank you! My name is Thomas Legardier, calling for Mr. Goswold, please. I'm at the London Exchange, Desk 489 with items of enquiry..."

"Oh! Sorry. *ENQUIRY*. No, not delivery...Hello?"

He waited, his fingers white.

"Oh, yes! He is? Oh, I see....Of Course, I understand..."

He glanced at the time. "Yes. I'll hold...Yes. I am sorry to disturb, calling at this hour..." he nodded.

He searched the ceiling of his office for all the patience he could muster. It was two in the afternoon Eastern Standard Time. And it was *he* who was inconvenienced calling from Greenwich Mean Time at seven o'clock at night.

 He could almost hear her inaudible comment: Most American executives liked to have their work done by 11 a.m. Then lunch, followed by an early exit for a golf game or Away meeting.

"Yes. I am calling from London...Yes, hold? I can hold..."

He was about to end the call when a stern voice jumped on the line.

"Mr. Legardier! How good of you to call. I'm Harry MacIntire. I'm sorry for the delay. How can we assist you?"

Well, at least the Americans were awake!

Calls from the London Stock Exchange did not come often unless there was an issue about banking compliance. So it was a fair assumption that they took their jobs seriously.

Legardier explained. Just as matter of legacy verification. He cited the bank account deposit from 1948.

"I'll have the matter examined. Yes, I'm sure it's on the ledgers for just *after* the war. We had changed the systems of deposit by then. Of course, I'll look up the account number and let you know. Err... An American citizen you say?"

Legardier was impressed. At least they hired intelligent young men over there! MacIntyre would look at the two accounts that Debien had cited in his papers - deposits made by Alpha just after the war,

MacIntyre explained that Certificates of Deposit with the US Treasury would have matured in 30 years. Plus, other bank account deposits may have become archived data.

Legardier trusted his client Debien, and he believed him. But he had to be sure and verify the details.

* * *

New York

Amanda was in the car when she took the call. She was on her way south on *Interstate 95*, near Philadelphia where traffic could not have been heavier.

Truckers, on this overworked freeway, handling heavy hauling routes and did not appreciate downshifting gears of heavy diesel engines. They treated their rigs with the vigor of a Chevrolet after dark.

For Amanda, the stopping distance was the concern. No time to consult a traffic image on an iphone - much less take a call from New York. But Barbara it was, and Amanda pulled off the highway and returned the call.

"I have NO idea WHY they called me!" Barbara beleaguered, "Except that my affiliation with your Research Firm a few years ago was legendary, mebbe?..." she groaned. "Do you *remember*?"

"Of course I remember! We did great stuff, you and the staff..." Adding "We had a lot of fun doing it!"

"Yes" Amanda consulted her watch.

"Remember that awesome evening at the Kennedy Opera Center in Washington DC?" continued Barbara.

"Yes." A string of trucks roared past

"You are lucky to have such a wonderful family Amanda. Your son, well...he is *Soooo-good-looking* My God! What stardust did you put in his Wheaties as a kid...He is *awesome!*"

"Thank you Barbara. I'll tell him you said so!"

"So, *where* is he staying, did you tell me, was it last month? Not that I'm prying..."

"He's arriving in Miami for a Summer Internship with Salaman's Group Office down there..."

Barbara didn't answer.

"Barbara? ...Hello? You still here...?"

"Yes I'm still here. So, just this then honey, tell him to be careful. They have sun and beach and girls and scorpions down there at Miami. And I don't mean bugs. I mean humans..."

Amana rolled her eyes. Always the Jewish grandmother was Barbara.

"Oh, so I almost forgot why I called. Look, the Metropolitan Museum was trying to reach you and they got me instead from a third party attorney's office: They have received something in the mail related to the Statue that you have with them. It's an accompanying item that was mailed in, apparently."

"Oh? Any clues?"

"They do take their security very seriously. Some of their collections are out of this world. Especially when insured with a Deed of Gift etc. Plus, there is their reputation etc. You know all of that, right?"

"Right"

"No. Just that it seemed to me that they would say very little. They want us make an appointment and go see them...It's *something* that arrived, I don't know what..."

Amanda checked her watch: Two hours to go for Washington DC. Mercifully, she was flying back out of Reagan Airport.

She took a deep breath, put on her sunglasses, and with hair afire she stomped on the pedal and headed back out into the mainstream of traffic.

* * *

Washington DC

The US Treasury was a stunning building of the 19th century, positioned atop a rise that overlooked the Tidal Basin of the Nation's Capital. It gleamed in the sun as a granite monument, an emblematic shrine of lofty aspiration. Marked by stone risers and Corinthian columns upholding the plinth, displayed a frieze sculpture of people in motions of industry and diligence.

Here, all policy was framed. All monetary matters were itemized and catalogued. All budgets recorded in archived ledgers. All archives recorded. All legislative Acts and Executive Orders filed by its parameters.

The rest of the building was well-patrolled by police as a federal building, an iconic place photographed by tourists.

Within its working walls however, little other than administrative functions occurred. The real work of the United States Treasury was elsewhere conducted, and its treasure elsewhere hidden behind secured premises, deep repositories, bank vaults and safe storehouses.

Sam Rider loved the building, even as he drove past it every day on his way around the Tidal Basin to cross the Potomac river to his home in Arlington. His office was elsewhere in the city, and for some reason today, with the sun painting marble and granite monuments on still waters, his mind was elsewhere.

It was about a routine call that he received from New York. The SEC had received an enquiry from a

Broker at the London Exchange about an account that had been held as a US Deposit since WWII.

Not often did the SEC call anyone at the Treasury. Those ways of doing business were long past. But this was a little different, and he was concerned because of its ramifications.

Goswald told him that the account had been opened in NY at the Federal Building. The ledger showed a vast deposit of gold held over from Europe, for safekeeping.

When Rider heard those words, he groaned. Those old arrangements had been a pain to monitor over the years, and had been silenced by their retirement long ago. What the hell was this one doing being aired, and for what possible relevance?

"The problem is, Sir, that we have checked with Poors, and there is no risk associated with the account, nor even an Evaluation."

Anticipating the next step in this ridiculous procedure, Rider asked if there was any movement on the account.

"None Sir! No activity. No movement."

"No verifications?"

"None. Poors said there was no need, since no risk was ascribed to the account. It just was listed with a balance sheet total, and archived. Forgotten."

The room was quiet.

"So?.."

"So we've checked Sir. In tracking the original deposit, we find nothing in the vault ascribed to the account!"

"Well. You know that's impossible. If it were a bona fide account, then there was a bona fide deposit!" said his boss.

Both men stopped talking, considering the possibilities.

Rider spoke. "Well, there has to be an explanation or a note as to its movement. Surely?"

"Yes Sir. We've examined the point of deposit from several angles. The deposit was actually never made in hard cash. Or gold, I should say..."

"Gold, you say?"

"Yes. Sir. Gold and Diamonds - As it says in the ledger."

"Diamonds?"

Another pause.

Now Gosnold spoke. "As you know those items were usually stored in the Fed Buildings of New York City since they were close to the docks for incoming cargo, or by rail...You've checked all old venues for possible depositories..."

Rider, clearly as perplexed as Gosnold said "Whose asking, did you say?"

"The LSE. A broker says is client asked him to submit a claim on inventory deposited during that time..."

"Obviously, we'll have to do some more digging. Any serious exposure? I'm sure we'll come up with an explanation, right?"

There was no answer.

"Is there something?" asked Goswold

"Yes Sir. The account was active at one time. It was used and reused as collateral for several large trading transactions over the years..."

 "Yet we show no history or deposit of this account?" Rider added "Nobody *checked* to see if the asset was in the account...?"

"No. Err...It was a long time ago."

Both men knew that what the US Treasury valued as a world currency was, amongst other things, its credibility.

If so much as a penny fell astray, they were backed up with guarantees and insurance instruments without question. Not often had it occurred that money was tapped through short-circuits. Only on occasion of a national crisis, or for foreign aid, an outbreak of a war somewhere needing reserves and assurances for risk guarantees..."

"Ok" said Rider. "So, err...How *much* was this account exposed to as collateral?"

"Over the years, I'd say over 2.5 Billion US Dollars"

Rider stared. "And there was nothing in the account?"

"Nothing."

"Who opened the account?"

"It was opened by a party named Alpha. He is long dead of course..."

"We uphold the world's currency for God's sake.. " began Rider. "We keep ledgers, not anecdotal histories: Reorganizing the gold-standard after a world Depression took a monumental effort. And we can't find the archives?"

"Yes Sir."

Rider picked up the phone.

His source would pick up without much chatter. Rider spoke swiftly, knowing that back channels for intelligence, if not always legitimate in a court of law, were faster than a Law Firm on K Street.

 "Yes?" came the anticipated response.

"Oh Err..Hello! I'm with the US Department of Treasury. I need some FOI information..."

"Your name, and your OPM Title position, please?"

"Rider, Sam. Director of Special Accounts since October 2012. My SS is 454 475 6784. My DoB is 12/30 1948."

"Have you submitted an official FOI Form with your query details?" came the terse response.

"No. Just a first feeler..."

The phone remained silent, then a listener came on the phone. "Yes?"

"So, ok. It's about a shipment of gold sent from Europe during WWII."

It wasn't really, but Sam didn't know how else to compress the intelligence.

"That's outside the Freedom of Information Intelligence protocol. Tell me what you need to discover..."

Sam told him. "I need some forensic research on an Alpha from WWII. I'd like his legacy connections if any, especially any transactions of commerce..."

"Are you at this number?"

"Yes."

"I'll call you back in a couple...Your Request No. is 4750. Stand by."

* * *

It wasn't until they were back in New York that Trevor asked Amanda if he could review the messages sent by their son from Spain.

"Of course!" said Amanda, sitting at her desk. She pushed a button and printed up the emails.

"Why...Is there anything that alarms you?"

"No, just looking..." he said, reviewing the messages.

"The shopkeeper said that the last time he heard from the Artist, the Diamond Dealer was when he placed an order for gold material. It was a large order: The gold supply came from one of his Mines and normally shipped out of Casablanca. But it never arrived..."

"The shopkeeper said he had not heard from the Artist since the war..."

Trevor returned to his study with a frown.

By profession he was a banker, and over the years had witnessed the traits of human behavior responding to the knowledge of treasure. Men had killed for such a thirst.

He was somewhat disturbed that his son had been exposed to such intelligence.

Why was the shopkeeper talking so freely? Why reveal this to his son Tray, to someone whom he didn't know, or to someone so young, he wondered.

Perhaps the shopkeeper was divulging information for a reason. It didn't seem logical to provide details of that sort so openly. Tray's queries were of a general sort, merely an interest in the artistry of the statue.

But the Ledger Accounts?

Surely, that kind of information had been kept silent for years...

In the wrong hands, such knowledge might incite misdeeds by an assailant, even if misinformed.

Had the shopkeeper somehow put Tray in harm's way? Unless the shopkeeper had a reason for revealing all...

It worried him.

"Anything wrong...?" called out Amanda from her study.

"No. Nothing at all!" said Trevor, adding "...when did you say Tray was scheduling Miami for his summer internship at Salaman's?"

"Umm..." said Amanda, checking, and humming a tune as she did so.

Trever was anxious.

Was the shopkeeper reliable? Tray had just imaged his Leger with records, receipts and history. Was that a liability now?

Did they know too much?

Especially if any item was highly valuable. If so, what was it doing in a shop-window for all to see?

He thought about it.

How could he forget. Barely had they purchased the statue when they were assaulted...

This was not a shopkeeper without a history.

* * *

New York

Trevor's head was bowed over a certified letter that had been delivered to his door. It was a Summons.

He picked up the phone and consulted with his attorney. Next, he made calls to the UK.

He spent the day in his study, and Amanda had to bring him a sandwich for a meal. She wanted to stay, but she saw the expression on his face. He needed room.

Finally Trevor consulted with a Minister in Washington to discuss the reasons behind the Summons.

At the end of the day, a clearer picture began to emerge. A case had been filed against him in US Court of New York, reference a Claim filed against him on two different continents. The allegations were insurance fraud, theft and tax evasion.

Later in the quiet of the evening, as he told it to Amanda, Trevor explained.

A ship that was supposedly delivering a cargo of Gold to the United States during WWII as payment for supplies, had been declared as sunk. The claim was listed by the Admiralty.

Now the plaintiffs claimed the ship was not sunk at all. It had made its way to New York, they say. But the gold was not included in the ship's manifest.

"How in the world does that have anything to do with you?" asked Amanda, her soft blue eyes filled with the horror of such a world.

"My father's company issued a bond of insurance for a ship commissioned in 1942 by the Canadians. I am the surviving executive company heir. The loss of the cargo, being now in question, is subject to an investigation by the cargo carrier's insurer. My Firm is cited, and I am called to testify as to the accounts..."

"But that was years ago...surely?"

"It's a forensic case, certainly. But apparently a murder had taken place. As you know, once that is proven, there is no legal Statute of Limitations on murder investigations..."

Amanda raised her hand to her mouth, her face distraught. "So who is the company that's suing?..."

Trevor handed Amanda the Notice of the Summons. "Derek Salaman."

* * *

Trevor was keeping notes. He had the entire set of images sent to them by their son.
It had been a few days now since Tray had installed himself in the office of *Salaman & Salaman*, Miami. They got a message from him.
"Settled in. 'Pitifully spoiled as a young man testing the delights of Miami' --as Sophie my Office Manager puts it... "
So. No ramifications there...Thank God!
Nor had Sam called him... Uneventful.
Therefore that meant that only a third party must be doing the filings.
Still, later than night, Trevor reviewed the images quietly. Was there anything to worry about?
These images showed old ledgers on the books of the shopkeeper. Yet there was more here that troubled him.
Tray had been exposed to proprietary information by the shopkeeper. Why?
The old ledgers were sobering, listing vast quantities of raw materials. Such ledgers were usually locked up in the vaults of Europe. The facts before him were fragmented, and though he couldn't quite tell why, something about them was worrying, and he checked them off as a sequential list:
He started with the statue. Firstly, the sculpture had showed up at the shopkeeper's shop in a small straw crate arriving just after the war. The Spaniard held it in his shop, thinking the Dealer would come along for it...It was catalogued and listed.
Secondly, they had done business, these two families, since before the war – going back generations, possibly to the middle ages when Jewish artisans worked in Spain...

But of course the Artist didn't show up. The statue never left the shop. The elder shopkeeper and his wife had long ago died of course. That's how the statue remained in the shop for the son to inherit, along with all the rest of their stock an legacy...
 Further, in the 70s, tourism being the only trade of the region, the shopkeeper's son put up statue in his shop for sale...
Finally, and perhaps most significantly was one detail. Apparently, someone had already visited the shopkeeper, arriving just one week before his son Tray came. Someone called "Debien."
The shopkeeper who knew the parents...long ago. Yes. Yes. They did business together...

No. He didn't like it at all.

* * *

Morning sunlight filled the apartment.

Amanda folded back the shutters and wedged open their building windows of the 35th floor. From their vantage point, they could view a river emerging from pre-dawn mists and wheeling birds. She brought out their breakfast tray and laid it on the white damask tablecloth of the dinning room, English style.

Trevor opened a newspaper, delivered daily to his door, and together they sat for breakfast.

In fact, Amanda had earlier peeked into her email, and she told Trevor that she had received an email from Jacques de Torraine.

Trevor looked up from his paper with interest. "Oh yes?"

"He said its entirely authentic, and he'll be sending us a Provenance Report."

"Well Done! How much does he say we should insure it for?"

"That depends on who owned it..." grinned Amanda facetiously. "And I'm not telling...*yet*."

"Umm" he said, amused at her non-salutary remark of intrigue.

 She picked up the tray and returned from the kitchen with a wooden spoon and a pitcher to ladle water for her house-plants.

"Meantime... the Museum is preparing the statue for Auction. Are you sure you're ok with that?"

"Absolutely. It was your call, and we discussed this carefully. So go ahead, I'm still onboard for you all the way..."

"Really?..." asked Amanda, holding up her witches' wooden spoon. As in...my... latest Museum *Donor*?"

He peered up, his eyes following her waving wooden spoon "Err...is that a threat?"

She dissolved into laughter.
He reached for her waist-line and pulling her closer.
"As in your *Forever* Fan!"
She kissed him. Then added "So, Jacques says he has been unable to locate the shopkeeper in Spain for more information about the statue for the Auction, like what year it was made etc... Apparently, the shop may be going out of business."
Her eyes clouded for an instant.
"Jacques says the local police fear he may have come to harm...Its unknown."

* * *

The Inspector Superintendent from New Scotland Yard was informed that the body had been found by the Hotel Housekeeper.

Debien was dead.

 A stockbroker, Thomas Legardier told him, when they found his card.

Days later, Legardier called the Superintendent for an update. The answer was simple. According to the forensic coroner, the subject died of a heart attack. This being a natural cause of death, and without suspicion of any irregularity, a report was filed and the case was officially closed. His family were to make all necessary arrangements...

"May I have their name? I mean, I'd like to send my condolences to the Funeral..."

"Of course!" said the Superintendent.

Thomas was informed that all mail was to be delivered to his house through a Forwarding Agent.

"Is there anything else you wish to add in the way of information Sir?" asked the Superintendent.

"No. Not at all. He was my client. It's just that I had some fresh information I wanted to give him!"

"Perhaps you could pass it along to his Forwarding Agent. If that's a suggestion that helps...."

"Yes Sir. Thank you! Perhaps I should. Again, thank you!"

"*Regarding you query...*" began the letter he held in his hand with the seal of the US Treasury, Office of Special Accounts. Thomas would have liked Debien to know about it.

He pulled out the file of papers that Debien had given him.

Regardless.

There was work to do, he decided. He had made a promise - as if needing to find redemption for his own life. He wanted to pursue the matter as a debt of honor. After all, Debien had made him a rich man on a number of occasions...

He made his own list of Notes.

Debien's father was a man called Arran Klein who had been betrayed by a partner, Alpha, a man whom he trusted.

Question: Known only as Alpha, his true identify remained a mystery.

Second: Alpha acquired wealth shortly after the war.

Third: He traded it through a stock brokering agency, (even as Debien thwarted the gaming and betting he made over the years.)

Fourth: Debien had his own wealth, which over the years, Thomas had invested for him in trades on the stock market. And they had profited handsomely.

Debien told Legardier about Alpha. *Why?*

Alpha supposedly deposited an asset into a bank in New York following WWII. This was part of a shipment sent to the United States from Europe for safekeeping...

Alpha went to New York.

That asset was used as collateral and basis for much of the wealth that Alpha had traded upon.

Thomas discovered from the SEC that in fact the assets in the account were not there.

What was Alphas's legacy.

There was only one lead, a widow who claimed her husband knew Alpha.

Chapter 5

Trevor was worried.

His attorney called and told him the Second Circuit Court of Appeals had received a case regarding Admiralty Law. The New York State-Federal Judicial Council was asking for explanations regarding a claim filed against him. They needed to make a recommendation as to territorial issues, and possible revision of venue provisions. A meeting was scheduled downtown.

In the report, the claim before them contained a copy of a ship's manifest. The ship, which his company had insured at the time of its sinking following the war, was claimed as a Loss to its Cargo carrier.

In addition to the ship's manifest, there was one item on that list that appeared to show evidence of alleged foul play and fraud.

Both the manifest and the item was cited and attached by a widow in her Last Will and Testament now being deposed by the Orphans Probate Court of New York. Because of those circumstances, they had deferred the matter to the District Attorney for a decision about what to do.

"How does an Orphan's Court Probate case get to be the target of a filing against my company?" asked Trevor.

"More like, how did the Prosecution even get to *know* about the Orphan's case and find a relationship with you?"

"I have no idea."

"Or why?"

"I have no idea."

"Or even, why now...?" said his attorney. "Ok. You have no idea. But think hard, is there any reason that anyone finds it necessary to prosecute at this time? This is a case without a statute of limitations, remember. By tying it to a murder, the allegations are quite serious..."

"Sorry Paul. I'm honestly baffled. I will check all my records, documents and see if anything refers to anything...Maybe a link or something?"

"Or a Leak!"

"How do you mean?" asked Trevor.

"Any business transactions? Any development that is new that might have provoked or motivated something else?

"No." said Trevor.

"O.k. So, when you testify, just speak the truth, and tell them what you know... Got it? If you've nothing to hide, there is nothing to be afraid of. This is just some questions."

Trevor and his attorney arrived armed with all the documentation needed to show the full claim and report. The Sinking Report. The Loss of Cargo and Ship's Manifest. The Cause for the Claim. All was in order for its time.

Finally, they offered the name of his Firm's councilors offices in London to verify and cooperate with any further enquiries.

The Council seemed satisfied and thanked them for their cooperation.

But as they left Paul turned to Trevor. "They seemed as puzzled as we are. That means nobody knows what's coming..." They walked. "I'm a little concerned" said Paul.

Before parting he added "And err...better speak to your government since you're on US soil. Just in case you need them! At least be prepared for anything..."

Later that night, Trevor and Amanda had drinks at a rooftop café. He explained the events of the day.

"The ship... had indeed been sunk after leaving the port of New York on the 12th of June, 1942. The case was cold." His eyes looked down into his drink, his thoughts far away. "A sad and desperate time it must have been..."

Amanda squeezed his fingers.

"I can't imagine what ties that to the District Attorney case from the Orphan's court managed by Karen McCullock" said Trevor.

Amanda looked out across the traffic and pedestrians that filled the streets of a busy city, so many interests and so many histories. She had an uneasy feeling.

"I'll call Karen McCullock tomorrow. She may not talk to me, or she may find the case too proprietary to discuss...But I'll ask her if she knows of any connection."

* * *

"The thing is.." said Amanda when she called Karen "we're trying to find out the facts."

"I understand" said Karen. "I cannot speak to your case. Nor do I know if there is any connection. But in her Deposition, the widow in question claims that a ship was docked in NY. In fact, it alludes to the fact that the ship was carrying precious cargo, and that it was unloaded illegally. Her husband, she claims, was made to hide the precious cargo for a week before he disappeared."

"Is the case open to the public...Do you have attorney's with exclusive proprietary access to this information? If so, who?" insisted Amanda.

"No. Well. It *is* public, or rather *will* be in the public record when we've decided the finding. So far, it's still closed - not open to the public yet. But remember, this is Public Defender's Office. I have attorney's in here all the time...Why?"

Amanda paused. "I'm not sure. It may have triggered a case against my husband's company. I'm just doing some homework. But thank you Karen, you've been helpful. And I don't want to take up another minute of your time." Then she added, "I'll take the normal channels of enquiry in the future. It may all be just be coincidence. That's all... No worries."

Amanda told Trevor this.

"That's the most incredible thing I've ever heard!" he said. "It would have been so much easier on us all - the ship's owners, the insurers, the governments and the Trustees involved had we known the cargo was not onboard when the ship sank!"

"Why?" asked Amanda, still incredulous.

Clearly, someone in Karen's office had an opportunity to file a case against Trevor's Firm. Somebody holding judiciary privileges. And someone with something to defend...

* * *

Thomas Johnathan Legardier II was standing in his dark suit and clearly overdressed for May. He was hot, sweating profusely in the heat of New York City. He examined the tourist brochure, briefcase in hand, and he stared at the painter's drop-cloth on the ground; the trestle and workbenches. Two men were making preparations for the museum exhibit. Or so he was told by a woman in the Administrative office.

A security officer approached him and asked if he needed help. No, he was fine he said.

A large delivery van pulled up, the rear opening up, and workmen hauled out a covered rig. They unraveled the packaging and deployed the apparatus to become a Visitor's Security Guard rail. They affixed it to support posts and placed it around a large perimeter.

Thomas drifted into the Library Museum of Downtown, one of the oldest and most venerated buildings of the metropolis. He read its history. Through two centuries of American enterprise, this building had housed memorabilia from the eclectic to the very ordinary - owned and variously donated by affluent celebrities and industrialists, including works of art, portraits, inventions, rare-earth gems, relics and statuary from far-away castles famously displayed at 19th century World Fair.

Neither this Library nor the Museum were struggling for funds, as were most Exhibitions of the non-profit world. No. This was a staid and traditional museum, even as other Collections were falling into disuse and neglect for the lack of interest.

Thomas made up his mind. He would make a generous contribution when he returned to London, and he would want to be kept on the list of contributing membership. He hadn't been to New York since he was a boy.

He remembered that occasion. His father was delivering Railroad Bonds to a bank as a courier from Europe, and he brought with him his wife and son for the vacation. Thomas remembered it as one of the highlights of his youth. His mother, he recalled, was enchanted with it all, his father pleased to show them the sights. All but this one, evidently. He knew it from general literature and tourism, but never had he visited the Library Museum of New York.

This was it. He had promised his father to follow through...

"Excuse me!..." he called out after the Administrative assistant, now at the end of the great hallway by the elevators.

"How can I help you?" she asked, politely.

"It's this event in the brochure - the display you are preparing over there?..."

"Yes."

"The statue of the *Kneeling Woman*...Is that exhibit opening *this* weekend?"

"It is. As the brochure says, she will be on display for a month, then she goes on a travelling tour across the country. She was commissioned during WWII."

"Yes! I...err... am familiar with it."

"Oh, please excuse me! Are *you* here to represent the agent's insurance coverage documentation for the display? I'm expecting him..."

"No. No. Just... an interested visitor in New York on other business, that's all."

The woman smiled.

"Here is my card" he said. "I'd like to make a contribution to the Museum. Can I call on your Development Gift office?"

"Thank you Mr... Legardier" she said, reading the card, "Yes, the *Kneeling Woman* was donated by a Mrs. Trevor McDonnell. That's on the plaque, when the workmen mount it..."

Thomas shook her hand. "Is there a way I can reach the donor's representative?"

The woman regarded him closely. "Yes. I have their office information. Ms Barbara Riggetti is their Manager there... We know her well around this museum. She's always a great help!"

She wrote the name and number down on the back of Thomas' brochure. "Do please call them!"

"Thank you!" said Thomas.

He must have sat outside in the park staring at the building for a good two hours. There was a breeze as newly budded leaves danced in the sunshine of Central Park, a few dogwood and cherry blossom trees peeping through the fauna...

He had to wonder. As to the statue shown in the brochure, of course he had seen it before! It was that of the sketch. The sketch contained in Debien's wad of papers. No question. This was a commission for work - drawn by the artist, approved by the signature of the buyer...

This statue was that executed work of art!

But who was the artist? And how did Debien have it? He made his decision. He had come to the New York to meet some colleagues and traders working on

Wall Street. Since his father's death, he made his task to become completely familiar with the dossier, as promised. Besides, he had other reasons for being in New York. It was his responsibility to continue the family brokerage. And this he would do.

Meantime, he was meeting with the US Federal Bank. He still had questions about a man named Alpha. Following his request for more information, the Fed had replied that they found nothing.

Debien, his client, had asked him to investigate. Even if he was now diseased.

The thing was, he felt Thomas Johnathan felt he was close to something. So he arranged for a meeting.

If the account that Alpha had opened was without funds, as the Fed asserted...then Debien was right.

Further, if Debien was right, his papers might additionally authenticate the artist who drew and made the sculpture. Even... who commissioned the sculpture!

Most importantly of all, he might shed light on a situation for the Fed. He might actually be able to identify Alpha by name.

And his sons...if he had legacy. That too...

Still, this museum captured his imagination. He would definitely make contact with the Administrator of the Donor, he decided. Even if to discover more about the statue...

* * *

Amanda was in a cab crossing the city when she took her call from Barbara.

"Say that *again*?" she piped into her cell.

Barbara, who could be terse at the best of times - let alone when one was crossing the city, was fading in and out of good reception.

"That's what I told him.... To visit the District Attorney's office with any information that might be useful to identify the man known as Alpha..."

"*Who*?" asked Amanda, baffled.

Traffic was loud. "You got that?" screamed Barbara.

"Yes!" managed Amanda, lurching forward with the driver to a full halt. An infant in a perambulator had just bounced onto the crosswalk, being pushed by a very pregnant mother as if testing the traffic with her child's life.

"She called me..." said Amanda. "I'm on my way into her office now..."

"Who...?"

"Karen McCullock!"

The wait in the lobby was welcome. It took ten minutes to recover from the city swirl of noise and aggressive driving. Amanda pulled her thoughts together.

Only two days ago she and Trevor been in here to talk with the New York State-Federal Judicial Council asking for explanations regarding a claim filed against him.

Today, Kare was meeting with the District Attorney about a Deposition and Testament of a woman claiming foul play in the death of her husband...

And, she got a call from a London stockbroker visiting the Library Museum who recognized the statue going on display for the Fundraising Gala.

As he explained, the Library Museum Director had informed him of the donor of the Statue. That was Amanda Wells. Barbara was listed as her Administration Officer.

Evidently, that was what Barbara was trying to tell her in the cab.

Amanda's thoughts were interrupted. "You can come in now!" said the clerk of the DA's office.

Karen McCullock invited her to take a seat in the lounge seating area of her office and offered coffee. They chatted.

As Karen explained it to Amanda, a Mr. Thomas Legardier was here in New York and had gone to see the exhibit preparations being made at the Museum. "It's a lovely piece" said Karen, smiling "Where did you find it?"

"A long story!" grinned Amanda. "I'll wait till you're not on government time to tell the tale!"

Karen smiled. She returned to the subject of Thomas Legardier.

"He was here to talk to the Fed on other related business for a client. That is, the Federal Reserve Bank and their offices at the Security and Exchange Commission. As you know, they oversee compliance regulation for trading on the New York Stock Exchange. They were asked to examine the collateral reserves backing financial exposure used to underwrite large investments...Sell bonds, stocks, raise capital by this man. But when he saw the statue, evidently, he recognized it as something his client told him before he died..."

"Here's the copy of a sketch. He says the Statue was commissioned by someone in the United States. He had the Ledger Page copy showing the down payment. It gives me probable cause to inspect and examine further..."

Amanda blushed, her hand rising to her mouth. Not only did she gasp at the sketch of her statue, but the had actually seen the Ledge Page showng the down payment! Tray had imaged it when in Spain and sent it to them. It was in Trevor's office.

"I don't understand the connection" said Amanda apologetically. "As you know, my husband is being cited in a case of claim fraud. And yes, I am the owner of the statue. But I still can't connect the dots..."

Karen took her place at her desk to consult some files. "The Fed's sent him here to me because Legardier's client claims, or claimed, that he knew the man who operated in stolen goods, spying, sabotage, profiteering and murder during the war."

Amanda looked at Karen.

"Legardier said he couldn't divulge all the details, since he had to talk to the UK Authorities about it. But that he had information about the man's identity known as Alpha..."

"How?"

"He says he has corroborating evidence from a client who claims he knew him. It parallel's that of the statue's identity."

Karen paused. "But more importantly, the Fed informed me that it was this man who had a bank box which he had opened in 1942. He asserted he held assets as security and collateral in this account. In the box was nothing but a few personal

mementos, including a locket with an image of his mother, and encased hair locks of his hair at birth. The contents of the bank box have remained untouched and preserved for over seventy years...His hair locks sample survives."
"But surely, the parties would have all died by now?"
"Yes. But today we have DNA. It might trace familial signatures into the *next* generation..."
"Is that admissible as a procedure?"
"That's why I called you in Amanda. I need your permission to use the data related to the statue to further our investigation."
"Why?"
"Because if there's a forensic connection to a second generation - who might not even have yet been born – then we can trace the perpetrator! The identity of the original perpetrator might be discovered, and his story revealed. His whereabouts, his movements, his addresses at the time might be of relevant to a case I'm dealing with. It is allegedly related to assertions made about Mr. Greene's alleged murder..."
Amanda was appalled. "A *murder*?"
"Well. As in all cold cases, nothing can be certain until it is proved beyond a doubt. We do have an obligation to make every effort to identify a murderer. Again, as you well know, there is no statute of limitations to crimes of murder..."
Amanda looked down, wondering what a crazy, unsettled and terrifying world it must have been during the war. Still, finger-pointing was not her favorite pastime. Even if it related to her statue.
"You're hesitating...?"

"I am. I'd like to think that we've come a long way since the era of war-time Quisling and finger-pointing for the police!"
Karen looked down, almost embarrassed. "Accountability" she said quietly. "I'm sorry. But yes. It's a world that cannot forget the crimes of the past...no matter how distant, dark or forgotten. That's what distinguishes us as *survivors* of wars."
Amanda paused. She took a deep breath. It seemed so very sad. Time, if laced with foul play, could leave no evil deed without redress. There were no good options here, she knew.
"I understand" she said finally. "Here, let me take the Permission Form. I'd like to discuss this with Trevor if I may? I'll be in touch shortly...."
She was almost out the door. "Just to be sure, are you saying that evidence from old hair samples, those baby locks of hair ... provide inherited DNA tracings into the next generation of family relations...and can identify the name of the original perpetrator?"
"Yes."
Amanda looked at her.
"Technology can!" said Karen, closing the file.

* * *

Bill Wickowsky set down his brief case and pushed back into his chair at the conference table. A suited young man followed him in and took a seat beside him.

They were at the top floor of the building for a scheduled management and sub-agency performance update.

Roberto Fernandez CFO of the Firm sat at one end of the table, Derek Salaman at the other end for 'just a sit-in' as he put it.

"My associate Mark Ruttenberg..." said Bill as introductions came around.

Following the presentation of facts, figures and charts showing excellent performance for the month, the CFO offered a few words of thanks and congratulations, and the plasma screen went dark. With few questions proffered, and only general chatting there was little new business to discuss, and the meeting was concluded.

Derek Salaman stood, then looked over at Bill as the meeting ended

 "We're on our way out to lunch. Care to join us?" He was smiling.

For the CEO of the Firm to be inviting someone to join him and his party of executives to lunch was an privilege.

"Yes Sir. Thank you!" grinned Bill Wickowsky. Mark went down with an elevator the others.

They entered the next elevator and Derek turned to him and said "Your young man, Mark Ruttenberg...he's learned his lessons of sobriety by now, yes?"

"Absolutely Sir! He's been quite penitent, doing dogs work around the offices. Actually, we'd agreed to have a quick lunch together and review his re-instatement as a Broker for the Firm. He has a good business sense. Many of those accounts were his…"

"Good!" hailed Derek. "Tell him *Welcome Back* from me…"

"Yes Sir."

The elevator doors opened, and in fact Bill spotted Mark Ruttenberg across the Lobby in the seating area, waiting.

"We need a good Trader back on our floor!" said Derek Salaman "I'd like to see him in our Miami Offices!"

Two men flanked him and drew him quickly away with the others to enter a waiting limousine outside the building.

The glass doors that blocked out city sounds closed behind him and left Bill standing alone without knowledge as to the venue of any luncheon.

Bill swiveled and walked across the great Foyer. Clearly, he was left to fend for Mark.

He was hot.

"You're on again… But in Miami" he said sharply.

Mark looked both puzzled and elated.

Bill snorted angrily, words brimming from his mouth that might have otherwise remained sealed.

"And…I doubt that's the last of the favors you'll be asked to do for the Firm!"

Then he paused and eyed Mark carefully, realizing that Mark had arrived at his predicament not without coincidence: There was more in stall for Mark, he felt sure. And he didn't want to know what…

"*Come on!*" he said grudgingly. "Let's have lunch!"

Mark had just been discharged of all penalties following his arrest for illegal possession of substance abuse. Now he was being reinstated to trade as a Licensed Stock Broker? He was being kept on at a Firm when a hundred more qualified and unblemished candidates stood in line for his position...

Why?

Clearly, Mark Ruttenberg owed the Firm a debt of gratitude for his release, and for his reinstatement as a Trader...

No mistake. There was a reason for his re-instatement, Bill felt certain.

No. He definitely didn't want to know what Mark would be expected to do in Miami for the Salaman Firm of Stockbrokers.

Thank God!

* * *

Philadelphia, Pa

Derek sat at the podium of a media center in one of Philadelphia's newest buildings. For an historic city this was a remarkable accomplishment.

At 1,121ft height and a cost of $1.2 billion, the 60-story structure in Center City was designed to be one of the tallest buildings in the country. State-of-the-art innovation at the Comcast and Technology Center was the global headquarters for the corporation's satellite and communication businesses.

Top floors were dedicated to Hotel accommodations for visitors. Plaza functions that spanned the entire 1800 block of the old city's Arch Street.

From his seat at the 35th floor, Derek Salaman could see across the Delaware River, known to have spirited George Washington and his colonial army across the river to defeat the Crown.

Then, barely a remote trading outpost for tobacco and fur-trading ships, the old town of Philadelphia was where Founding Fathers, their hearts in trepidation, framed the constitution of a new nation. Since then, tourists flooded into the iconic city. Here, young families walked on cobbled-streets and viewed colonial structures held fast by morticed and tenon beams built at the hands of masons, carpenters and planters.

Derek Salaman smiled. Not quite the building of Miami, but just as gratifying. Especially since his company had brokered the deal that resolved incursions against his mega-corporation by a number of fractured entities willing to unite and compete for the core workings of his global company. Not only had he brokered the deal, enjoying fees in the millions of dollars, but he had for himself attained a seat on its board of Directors. This would give them a long and sweeping reach into the field of communications. That was after all, the plan. The plan of his brother, at least. And he had followed instructions.

"I can't tell you how proud the Firm of Salaman & Salaman is to be a part of this deal. Frankly, gentlemen, it's a winner. Here's to all of you for making it happen! Well Done..."

They stood up to applaud.

Philadelphia was charming, indeed. But replete with moral overtones that made him uncomfortable. From daytime meetings to nightime entertainment and especially gaming options.

No so in Miami, thank God!

Business concluded, they had lunch at the newest and finest Restaurant at the upper levels of the building where the view stretched clear across the state of New Jersey and into the Delaware Bay. They toasted their deal with Champaign and a couple of speeches. With all business complete, Derek Salaman stood.

It was indeed the Acquisition of a lifetime. It might even be ... they were told, large enough of a stake to solicit review by the Federal Commission of Communications. But he felt confident that his attorneys would fulfil all compliance requirements, easily. More importantly, profits for stockholders would thrill Wall Street.

Sitting now in the back of a limousine that would take him to his Jet at the Airport, he felt relieved.

Outside he now saw the real city that had survived the ages of American development, much of it sadly in disrepair and need of rehabilitation.

Still, the business world needed a satellite communication network with this kind of reach. They could only imagine its potential, soliciting new Internet, communications and broadcast to sway consumers and increase revenue, but more importantly, influence a population.

Yes, he decided. His brother would be pleased. Two years in... and then they'd refinance their way out of their exposure to all that financial risk. Someone would be begging to take it over. It was a win-win proposition all around. Especially for Sam, his brother.

He took his seat in his jet and accepted a drink from the steward.

That's all he needed. After that, it was a question of which political candidate to finance. Someone with the ability to shape the landscape for his interests, and create havoc for the rest of the markets. His influence would be unstoppable, his aims clear, and his ambition unlimited.

The politician now on the ballot aimed to win the next election was against this merger. He had run on a campaign to alert voters and post advertisements to get himself re-elected.

Ha!

Yes. He would have to be taken down. Sam had warned Derek countless times. *Family interests came first and at any cost, ethics be damned!*

God, thought Derek, Sam had dogged him all his life, as had his father. Somehow, Derek was not entirely sure, but his brother and father were certain that money should be made free of regulation. His father, he knew, was a survivor...

His father's defections were made public after the war; his "profiteering" as they were called it then, was   cited in the newspapers in London. His license to trade on the stock exchange was revoked. Especially after he had bet against the English pound sterling. It fell in value as a result, and he made had made his fortune on it. But he was exiled from the European Exchange and forced to start again. He did. First in Canada, then in New York, until his death.

Now his two sons had taken over the Firm. Sam was committed to block bureaucracy and governance that probed or guided investors away from certain traders and into the arms of others...

That's what all this deal was about. But for Sam there was now one thorn in his side. A name from unsuspecting quarters that, if left unchecked, might unearth some old stuff against their father.

Never mind all that, thought Derek. It was all over, his job done. Sam told him that he had made special arrangements. In Miami, of all places....

"Your flight Mr. Salaman ..." said the steward. "We are taking off now Sir!"

* * *

"You'll never guess what he told me" said Barbara.

"What?" Amanda swallowed her hot coffee and sat back in her seat. She listened on her cell phone.

"He told me he wanted *your* information from the Museum when he saw the exhibit. What he got...instead, was me! Since I know you're running around with Trevor these days, I asked him to disclose his business with you..."

Amanda rolled her eyes. How many people, she wondered, put up with a Jewish grandmother for a best friend.   Barbara was her former personal secretary, if not her office manager when they worked together professionally. Barbara had privileges that nobody else could have. Fielding calls was one of them.

"Well..." began Barbara

Amanda waited. Barbara took her time. There was something about the call that made Amanda listen a little more carefully. "Barbara?.."

"Yes. I'm here. Actually, perhaps you should see something he gave me. He left if for you and wants to get in touch with you...I'm not sure...well... what I mean is, I don't quite know what to make of this ?"

"What did he say?"

"He said his client gave him information that related to the statue he saw, or rather, he thinks it's related to his client's business...He's not sure."

"What information?" said Amanda, still sipping her coffee.

"I'll deliver it to you!" said Barbara, her voice decisive.

Amanda knew better than to push. There were quirks with some people, and then there were underlying reasons. Barbara certainly came under the category of both. But she was not stupid. She was an extremely perceptive individual, that was what had made her such an excellent Associate over the years...

"I'll be over in the morning" she declared, and hung up.

Amanda had to smile.

Never lost her edge...

Barbara showed up at the door of the apartment. She wearing an Umbro scarf wrapped around her neck and a black leather miner's hat perched over her brow.

Amanda laughed. "Come in before they arrest me for entertaining a Radical Fringe Element!"

"Damned right!" chuckled Barbara.

Amanda had coffee set up. They sat in the Study. Trevor was out with the dogs.

Truth was, there were few people who could be trusted more than Barbara with private information. Intelligence of a sensitive nature had often been the case when they worked together in Washington DC as a Research Team.

"I wrote it all down..." said Barbara. "He made me meet him at a Café – not far from the Museum. He wanted to explain himself, he said..."

"I'm not sure I follow..." said Amanda "This was a man visiting the museum...and seeing the statue, asked the Museum who the donor was?"

"Yes"

"So...err, why on earth couldn't he just make a donation to the Museum directly, if he so liked the statue?"

"Because it's not about making a donation. Nor about the donor of the statue, really. It's about the story that went with it. He recognized it as the same as a sketch he had in his possession. But he's uncertain..."

"Who exactly was this man?" asked Amanda.

"He is the son of a London stockbroker who managed the affairs of a German client with a past..." she paused. Adding "he says the client met with his father and gave him the story of a fortune that might well have included the statue in its portfolio..."

"And his father is?" interrupted Amanda, expecting the name and address of a licensed brokerage firm.

"Dead" Barbara, nervous, hiding behind her cup of coffee now raised to her lips.

"Ok" said Amanda, sitting back. Barbara would need to be given a chance to explain in her own way.

"Well..." said Barbara, pulling from her bag several sheets of typed notes.

"The man who spoke with me was Tim Legardier, son of Thomas Legardier, a London Financial Broker. Tim now runs his father's Brokerage firm."

"Apparently, the German client was only known as "D" to his father, Thomas Legardier. But they met once. His name is Debien."

Over the years, Debien gave his father a lot of business. Mainly from Frankfurt. He evidently had lots of money to invest on the London Exchange."

Amanda listened.

"Then when Debien came to London to meet with Tim's father, he disclosed details about a theft following WWII, and he asked Tim's father to look into the matter and rectify a wrongdoing."

"What kind of offense?"

"An egregious one. It was theft of his father's assets by his partner... His partner was known as "Alpha" back-in-the-day."
Amanda put down her coffee. "A war crime?"
"Tim said that when Debien met with his father, he explained that Debien was his mother's name which he adopted after the war. His true name was Klein. Klein's father, before the war, was a known goldsmith in Europe. He had a partner..."
"Klein and Alpha were close friends before the war. Then Klein went missing, and his son - as *Debien* - pursued a lifelong quest to find answers...
Debien asserted that his father's assets included treasure and arts which Alpha had stolen, used in exchange for his own life, then plundered after the war."
"The statue was one of the assets?"
"Yes"
"How is that possible?" asked Amanda. "Can it be verified?"
"Tim's father did make some enquiries. But Debien was soon after found dead. Then Tim's father had a fatal heart attack."
Amanda gave Barbara a look of query. Coincidence was not a word they ever felt comfortable with.
 "So. Tim Legardier is doing this on his own, flying blind if you will...He's onto to something, he thinks. The statue triggered a link to his enquiry...."
Amanda gave Barbara a questioning look.
"I swear. I didn't say a word to encourage him!"
"Hmm..."
Woof, woof, woof came with rattling and excitement.
"Hello!" belted a voice from the lobby. "Its me..." said Trevor, returning from his excursion with the dogs.

Adding "Hello Barbara, Hello-Hello. How've you been?" He proffered a big hug.

"I'm doing good Trevor. Thanks for asking..."

"Coffee?" asked Amanda.

Trevor nodded. "Please!"

"Your statue...It's a big success at the museum!" said Barbara.

"Thank my beautiful wife...It's all her idea" he grinned.

The dogs raced to Amanda, then recognizing Barbara as a family friend, settled on the rug at their feet.

Trevor retreated, and Barbara resumed her account.

"Tim Legardier claims that there were precious gemstones and metals. Chiefly used for jewelry-making of the early 20th century style and importing their materials from South Africa...Especially diamonds. In fact, the Klein family owned the mines."

"How were they disposed of during the war?"

"This was before the Allies forged their Agreements. This happened somewhere between 1939-1942"

"They had a pact, the partners: Alpha vowed to attend to the interests of the Kleins. Alpha was supposed to send all his father's assets to the United States. Their arrangement had been made"

"Go on" said Amanda.

"Debien searched for his father, Klein, for years. Then he met with Mr. Thomas Legardier in London and explained everything..."

"Alpha..." continued Barbara "betrayed them instead. Especially when Klein went missing..."

Amanda waited, putting down her cup.

"Alpha informed the Germans which ship the assets were on...and they let Alpha go free."
Amanda looked down. Too many ships had tried to deliver goods to the Allied front lines, and too many had perished in the effort. "The ship sank?"
"Yes. With all hands." Pause. "But there's more..." Barbara continued. "Alpha *did* come to America. He apparently *also informed* the Allies which ship the assets were on!"
"A double-spy?" asked Amanda.
"Yes. So presumably with that intelligence, the Allies intercepted and sank the German U Boat who thought they had attained the delivery supply."
"And the cargo?"
"The cargo was sailed into Halifax. Then, it was coming out of Halifax and heading for New York where it was to be deposited into the US Treasury..."
"My God!" said Amanda. "One of Roosevelt's gold shipments for payment of US Arms..."
Barbara looked down at her notes.
"In New York...Alpha *waited*. The cargo arrived and he arranged for its disposal..."
 "He double-crossed the enemy, and he kept the cargo?" asked Amanda.
"Yes."
"How could he do that?"
"Easy. The world was divided about entering this war, remember. There were spies everywhere. Especially at the docks..."
Amanda's hand flew to her mouth.
 "Apparently, he hid the cargo in New York somewhere at some construction site. And he kept some..."
"Were they recovered?"

"That's the problem. Tim Legardier doesn't know."

"So. Who was Alpha?"

"Only Debien knew his true identity. He tracked every investment that "Alpha" made, and tried to negate it with one of his own investments – using Thomas Legardier as his broker."

"What happened after the war ended?" asked Amanda.

"Alpha returned to London for a normal life. He opened a trading license. Finally, the British authorities challenged his trading practices and banned Alpha from the London Exchange."

"Let me guess. He came to New York...city of hope and opportunity for all?"

"You got it."

"So, who was "Alpha" when he came to New York?"

"Nobody knows. He used an alias. He died of course. But he made a fortune in the stock markets! It is presumed that his heirs run his business. Apparently, it's a standard business today. But we don't know which!"

"Tim Legardier told me that his father made enquiries for his client after they met in London. He asked the American Securities and Exchange Commission for information on the holdings of a possible Alpha trader in New York. But they came up empty...It was a false deposit."

Amanda stared.

"Tim gave me his card when we spoke. He says that he'd like to meet with the donor of the statue. He had a sketch of it. Plus a Deposition from Debien - made when he had talked with his Dad in London...."

Barbara turned to her notes in her bag. "Tim says he has records sealed in a vault in London about the case which his Dad left to him."

Amanda took the card. It was a business card from a brokerage. She wondered whom she should inform about it. Trevor? Jacques? The Museum? The Fundraising Chairman, Mr. Salaman ?

"Look. I say that...maybe you keep this to yourself for a while, until you are sure. Are you scheduled for London any time soon?" said Barbara.

Amanda nodded. "I could be."

"Then wait a bit ...Perhaps more will come to light by then" recommended Barbara.

There was something nagging Amanda, and she couldn't determine what it was. A familiarity with something similar...She couldn't decide.

"You let him burden you with all this Barbara?" said Amanda.

Barbara looked at her with a wide imploring expression.

"What? There's *more?*" asked Amanda.

Barbara returned to her bag and riffled through it. She hesitated.

"He gave me this..." said Barbara retrieving an envelope.

"When I told him that you had been tracing the authenticity of the statue, and that we were...well, researchers as working professionals a few years ago, he wanted you to have this."

Amanda took the envelope.

Inside was a white velvet rectangle pouch folded, tied with a small black silk ribbon. The dog came over to inspect the item now on the coffee-table.

"Sit!" she commanded.

She laid the fabric pouch down and untied the ribbon. The pouch unfolded and revealed a gemstone, a small diamond.

"A down payment, he said, for our services to discover the true pedigree of the statue!" said Barbara.

Amanda looked at her, then returned her gaze to the table.

They were mesmerized.

The diamond glittered against the white velvet lining of the pouch like a shy lodger, its unmistakable blue glow clear.

Finally Amanda spoke. "Of course we can't keep this." She peered at Barbara, who nodded.

"I told him..." said Barbara "that we were no longer working on any Research. We could not accept any payment as commission for work. We were not bonded or insured...He understood. And I explained that this was a Museum Charity event, with the statue discovered by you, valuated by an antiquities dealer, and then donated to the Museum as a fundraiser incentive."

Amanda agreed, nodding. "If he consents, we'll give this gem to the Museum as *his* own donation" adding "even if we are lucky enough to discover more about the statue!"

"I understand. But he insisted I give it to you!" said Barbara.

"Is this even legal tender?" posed Amanda. "Perhaps he meant it as a sort of evidence...Or *identification*?"

"I'm not sure. It's probably something the Museum is better suited to process?"

"Definitely!" said Amanda. "I should write to him and acknowledge his gesture. Please tell him to expect a letter, Barbara. Perhaps he can amplify what he knows with further information. I'll ask Jacques, too."

Amanda got up and made fresh coffee.

It was agreed that Barbara would stay for dinner and spend the night at their apartment.

Trevor joined them for dinner. Amanda prepared salad, croutons and mashed potatoes. Trevor grilled up a steak, and Barbara added a shrimp cocktail to the table setting. They opened a bottle of wine and thawed a frozen sarbonne for dessert. Together they spent the evening sharing recollections, toasting victories, and chuckling at their many funny incidents.

Barbara was up and ready to leave before breakfast – she had a car waiting downstairs.

"I'm glad I came" said Barbara, standing at the door.

"Me too" said Amanda. "Thank you for being... alert!"

"Of course!"

Barbara was a loyal friend, thought Amanda. New York habits notwithstanding.

* * *

Chapter 6

It was a glorious day in New York City. From their apartment they could view the Hudson river. Today, the sun glittered across the city as if dispensing its morning blessing.

It had been a week since Barbara's visit.

Amanda took her coffee and walked to her desk. Opening her e-mail was like reading the morning paper. Print remained Trevor's favorite way to read the news, but for her, it was digital all the way, she told him.

Today she found items of interest. And she received a response from Jacques de Torraine, the email had quite thread.

Following Barbara's visit, Amanda had drafted an email to Jacques, trying as best she could to explain the parameters of the situation without entirely disclosing the details.

Based on presuppositions, as she put it, and given that 'a gesture of trust by a donor to the museum' was on the table, she needed to discover the true story behind the statue, even beyond its valuation and *provenance.*

His answer to that email had came back affirming that it was authentic, as they knew. It had been certified and verified as an original work. Certainly, it was made by an artist of some renown amongst collectors and museums who knew Art Deco design and jewelry. So, it had a field history and artistic integrity.

However, its currency had not been well documented because it was considered contemporary work. It might have been commissioned for any workshop by any wealthy patron! Thus, the question of who the artist made it for, or why the artist had deviated from any known path and sculpted a statue was still a mystery.

She wrote back asking if it might have been insured. Jacques responded saying was liked and given a strong valuation. Based on the interest by Auction Houses for the piece, it was deemed able to solicit quite a lot of money in a bidding process, if necessary. But there was no record of previous value by any insurance company. Did the Museum have interest in its monetary value?

Amanda wrote back explaining that the Museum was to dispense all proceeds from the fundraiser as they saw fit. The Deed of Gift specified that it could do with it as it wished in order to achieve the highest donation. They could sell it, or they could simply store it. Naturally, they would incur cost in its management, storage and documentation.

Jacques added that the shop had gone out of business: Neither he, nor his son could be located. He reported that he was still on the hunt for the owner, and that he had possibly located the old aunt of the shopkeeper...

Amanda was deeply absorbed over her laptop and was about to hint at some new information from a source in London when she felt a kiss on the back of her neck. She looked up and smiled. Was it an hour already?

She signed off.

Like two newly-weds, she and Trevor made it a habit when in town, to dash out for a mid-morning break at a neighborhood Cafe. And of course, they took the dogs with them, both of them wagging and waiting with great anticipation until down the tree-lined street they all went...

Trevor would read a copy of the London Financial Times, and Amanda would pick up the Wall Street Journal. Today's treat was a croissant for Amanda and a cranberry scone for Trevor with coffee.

Later, with business pending, they would return to their desks for the day. That was the pleasure of living a retired life, they chuckled, their 'happy-hour' as Amanda put it.

The clock was advancing on them, they noted, as they returned to their building. Trevor was negotiating frisky dogs and refusing to surrender his paper, and they laughed. The Concierge gave Trevor a message. There was someone waiting for him in the Lobby.

Amanda grabbed the leashes, pressed the elevator button and tumbled in with the dogs, going up ahead. Inside the apartment she untied the dogs and patted them down with a towel. They'd had a good run.

She noticed several messages waiting on the house-line, and she went into the kitchen.

Tomorrow they were entertaining. She had made arrangements with her housekeeper. The event was for a small cocktail party of guests coming up before going to the theater together. The plans were not complicated. They agreed on *Hors d'Oeuvres* to include a shrimp tray; creamed spinach dip, a service of date-olive-goat cheese tartes, and some sausage cheddar balls and crab croquettes on a platter.

Also on the buffet would be hot cider with ginger in the punch bowl with a good tot of rum, and some small sweet-tooth servings of carrot-cake squares would be on hand.

"Oh... and why not add a loaf of good bread and cheese on a cutting board for starving men?" she added, laughing.

Mrs Carlos her housekeeper had said it was no problem. She'd like to prepare all at home, and bring it in at about 5 pm the following day, if that was alright.

Amanda heard the front door open. Trevor had returned. She concluded her conversation with her thanks, adding a couple more details – including the promise to leave an extra check of money for her housekeeper and her assistant on the kitchen counter.

Amanda went to the study, snatching a glance at her desk for any new email. She expected Trevor to have changed and be at his desk in his Library where he routinely checked his mail and took calls.

Instead, she heard his voice in the bedroom. He'd been back for over an hour, and he was on the phone.

Amanda walked down the hallway and leaned against the door frame, coffee in hand.

"Going somewhere?" she chuckled in a teasing tone. Having raced home with the dogs together, all of them giggling and out of breath, there were in a festive mood. Downstairs he certainly was relaxed

when he checked in at the desk of the Concierge, and coming up behind her, it was clear that he'd had nothing scheduled but a casual day's work in his Study at home...
On the bed was a suitcase, the back-pack and a travel duffle. Also his heavy coat, she noticed.
He looked up, as if frozen. "I have to leave" he said.
"Huh?"
"I'm flying out of Boston. It's complicated...There's a car downstairs now!"
In two strides he embraced her, the coffee spilling, and he kissed her.
Just as suddenly, he jammed a few more clothes down his back pack, zipped his case and dragged them to the front door.
She trailed. "Err...You're going to London? What on earth..."
He lurched into his study, unplugged his laptop and, collecting the cords, stuffed them forcefully into his briefcase. He paused for just a second, searching for words. "Emergency!" he blurted, a shortcut.
"Why so sudden... I mean, what's in London ...?"
He paused. "It's not that I have to be in London. It's that I have to leave the United States...Gotta go!" he exclaimed, pecking her on the mouth. "I love you!" he added, his mind distracted.
He was out the door before she could get anything more out of him. The elevator pinged, and he was gone.
She stood there, stunned.
Surely, an explanation would arrive?
It's not that she had not the opportunity to confront him. It's just that they did not have that kind of relationship. There was always respect for privacy

between them.   They had a gentle and accommodating bond that would preclude such dominance. Clearly, he had his reasons...

The sun was just setting over the river, its glow reflected in a thousand city tenement window frames.
She went to the window, her thoughts a jumble. What about tomorrow's plans? Or his paperwork on the desk? His ...calls?
An hour later, she still felt numb. She sat in her study.
She was utterly confused. It was raining outside, drizzle, hanging on window panes like unsolved riddles.
She realized one thing for sure. He was running...
She felt motionless, bereft.
Later that afternoon, she thought he tried to call her, but she wasn't sure. It was a prepaid phone with an unknown number. The caller hung up.

* * *

At the British Consulate in Boston a phone conversation was underway between the British representative and an officer of the Court from the US Department of Justice.

The view from the ninth floor of the offices in Boston was splendid. One could see clear across the harbor, facing north and over up towards an ever busy Logan Airport.

In the distance, a plane was gaining altitude, its tail fiery red with the insignia of *Virgin Air.* It disappeared easily over the water and into the clouds above the Atlantic as he spoke.

"I'm sorry Lionel. He has left the country, I'm told" said the British official. "He is no longer on US soil. I'll keep you informed, yes Sir!"

He hung up, a breath of relief escaped his nostrils.

Bloody Hell...

Trevor McDonnell was a person protected.

The banking interests that he represented needed inventory evaluation in London.

It was a matter of priority that he deal with them as a domestic enquiry, and as scheduled.

There should be no cloud over their proprietary ownership. No question of poor administration like that of the US Treasury whose certain accounts remained unverifiable.

Precisely the kind of security that underwrote financing of the HMS Treasury and its investing branches.

Yes, he was needed at the moment. He could not be detained, or waylaid.

What triggered the action in the US was curious. Clearly someone had access to privileged information. And they had managed to create sufficient noise as to call in the Justice Department citing matters of procedure and regulation.

No. There should be no opportunity to detain and deter with endless questions a process that must take place on British soil.

Especially if there was any party seeking to challenge the asset held in Trust.

Trevor McDonnell was definitively under protection at the present time.

The head of the Consulate section sent his message to London.

* * *

New York

How did the statue end up in Spain?

"Sam" William Salaman　stood with his hands behind his back gazing out glass walls that defined his corner office. From this elevation at the top of his glass building he could see Long Island Sound, clearly a mark of his Firm's financial success. Ten years had passed since his father's tenure as head of the Firm, and the brand name had flourished. It was one of New York City's most celebrated trading houses.

Not a particularly tall man, he gave the appearance of stiffness, a square-shouldered man who held his posture straight and sharp.

Maybe it was attributed to his tailor who had dressed him for over three years now in *avant guarde* men's wear, including apparel for dinner jackets, sports clothes, formal wear and shoes, ever pressing something new. Perhaps it was his understated form that left everyone else in the room wondering why they felt like Guinea fowl under the gun.

He was looking away, but he was thinking of Trevor McDonnell. The call he just received from the Police Commissioner reported that the Sherriff's office had failed to serve papers, and the Detective made a direct call to the Consulate in Boston!

Trevor had left the country. No injunction or law suit could touch him now. But even that was not what troubled him. Trevor was clearly as wired and informed as he was. Sam had just exposed himself, and missed his shot.

Perhaps he should call Trevor's wife, Amanda. A lovely woman, there...But then again, she would have heard by now that litigation was in the offing against her husband. She would be cautious.

Unless he read her wrongly, she was avidly loyal to her husband, her good looks and delightful charm notwithstanding... Such women, at least those rare few whom he could name, were clever and discrete. One stupid or false move on his part, like untoward impropriety, would be spotted a mile away for what it was.

But he could offer his support for the Museum fundraising drive. He would wait for her to come to him.

Amanda Wells was too well disciplined to let business shade any charity or fundraising donations. She was on the board. So he decided that he would not pick up the phone and speak to her about his most recent donation. In due course, she would find out. And though she would not miss a beat, she would know that he was a man not to trifle with.

His secretary came in, then left the room with few instructions on how to proceed with her work.

Plus, there was the matter of their son, he thought.

The boy had accepted a summer Internship with his Firm in Miami. Too late now to withdraw, even with litigation pending...

There was too much to weigh, especially with the new information he had now. Trevor had eluded him. But he needed to think about it. This wound had been festering for a long time. In the end, it had taken down his father.

So again, how did the statue end up in Spain?

Clearly they had known each other since boyhood, his father and Klein...

Their families had intermingled since the middle ages of Spanish banishment, possibly. They had moved about Europe before finding refuge in a city. Frankfurt, Germany was where they settled their goldsmith business, and it became their permanent home at the end of the 19th century.

Trust between them had intertwined by marriage and by finance, by alliances through the generations. Even after they had moved to Frankfurt, Germany.

Yes. Those early communist and socialist revolutions of Europe displaced those who patronized their trades and introduced automated machine-made products for a domestic market.

Yes. The bourgeoisie bought trinkets certainly, but few could afford specialty items...

Then World War II swallowed up Europe with nationalism. Thus when Klein disappeared, it was no wonder his father took over his interests...

Still, as far as Sam knew, everything was accounted for. Except for this rogue statue that fell out of the inventory and remained in a shop in Spain!

Or perhaps it had never been picked up by Klein, as he did customarily with all his other supplies and shipments mined in Africa.

If ever the name of his father was unmasked, that would finish them all. Even his brother Derek was in the dark about half the story. Their father had trusted his Last Will to a good friend who executed the will in the presence of the one son, Sam.

First things first. If that meant taking down the McDonnell family, then so be it.

The phone on his desk tinkled through his speaker.

"Yes?"

"Mr. Bernstein to see you, Sir?"

"Show him in!"

Sam looked down. On his desk was a commemorative plank carved with the family name, it came from a ship decommissioned years ago. The plank was for crew and friends. He picked it up.

All but the mystery of the remaining cargo. That...which had eluded his father those many years ago. Oh certainly, he collected the bullion. That was the asset that made them great.

But there was something else that remained unsolved.

The door to his office opened. His secretary was showing in Mr. Bernstein. They had an appointment to go over a case together...

But his thoughts lingered on the plank. What ever happened to the missing cargo? Those supply shipments? He wondered. He turned to face his visitor.

"How is the litigation going against the ship that sank in 1942 with supplies?"

"We've filed the case for fraud in the Fourth District Court of the United States. The legacy owners were taken completely by surprise. It'll be one hell of a mess to unravel before we end it. Call it aggravation value!"

"Call it the loss of a precious cargo!" said Sam, sitting dutifully at his desk.

The cargo on his mind was clear.

Diamonds. Blue diamonds.

* * *

Hyde Park, 1942

The river flowed smooth and blue, softly shifting around bends and inlets and intermittently through opaque shadows and glimmering sunlight. The sky was icy crisp for an early morning hunt.

They watched. Geese honked and wheeled over the water, threatening to regain altitude and regroup into flight formation. They made landing screeching and filling the air with noise and commotion that echoed across the Hudson Highlands.

A shot fired through the bush and two birds dropped into the shallows. A hunting dog raced to retrieve the fallen game and placed first one, then the other flaccid bird at the foot of the concealed duck-blind. It was winter, and the game would be eaten for dinner at a sumptuous event in the great house tonight.

The President and his staff were entertaining officials from Canada for the weekend. The hunted game would be a buffet delicacy.

A state flag fluttered inside the porch, its colors representing the family that dwelt within. A decorative emblem of Revolutionary blue flanked by Liberty and Justice depicted two boats sailing on the Hudson River toward the sun, hills, mountains, and a Bald Eagle clutching the world – a family that had captured the early colonial trade through centuries of expansion, exploration and independence. Today, the flag fluttered in defiance. No flag or banner, or night-time headlights, blinkers or waving articles was allowed lest it catch the attention of unfriendly eyes in the sky. America was at war.

The dinner was a success. The President's home was an ideal place to hold a meeting with the leadership of its Allies. The Ladies had retreated to the drawing room for cards and a jig-saw puzzle, allowing the men to remain assembled for further talks.
Moreover, a service of dessert, coffee and even brandy had been spread out for those staying overnight.

The men had developed long and lasting friendships. From both sides of the Canadian border – families were sending sons to battle.
Already the Canadians had deployed men, supply and planes. Many soldiers billeted with British and Australian troops. But truth be told, the war was not going well for the Allies.
As the President explained, a consignment of tanks were in manufacture. Roosevelt had promised them to Churchill. hey should arrive in secrecy and serve to drive back the enemy from Tobruk, he told them. But shipping was the problem.
Air support was needed. The Germans were sinking supply ships. Especially supply ships approaching the coasts.
They listened, the wind outside delivering a soft whistle of the night, and with only the fireplace crackling, the room was filled with silence.
According to daily reports, the RAF was taking a beating. Yet Air support was critical. British mortality rates were astronomical. Airmen. Planes. Trainees. Squadrons at a time...
The Canadians understood.
At all costs air-support was paramount to the successful landing of American ships. For that

purpose they would double production within two months and use the Railroad to ship them south...

That was agreed at the meeting.

Roosevelt nodded, his pipe in his hand, they all faced the glowing fireplace.

Filled now with new hope and a chance to relax, the President in his wheelchair and his guests were gathered in the Library, and together they chatted.

With the curtains drawn for blackness, they smoked their pipes in the dim lights of the house they sharing sobriquets, now that official business was completed, and they even laughed on occasion, offering encouragement.

It was a good meeting. Up here in the hills of New York, and not far from the Canadian border, the President's home was ideally suited to planning and discussions. He was pleased with their Agreements and commitments as Heads of State.

Two ministers were British, having flown in from across the Atlantic over the Northern Route.

The Canadians had been helpful, not only in their support to the Fronts, but in support of the maritimes. Also, in aiding social dissemination of information. They published English-speaking newspapers widely read in the United States. This, the President emphasized with gratitude.

But it was getting late.

The President swallowed his drink, the night event coming to an end. And sweet as the day's accomplishments had been, a bitter taste lingered, it's delicacy perhaps visible only across his brow. Had anyone noticed, he wondered.

The war not popular at home. This, he knew. Committing to Europe was bad enough, a logistics challenge that seemed infinite. But even that was not as worrying as the lurking social unrest that stirred. Activism, socialism and communism would soon be raising their ugly heads, he also knew.

In America, there was little patience for another world war. In fact, Roosevelt understood that lack of resolution from the first world war instigated uncertainty for the second world war. It enraged the hearts of Americans having to come to the rescue for European disputes...

But this was an old enemy.

In the course of human activity, selfless labor and devotion given in the service of others usually resulted in hope and opportunity for all...

 But organized-Labor, when orchestrated for doctrines of angry social reactionism would result in regimes as harsh and cruel as any conquering army.

The President saw it today in a letter he received. A letter from an American sculptor who had promised to replicate the statue in his garden.

"...her arms shall be stronger, thicker. They represent the Laboring movements of this world that must fashion the machinery of this war...and organize" *warned the artist.*

The President, surrounded by council representing the greatest military might in the world, felt like weeping. The words burned like a threat from within.

He would have liked to say something, but couldn't. All day he had been sad.

* * *

Miami

"Welcome to Tray McDonnell!..." beamed the Office Manager, Sophie.

They applauded.

Gathered in the Lobby of their 12th Floor, staff emerged from various workplaces. Several held Executive ranking, and they all smiled cheerily.

"Thank you" said Tray, politely.

"He comes to us from his University in the UK and will be an Intern for the summer. "Teach him all you can!" added Sophie. "He may write his paper about us..."

"Before or *After* he becomes a lawyer?" offered someone.

Laughter.

"That depends on whether he makes it past the Bar..."

"Oh, we can help there..." said someone else.

Laughter.

"Alright everyone..." admonished Sophie. "Back to work! It's official then. He's one of us now," she grinned, shaking his hand. "You're On!"

Tray's face flushed red from his neck to his Scottish baronial hair. With a wide grin and deep blue eyes, he said it all. He was thrilled.

Sophie showed him to his spot located in an open space setting with ample room for his desk and telephone. Pretty soon several on the staff had surrounded him, especially some of the girls.

So it wasn't until the next day that Sophie gave Tray an extensive tour of the building, along with instructions on work-flows and procedures of protocol for certain clients and their investments.

By week's end, Tray had been exposed to financial transactions that exceeded his wildest expectations, not only in volume and speed, but in the diversity of options and enterprise. As Sophie later explained to him, theirs was the Fourth fastest growing brokerage house in volume of trades, and coming up to the third largest in total assets and acquisitions for their clients on a daily basis.

Before long, he was barely could leave his work station without carrying his open laptop with him just to absorb the information that coursed for attention.

* * *

Chapter 7

When the Travel Agency called to confirm the arrangements, Amanda did not cancel Trevor's plans. She rearranged to fly down directly to Miami, alone. In fact, she made an excuse for "Dad" when she met her son in Miami.

Two cabs vied for her attention to take her to the Airport. And now she found herself in Miami.

They ordered pizza, Amanda and Tray.

They were at the *Turf and Grill Garden* off Miami Beach. Most people ordered Texas beef-burger in a basket, fries, salad or coleslaw added on the side. They chuckled with pizza.

They sat, mother and son, at a table draped in a plastic picnic motif, laughing and enjoying as Tray recounted his life in Miami.

Amanda was glad she came. Booked in a hotel that overlooked the sea, the sun had touched her face, and she looked like a well-cooked lobster, as her son put it. She chuckled, just as she needed to. Somehow, Trevor would have approved.

She had needed to get out of town, and the break here to see her son for a few days was good.

But the aching had not gone away. Nor had she heard yet from Trevor. Since the moment he left the apartment in New York - so suddenly and without explanation, there was a void in her life. But more significantly, an absence that he could not explain.
Yet the more she thought about it, the more she understood. She had heard from his Secretary in London.

Amanda was pleased. Tray was brimming with things to tell. After their beach-side dinner they strolled down the broad-walk in the warm summer air, and they found a place for ice cream.
"Sophie told me to stay for the Fall Semester" he was saying. "Sophie told me to take two courses at the local university and have them transferred into my program!"
Amanda asked him what courses he was taking, and how they would help with his present situation in Miami.
"Accounting!" he said, without hesitation.
"Well, no one can argue with that! I'm sure it'll be useful"
"Oh yes! Sophie says that I'd be surprised at the number of people missing those skills in their analysis of risk management..."
"Really?"
"Yes"
"Perhaps you could introduce me to your Office Manager, when you get a chance?" said Amanda.
"Oh Sure. She's great!"
"That's terrific for you. I'll be sure to tell Dad. Accounting?..."

"Oh, and there's something else Mum. Do you think I can go skiing to Canada during the Christmas holidays? They have a group package for all of us going up...."
Amanda looked away momentarily. Clearly, he had already accepted the invitation.
She smiled. He was still very young, she told herself.
He grinned happily.
Finally, Amanda and Tray took a cab to his apartment. Tray asked the driver to wait fifteen minutes. They ran inside. He introduced his mother to the Concierge, and he gave her a tour of his quarters on the 10th floor...
 She had to agree that the view was stunning. But the lease, he told her, was still under the company name. He thought of getting his own lease, he told her...

Amanda felt satisfied that Tray was alright. He seemed happy enough. There was little to cause concern. Trevor had planned to visit him, and her own appearance had served as assurance, if nothing else. Tray knew that his parents cared about his well-being.
Later that night, Amanda strayed out to the balcony. She looked out and saw a city vibrant with movement and lights, the dark sea shrouded by night, ever present and thrashing.
Did she have the deep and unsettling feeling that Tray was receiving more attention from his employer than one might expect for a student? In fact, if asked, she might even say that he was been coaxed into staying longer than planned, as if by design. It was a lure any young man would fall for.

The phone rang in her room. She knew the voice.
"Mum" said Tray "I'm sorry I neglected to ask about cost...Dad is generous, I know. Excuse the oversight?"
Amanda smiled. "Thanks dear. It's good that you ask... We'll budget your ski trip from your Christmas allowance. Canada is a lovely country. Enjoy yourself!"
"Yes, I will. And thanks, Mom."
It was a nice way to end the day, she thought.
Tomorrow she would be flying home.

* * *

New York.

It had been drizzling in New York all day. She was on her way out, then reached for a cover from her wardrobe. It wasn't exactly cold outside, but it was damp and in mid-range for temperatures. A cold gust could leave people standing on the curb looking underdressed.
She pulled a short-length camel Wrap Coat and tied a knot at the waistline.
With a Nubuck Leather Hobo Bag, and glossy Kierstin Vachetta Sandals, Amanda stepped out of her building looking like a well dressed woman. Amanda was quite surprised at the crowd that showed up for the Museum Board Meeting. In retrospect, she was glad she had dressed appropriately. What should have been a quiet round-the-table talk amongst staff and Administrators turned out to be a small Public Hearing.
She and a few other principals were seated at a higher central table, and a small crowd of two dozen or so had gathered for information and questions.
"Amanda..." began Marianne Williams, her eyes full of remorse and confusion "I had no idea they were going to bring this lot along..."
"Err...Ms Williams!" called out the Senior Curator from the Special Collections, "can we count on any microphones out here, do you think?"
"Oh, yes Mr. Torres. I'll see to it."
There was no shortage of representation. Less than an hour later, the Museum went Live.

The Media were broadcasting the announcement of the exhibit by Museum Administration; the police Commissioner's office was offering consultation for security, traffic and scheduling; the Mayor's Office Advocate spoke to position itself for advantageous tourism,   public   safety   and   commercial opportunities; the local construction company were represented to show their contribution to the public event, and the news media had questions that sounded more like political challenges than practical questions.

Demonstrators who opposed the exhibit, appeared at the entrance, sometimes less than quietly.

When the spotlight came around to Amanda, she wondered how she should add to the information in any meaningful way.

A man wearing a dark silk suit leaned over and whispered "highly politicized for votes, looks like to me..."

Amanda had to agree, especially since her intent was to focus on the logistics of the display and its narrative.

In as few and simple words as possible, she told of the statue, and how the effort behind the work was appreciated,   with   thanks   to   the   many   who contributed.

Outside there was more shouting. Police rushed through the doors, and now Amanda couldn't help wondering if the place was safe. Certainly it looked as if the meeting had been ill-advised.

"My God" she muttered, as the crowd rushed through the barriers for viewers only.

Ten minutes later another disruption occurred. This time the police came in and asked everyone to stand back at the far end of the room, for safety.

They shuffled around, and the agitation in the crowd grew – some camera men seeking to exploit a potentially incendiary situation, and training their lens into the mob.

Police announced that they should leave the building by the East side entrance. Shrieks of alarm led the way as a stampede followed, tossing chairs, boxes, a lighting fixture and a table desk in their wake.

Amanda's position was not distant from the door, and her fingers were slammed by a folding chair that collapsed. She was shaking off the sting when a man beside her gripped her elbow and ushered her out. She glanced up and realized there was no negotiating. She managed to lurch sideways and grab her coat and bag as they fled.

Outside and safely across the street, he identified himself. He extended his hand, his eyes warily scanning the street for disturbance. "I'm err... Bill Wickowsky from the Salaman Firm."

"Oh!" said Amanda, recognizing Sam's firm. "Pleased to meet you."

"That was some meeting..." he said, rubbing dry dust off his knee. "Jesus! If I'd known we'd be in a public safety training exercise, I'd have worn my fatigues to work!"

She put on her coat. "This is New York...Abundance of caution, I suppose."

He grimaced "An *over*-abundance..." he added.

The wind blew. He cast about, still nervous, "Look. It's nasty out here. Shall we grab a cup of coffee?"

"Sure."

They crossed the street and found a window-seat at a Dinner. Coffee calmed them. He ordered a bagel with Lox and cream cheese. Amanda asked for a small slice of coffee cake for herself, and a baker's dozen box of assorted pastries to take home. Barbara would be around in the next day or two, and Carla would be happy to take several pastries homes for Emilio her husband...

"Wow. That was one hell of a morning!" said Bill. "Too bad we never got to hear your report...How's your hand?"

"Oh its fine now, thanks. Besides, I wasn't exactly presenting any report. It was a casual consultation about the exhibit" said Amanda, sipping her coffee.

"Ah!"

The waitress came to set down their orders.

"So. Tell me more about that statue. How did you acquire it and how do you know where it came from?"

Amanda smiled. She told him. If he was on the Board of the Museum, then he was entitled to an explanation – meeting or no meeting.

"And, who is it exactly that verified it as authentic?"

"Jacques de Torraine. He had it appraised and examined. He is one of Europe's most recognized dealer of Antiquities"

"A friend of yours?"

"Yes. Both Trevor and I trust him..."

The hour was passing quickly, she noted. He asked about their trip to Spain. He wanted to know what else was known about the statue. He quizzed her on its authentication and asked about any research that would shed light on it.

"Well. Let's make sure it has appropriate Provenience, certification, and more importantly, insurance! How much is it worth?"

"That, I cannot guess..." she said, beginning to wonder about his questioning. She pulled back her hands and let them rest on her lap.

"I'll write it all up, for an official report then," he nodded.

Finally she said "we do of course appreciate Sam's interest in the exhibit and his Museum donation. I know he's been particularly generous and involved with this event..."

Bill's mouth was full. He nodded vigorously. "Yes" he swallowed. "He asked me to come over and check it out...I mean, to represent his interest."

Amanda smiled.

He drank his coffee, fully revived from a robust plate of food. Then he totally surprised her with a different tack of questioning.

"I understand that your Assistant Barbara received a visit from a Mr. Legardier?"

Amanda looked at him. "Yes"

"He was in town, from London?"

"Yes. He noticed the exhibit at the museum, and the Museum contacted Barbara. He wanted to know more about the donor, apparently."

"Do you know him?" asked Bill.

"No. He did identify himself to us."

"Why?"

Amanda paused. He was clearly straying beyond his boundary. She looked up for the waitress.

"He... didn't say what his interest or connection was to the statue, did he?"

"No. Why?"

"He didn't ask you to investigate anything relating to the statue, or anything...?"

Amanda decided to bring the conversation to a close. "He left us his calling card and..."

"Did he know anything about the statue?" persisted Bill

Amanda looked at him, adding calmly. "I was going to say 'and his pledge of support to the Museum.'"

"Are you sure? He didn't pay you with any kind of money, or *asset* on deposit?"

"Mr. Wickowsky..." said Amanda, raising her hand to pay the bill "our meeting this morning would have been about the Exhibit. As you know, we do not discuss donors!"

"Oh yes. Absolutely!" he said apologetically.

Amanda paid and reached for the box of pastries tied by string. "Well thank you for the coffee. It was nice to make your acquaintance." She got up to leave "Please give our best to Sam Salaman ."

He did not move. She was about to step away when he grabbed her wrist and held her fast, his voice quite audible.

"Certainly Ms Wells! Of course, we wouldn't want anything to happen to Trevor in his court case, now would we? Trevor's firm is embroiled in litigation at the moment, is it not?"

"Excuse me?" she said softly.

"Well. It's just that we have friends at the DOJ who keep us informed about our friends and investors and their assets..." He released her wrist. He got up. "Let's just say, we'd like to be kept abreast of all that you know about your statue Ms Wells?..."

On the way home in the Taxi, Amanda could hardly breath. She felt fearful. She wondered if she'd been set up for an encounter with a veiled threat. She knew Sam's imprint was all over this chance meeting.

Trevor's firm is embroiled in litigation?

She shuddered.

She stepped out of the cab, glad of the cooler air. She walked a block, her thoughts distracted, and she bought flowers from a florist nearby. If she were being watched, she refused to show any sign of intimidation.

She entered her building and smiled calmly at the concierge with a wave, her heart drumming.

More than a coincidence, she and Trevor had just received a threatening warning.

Of that she felt certain.

* * *

Amanda found Barbara in the Dorot Jewish Center sitting at a large table beside the window.

Surrounded by carved paneling that rose to the ceilings, and chandeliers from overhead oak carvings Barbara was lost in thought. Except that the highly polished floors could not mute the tread of her high boots, Amanda managed to surprise Barbara.

"What's this?" asked Amanda, sitting beside her with a big smile.

"Oh Yes...it's a catalogue of the collections said to be missing following the War. Mostly owned by craftsmen and skilled artists. Look. Look, here's the Faberge Egg that nobody knows about. Only sketched by an artist from memory. Huh?... And over hear, look at the cut-crystal necklaces and jewels found only in museums..."

"Wow!" said Amanda.

"Amazing, huh?"

Amanda couldn't argue. The colors of gemstones, and the collections that attended were stunning. Especially sacred collections of religious icons. "Strange, this, isn't it? ... That we should only be able to find these things as catalogue items? Nobody knows where they are, you say?" said Amanda.

"Well. If they do, they're not saying! As you know, the Jewish people refuse to call themselves victims..."

"What artistry!" murmured Amanda, running her fingers across one page.

"Oh, wait till you see the artwork on books!"

"Come here! Look at this..." said Barbara, too excited to have a systemic plan in mind.

It took a couple hours, but they ended up at the Bryant Park Grill on 25 W 40th St.

"I'm famished!" said Barbara, tossing a table napkin across her lap.

"My treat" said Amanda. "What'll you have?"

They settled on an assortment of quiche, salads and a rustic burgundy wine followed by chocolate cake and coffee.

Barbara was having a crisis. She couldn't sort her thoughts, and she was deeply disturbed.

"Here's the thing. I never uttered a word. *Not at word*" she said stabbing her fork in the air. "I swear it!" She stared at Amanda sitting across from her.

Amanda spoke finally. "What happened?"

"He called me...Late in the evening. After 7 pm, right? To talk business...*Really*? I have to admit, I was a little tired and not totally paying attention. You know, one of the calls soliciting business, I thought. I was about to hang up, but he said the magic word. So how'd you figure?"

Amanda chewed. If there was one person she could trust for discretion it was Barbara. More than the event itself, she was wondering how to assuage her friend. It really wasn't that serious, she kept telling her. But no. Barbara made no errors. Period. This ...*thing* that happened, was truly upsetting her.

"Put it behind you, will you?" said Amanda. "We'll get over it! Truly, it's not the end of the world. Relax!"

Which was why Amanda ordered wine. Barbara needed to unwind about an issue that was not the biggest mistake one could make when taking a message... Besides, there was no answer to her question.

How did he know?

Barbara had received a call from the Museum Library. A man had introduced himself as a mid-level manager in charge of Evidence and Cataloguing Department. He cited the possibility of expecting to see a blue diamond.

"Well, don't worry" said Amanda, sipping her wine. "It's locked away in our Safe."

Barbara's eyes remained mortified. I'm so sorry, she mouthed.

"Look. We agreed to keep it to ourselves for the moment. And yes, we shall present it to the Museum. Perhaps it was Tim Legardier himself who told them he had it, and perhaps...he even anticipated that we would..."

"No. Tim Legardier definitely intended for you and Trevor to keep the thing!"

"So why didn't you ask him *how* he knew?"

"I did!"

"And...?"

"He said he was having lunch at the Blue Bottle Coffee Shop on 54 West 40th St, just a block and half away from the New York Library. He has a buddy there that he occasionally finds sitting. He reads the local paper and he saw a police report citing the loss of 'period pieces' from the 1940s. Part of an investigation by the New York Assistant District Attorney.."

"Period pieces?"

"That's what he said. Precious metals and gems, to be precise, and he recalled that I had asked to speak to their specialist last week asking about diamonds...from the period..." said Barbara.

"He could not have suspected you..." said Amanda.

"He might have been fishing, even placing the

advertisement as bait for information. Besides, the name of donors is privileged information."
"But he did ask!" Barbara looked frustrated. "Oh My God!" wailed Barbara. "Now *we're* the ones under investigation?"
"Nonsense!" assured Amanda.
With the meal behind them, there was one decision she did make. They needed to find out more, and to speak to the New York Assistant District Attorney.

* * *

Karen McCullock showed up for work with a cup of coffee in her hand. She'd taken the subway today, and whereas her hands were normally too full to handle much more than a briefcase, pocket book, scarf and gloves – if not an umbrella while punching train tickets through turnstile, and all to keep her balance when standing on a rocking train, today she felt liberated and enjoyed walking the full length of the hallway in dress shoes and a black skirt and blouse.

"Good morning Susan!" she said, passing the central floor desk where detective Andres Dillon manned the phones.

"Hi Dave..." she waved.

"Morning!" he hollered back, unsure of who had addressed him.

Paul Talbot met her outside her office, grinning. "Good Morning Madam Assistant District Attorney! How are you today?"

"Hello Paul. Come in" she said, opening the door and landing the coffee cup on her desk with some success. She walked to the hanger and unshed her mackintosh raincoat. "How's everything?"

"Oh, pretty good thanks. Family's doing well. Laura has a hockey game this afternoon after school which I'd like to make, if that's alright..."

"Sure! For as many long hours as you put in for this office..." She took her place at her desk.

Amanda settled in. "So. What've we got?"

"Right" With several file folders on his lap, Paul sat facing her.

Dave Thomas - the new recruit, appeared at the door and tapped respectfully at the door jam. "I have a message for Mr. Talbot" he said "Umm. From the Evidence Locker..." and he handed a note to Paul.

Susie came next, tapped the door jamb and walked in with a stack of files. One pile consisted of cases 'Approved' and signed-off by her boss the District Attorney for Karen to follow up. Another pile New cases.

Karen grimaced.

"Oh..." added Susie "and the Commissioner wants a Press Conference 11 am this morning. He wants you there. His office asks that you stay behind to meet with him..."

Karen looked apologetically at Paul who had been interrupted by both people vying for her attention.

 "Thanks Susie. Got it!" she said, sipping her coffee. Then she said, "what's up?"

The look on Paul's face was incredulous. He was shaking his head, "I've gotta go downstairs...I'll be back. Excuse me!"

Karen settled in the for the day, her eye keenly on the watch. Minutes before getting up to leave for the Commissioner's meeting on the 10th floor, Paul walked in.

"You're not going to believe this. But the evidence on the Green Case has disappeared. Even the Coroner's Report and file have gone...There's no trace of who logged it out!"

"That's impossible Paul. Someone has it. We just need to track who signed it out ..."

Paul followed her down the hall. "There's more. A complaint has been lodged with the Commissioner of Police. The DA wants to talk to you about it this afternoon. Apparently, your investigation about a cold case is trespassing on secure intelligence held by the government. There's an operation of law at the Federal Department of Justice relating to one of your contacts - the husband of Karen Wells, Trevor McDonnell. He has fled the country. He's a resident of New York. There's a Summons out on him..."

Karen stopped. "You are *kidding*, right?"

"No. The British government claims that he has Diplomatic Immunity. They say he hasn't fled the country. He's in London. They deny that he's withholding critical evidence wanted by the SEC."

Karen pressed the elevator button. "Explain?..."

She stepped inside. "What are the allegations, exactly?" then adding, "and where's the State Department on this?"

Talbot shrugged. "Where they always are. Out-To-Lunch."

"Fraud?" Karen asked.

"Unknown. But it undermines any credibility from one of your information contacts. We've got missing evidence, and a case under investigation by the Security and Exchange Commission fixing on a financial audit...I'd say Fraud."

"God! That's probably why the Commissioner wants me at the Press Conference - to field any questions that might arise ..." The elevator doors began closing. "Get me all the info you can Paul..."

"You got it!" Paul turned on his heels. "Especially if it's been politicized and leaked," he muttered.

     x x x

Barbara called Amanda at 7 a.m., giving her exactly three hours to prepare.

"We're in!" she said. "10.00 o'clock this morning. I'll meet you there," then hung up.

Amanda was up, coffee in hand. Since Trevor had left, she was no longer as formal as she used to be. Theirs had been a busy life that required early starts most days. But Amanda had shut down their agendas. Her days were simpler now. Full of work, certainly, but less rigorous.

She opened her closet then closed it again. Without Trevor around, it just wasn't the same.

But Barbara was expecting her. She'd take the dogs out for a quick walk - pick up a fresh baguette from the corner bakery, and jog back just in time to get dressed – plus check her mail for any word from Trevor. Then she'd hail a cab across town.

Why Barbara couldn't have called last night was annoying. Amanda knew the answer she'd get. *Didn't want you up all night on your computer, working...*

Barbara was right of course. But what the hell?

Amanda spotted the cab from the lobby just as she walked out the elevators. She stepped into the rear seat, briefcase and laptop in hand.

"163 W 125th Street. Please!" she instructed the driver.

Clearly, Barbara got word late yesterday, possibly after- hours when the ADA tossed out one last call before leaving her office. A brief appointment had been scheduled.

Barbara was waiting for her in the Lobby of the New York building. With State Courts, Police Metropolitan Headquarters and other government offices listed in the building, the place was teeming with professionals and blue-uniformed policemen.

Barbara looked sharp, if edgy with the boots and the miner's hat. "You look great..." she said to Amanda in the elevator to the seventh floor.

"And you could have given me more warning" retorted Amanda.

They were shown right into Karen McCullock's office. Evidently this was an appointment slotted just before a Court Appearance for the ADA who was already reaching for her papers and closing her laptop to place into her briefcase. "Come in" she said cheerfully.

A Detective tapped at the jamb and signaled he was ready to go with her, clearly wanting to divert these visitors to someone. The ADA looked up at him, about to speak.

"Thanks for seeing us!" charged Barbara, her hand extended out for a handshake. "Ms Wells and I are pleased to discuss the case of missing period-items, if it's helpful..."

The meeting lasted fifteen minutes. Long, by most standards of verbal exchange in those offices.

What's more, a second meeting as follow up was deemed necessary, and it was scheduled for later in the week at the end of a workday when they could talk more largely about the case in general.

Obviously, there was more here than met the eye. And it was a delicate matter.

Just as importantly for Amanda, was a comment made by Karen before they left.

"I understand your husband is under investigation..." she said, "I hope it won't be long before your party

can shed light on the matter and clear up any misunderstanding..."
Misunderstanding?

* * *

The numbers pleased Derek.

The room was full of IT specialists. All of them pleased to be introduced to a client who wanted their services. They had been specially selected, and the seating for them was ample and comfortable.

What he wanted, he had told them, was *direct* access to customers to buy his company products.

They nodded.

The room was his, he knew. And he paced for effect. How often did such a lucrative client ask them for a special meeting, after all.

He continued. And just as importantly, the *speed* with which his customer could be reached, he told them. , was a marketing advantage for his firm. He wanted. He looked at them, his hair wavy and straying down his forehead like a man impassioned by his mission.

The best advertising for his company, he insisted, was targeted to special clients!

Of course...

Further, being in the investment banking business, his company had lots of instruments and financial products to offer! And he told them.

From license franchise products to Internet subscription accounts...Clients could *bank* with his Firm. They could *invest* with his Firm. They could get *mortgages* with his Firm. They could open *savings* accounts with his Firm...

He turned and squarely faced the team.

He wanted to challenge them to produce the best Advertisement gambits on the internet! As he put it, he wanted his brand to be the online advertisement posted on football games - from the Super-bowl to the Olympics...

To achieve new prospects for his firm, he told them, they should expect to engage in data-mining on demand.

Now he paused.

'Cyber plunges' into data-mining was it the best marketing strategy, he wondered...

If anyone could come up with suggestions they should let him know, he said, assuring them of encouragement.

One man shot up his arm.

There was the 'viewing audiences' to be found within the entertainment industry, he volunteered, including those online, or watching shows – from family viewing to the fringe elements...

And what about audiences who were News viewers - from fake to real of any kind.

Anything was game if it held the attention of his potential customers.

What he wanted, he told them, were Metrics of those consumers, he told them. Audience data. Public data. Private data...

Business was business.

The room was full of excitement.

With such encouragement, programmers and code creators of software would enjoy this lucrative Advertising account, he assured them. They could accomplish the task easily - unleashing the very most probing and wide ranging options for searching, metrics, robotic-calling, data-mining that any IT expertise could create...It was a global market, he told them.

They applauded him.

By the time the meeting was breaking up, they had become an informal fraternity of software talent.

"Oh, and keep it legal!" he joked before leaving the conference.

They all laughed, thrilled. .

Most had rights to work in the United States. Few were lawyers or even understood the laws of consumer protection, intellectual property or personal data infringements.

Two of his team of specialists, Ned Taylor and Jesse Stromy lingered. They were not smiling, and they discretely tapped the elbows of a few other to remain behind. The rest could go, and they vacated the premises.

Ned Taylor and Jesse Stromy knew this account and were the managers for the task.

Here, they discussed other data that could be used for the harvesting of clients – or, as they tacity understood, the discrediting of competition! Not that they should foresee such a day, but it might come in handy...

Finally, the office secretary tapped on the glass door and signaled that there was other business...

It fell to Taylor and Jesse then, to be clear. They needed probing information and intelligence gathering. They needed inside material on *every* customer.

"For what?" asked one of the younger men in the group, Sati, from New Delhi. His uncle Salim nudged him hard in the ribs..

Quiet!

Outside, Sati was told. It was probably for election time. Eves-dropping. Surveillance. Re-dating. Re-routing and network-connections were also necessary. Maybe even for deep-state insurrection, foreign affairs, national interests or even defense hacking...and their coordinated tie-ins.

Business was business.
Besides, this was America. They had no allegiances here!
Sati got it.
The meeting was over.

* * *

Derek was fed up with his IT.
They failed him.
They provided very little that was aggressively viable. Why? Who was advising them?
What part of 'hostile investigation' did they *not* understand?
How exactly did they think business was being conducted, these days? By asking permission to leak intelligence to the competition? Is that what they thought tech companies and software was solely engaged in? If so, who the hell did they think was paying the bills?
He'd cancel the Advertising account, for sure.
He called his broker. He had a bet to place on the stock exchange. Yes. Yes. He could wait a day. He'd like to hear about more options. Yes. Yes.. That's fine.
He'd need to search further afield for what he wanted.

x x x

As hacker, Dimitri was as good as it got.

An orphan in his grandfather's household, he aspired to be a musician just as his grandfather admonished. In Austria, there was that city of great musicians, he was told. He travelled there. But as a young man without labor experience he found little work - and even less charity in the alpine regions which today served as suburban districts of modern living for financial corporations and global wealth managers. He worked in construction for a season, but returned to the delta regions of Croatia.

Now he had some experience. One local construction contractor hired him for projects on a consistent basis. And Dimitri learned things. He understood things. He knew how to load a truck with timber. He could dig an even ditch, and he knew when to speak and when to keep his mouth shut to those with the power drills. They called the shots.

He was good with cement. He learned masonry. He even learned how to operate a crane for small lift platforms. He could drive, now. He could back a trailer. He learned some carpentry, and soon it was "Eey Dimitri...do this! Dimitri that!..."

His contractor was an easy man to please. Being upwardly mobile, he asked Dimitri to do odd jobs at his personal home, a rehabilitated farmhouse.

Dimitri was expected to do this for free, being as he was invited to stay on the premises for the season. He slept on a cot in the warm kitchen, beside the foyer of the main hall. They fed him well at the kitchens. And since he would drive the tractor around for farm work, he was rewarded with cordiality by the landlord's household.

His tasks expanded. He kept the kennel and tended to some goats. A horse or two was occasionally brought in for sheltering at the stable, and he kept the courtyard cleared of clutter for deliveries and business supplies.

Inside the household, the family pets were fed and exercised by Dimitri. The dogs, five Irish setters, came to know him, and while they gave to their owner the social distinction of a rising suburban businessman, it was Dimitri they responded to. Occasionally, when the household engaged in a community Squire's Shooting in the meadows of their township, Dimitri attended the hunt to attend and he dressed the game. He came to know hunting rifles.

Dimitri and his efforts were soon considered indispensable. At night as he lay in his cot, he imagined what it must be like to be the proprietor of such a place. The wife, a good looking woman, never lingered or showed him attention. A good wife, he decided. Even the children were playful and sweet. But his grandfather had taught him long ago never to look at the women. Play the Joseph of Egypt and earn the respect of the boss, he grandfather told him. So Dimitri was considered a trustworthy worker.

There was no piano in the house. But there was a computer. And just as the lights went out, Dimitri tiptoed into the library and switched on the monitor.

He learned. It was only a matter of time before Dimitri found his way into chat rooms and fringe elements who actually became his tutors.

He followed the Auctions of items on the world wide web, including musical instruments and collectibles. He placed a few bids, then bought and sold on bets. He exchanged money and even discovered how to make money on a few sales with little more than an image.

Within a year he had discovered the dark web where he could purchase and resell illegal, illicit items. And he then monitored messages on bulletin boards where money could be made.

He bided his time. For now, he was still learning, and each day his head thought of plans about what next he might master on the Internet...

He continued to work hard on the farm. The seasons changes, and he was predictable and needed...As the nights came earlier, with the household in bed, he strayed out to watch some television in the kitchen. This he could do, they told him. To pass away the long nights.

They never knew that he often stepped through the foyer and across the great hall and into the Library at night.

He understood firewalls and encrypted messaging. He even picked up the tit bits of code that would be necessary to operate a substation for himself as an operative. There during the night, he had his own pages on a hidden archived cachet within this boss's computer. The trick was to access it in full privacy, and without leaving traces of his presence on the monitor for the next morning...

He earned three thousand dollars US, and he put it in a bank account online, having never stepped inside a bank in his life.

From open forums where he posted as an outsider, he strayed into international communications between operatives and cyber espionage. He read the news, and he followed the geo-political movements of the governments. He watched and traced markets on the Internet, including bulletin boards of activism and actionable movements. He recognized those in resistance movements, their linkages, their rewards, whether in moral capital or monetary. He discovered how to make money with the purchase and selling of intelligence; identify theft and crafted negotiations. Then always with chat rooms, he discovered the world of finance and international banking trades.

Pretty soon he had collected thirteen thousand dollars US. And he started to wonder if there was more new stuff to learn. He already had his handles and passwords; his User-names and he discovered he could purchase information and intelligence on Bitcoin. Soon, he was trading, and he could play the stock market like a fine tuned piano.

No one could track his identify on the Internet, he used virtual private networks that no one could access.

Thusly, he returned for two hours each night to the Library of his contractor's house.

By the time he was making bets on arms deals, he realized that the world was not at war for territorial domination, nor even in wars of espionage or cybersecurity or technology development. It was engaged rather, in economic warfare.

That is, until an unexpected event occurred one night.

Dimitri was in the middle of a transaction. He had made some money. He was now in the three hundred thousand dollar range, US money. He started his next transaction, and the negotiations were underway when the light switch made him jump.

Standing there was his boss with a shotgun.

Dimitri was caught. A flush of hotness filled his face, his fingers still at the keyboard.

Actually, it was the child who had told her father that a thief was in the house. He came down with a shot-gun, and now he was standing at the Library door. Behind him it was dark. His fingers gripped the shotgun.

The look on his face was utter astonishment. Not only was there no thief in the house, but a laborer he hired was sitting at his desk and working on his computer.

"Dimitri? What are you doing?" he said incredulously.

Dimitri was alarmed but adjusted quickly. He had imagined, in fact, that one day it might come to this. He knew what to do.

"Oh, Oh, Oh, Mr. Sergev..." he pleaded, standing, "Please...*please!*" he implored, advancing a few steps. "*Forgive my insolence*...I beg that you see...I just want to look!" He closed distance between them, the shotgun able to be levelled.

Dimitri came close enough to embrace. Then he plunged the silver letter-opener into the throat of his boss, twisting to sever the artery. He held the body as it buckled, and he glanced outside the door to the darkened house. He softly shut the door, and reached over to turn off the light switch. He left fall the body, now choking and spurting blood.

Dimitri moved quickly. He wiped his bloody hand, and returned to the computer to add a few phrases to his transaction, then closed out his posting with eyes aflame and his fingers flying. He broke a window and he stepped over the body, still alive, and out to the hallway where he tiptoed to his quarters.

The next morning it was the wife who discovered the body. The household fell into a commotion, and it took a week to settle down to the awful reality of an intruder who killed his boss. The police authorities came.

Dimitri denied any knowledge, nor did he hear any intruder. He never knew that his boss was attacked, he told them.

Two weeks after the funeral, Dimity collected his belongings and told the Housemaid to explain that he found work across the border. He left his laborer's hat as a token of thanks to the Mrs for respect to her husband. He left with good graces, and he was given food and little change for his journey.

Dimitri left no trace of an account on the computer, having erased all his posts. He had four hundred thousand dollar US in his account when he left.

He took the ferry from Croatia to Italy, just as he'd said, if only to walk about and discover what it was like to breath the air of a free man with money. He stood at the rail of the boat crossing the Aegean, a sea full of blue, full of myths... that much he knew.

Quietly waiting, he pulled from his pouch a letter-opener which he tucked up his sleeve. Then leaning over the rail, he let it slip to the deep.

x x x

Chapter 8

The street belonged to a bygone era. It was an old building in Eastern Croatia where houses had been built for those ascending to power. The structures survived. Shutters and timber frames, old world ornamental woodwork carved by hands – a Luna set of windows here, or pair of hearts there or a cluster of grapes, if weathered.
Here, at the margins of the Franco-Austrian Empires had been a Victorian world unleashing new trade and industrial mass production of goods, such that the bourgeois classes blossomed with factory production, electrification and domestic markets. It was supposed to be the end of the agrarian subsistence economies. Instead, a new dawn broke out in grey and granite, and in the construction of tanks for socialist communist regimes.
Now, with shutters torn off and the carvings decayed, a warehouse or stock house could still be found.
A large rusty chain and padlock was mounted across wooden doors once made for courtiers and carriages, now reed-barred and rotten.
Dimitri had bought equipment and filled the space with gear and tables. Computers and wires, cell phone and transmitters, firewood and coal, and he

was surrounded by all that he needed, plus a nice big wood-burning stove in the middle of the barracks where once soldiers had been billeted.

He found his signal strength adequate. Beaming off a local cell tower erected on an abandoned military installation, it served his purpose. Mainly, it was remote, and rarely noticed on most grids.

From this shed, he had the time to cultivate his contacts and strengthen connections. He opened new doors and entered new deals. Choosing and learning, chatting and trading, he found pathways and passwords, portals and bulletins. He found access to funds and had knowledge to share. Twice he tweaked into sovereign intelligence. Once he discovered accounts of finance and treasury. He explored ways to communicate with players and cyber operatives all over the world. And now he was ready to play.

His transactions thrilled him, and his surroundings filled him with pride of self-achievement. Every penny he made was his own doing, and his prowess was growing with remarkable alacrity. He was close to a million in his bank, and one night he made more.

His back ached form sitting on wood crates. He kneeled on the floor, soft padding at his knees, and he stretched up to reached the keyboard. The sun had just set, casting long bony shadows, and he seemed like a man in a posture of worship.

He passed his first million. That night, he added eleven thousand dollars more. But a twinge shot up his leg, and he rose to complete his transaction-
Why kneel when you can stand?

It was a month before he found a good place, a nice urban apartment in Torino, and he came back to the warehouse only to pull plugs from the walls and pack up his van.
There was a café not far from where he lived, and a dear Italian lady with a phone and a basement for his office, next block. He had all he needed. He was an urbanite now.

* * *

Amanda sat perched on her swivel office-chair. She pondered the images and counted the documents strewn across her Study floor.

Her thick hair, swept up in a fierce knot behind her head, leaked a few loose strands down her neck and across her face. Leaning forward from the open neckline of a pale Marino wool sweater, she looked fatigued. Yet the firm limbs beneath loose clothes betrayed a well exercised and supple body.

She unfolded her legs and took a big breath.

"So, what've we got?" said Barbara, lying prostrate on the floor in socks, dark tights and an olive T shirt.

"Hm.." said Amanda.

Barbara waited.

A second later, a cell phone hummed. They both looked up. Whose?

It buzzed again. From where the sound?

Amanda dove across the room and opened a desk drawer. There is sat, lighting up with a buzz, a small digital device. Then dark it went.

Amanda examined it, less focused on its properties than on the strangeness of it being there. Yet there is was with little registered on it but a half dozen numbers. No contacts. No icons. No messages. No reminders or notifications.

"Hello?" said Amanda, the call long ended.

"Trevor's?" asked Barbara.

"It must be..." husked Amanda, appalled.

"Here, give me that thing. I'll tell you what zip codes..." said Barbara, her administrative voice in full command. "Overseas!" she said finally, returning the device to Amanda.

"What?"

 "Overseas. The call came from overseas!"

* * *

Actually, it was Trevor's Study.

They had set up ground zero in his office - a base camp to analyze all the information they could gather. Not the prettiest of working arrangements considering the clusters of crushed papers, spent coffee cups, abandoned dog-toys and snack sandwich wrappings, but hey, it worked. Amanda would clean up later.

The point was, as long as they could reach for information, they would piece it all together in this room, as if filling the void left by Trevor.

There were just too many gaps and too many questions at the moment. And they had to find answers.

It's not that Amanda could support this kind of effort at her apartment. She lived a torpid life. Bringing a case into her hands was hardly advisable. But that was the agreement. An office to work in that was secure.

 Certainly, their work-hours were not as consistent as they would have liked. Both she and Barbara had to consider their various appointments, travel schedules, social obligations and commitments.

"You do know.." said Barbara one afternoon "we are getting too old for this!"

Amanda chuckled, remarking that it was pretty steady.

"Oh Sure! If you mean starting early and ending at dinner time all cooped up in a tiny study with the curtains drawn and nobody to check if we had a pulse..."

"You forgot the dogs..." quipped Amanda.

"Oh yes. Walking the dogs! How I love picking up shit!"

Amanda glared at her. The dogs glared at her.

"Alright. Alright. It could be worse.." said Barbara, adding "The floor is a perfect place to work. *Jesus!*"

It had been a long day. Primarily, there was the provenance of the Statue to attend to. Both the Museum and Jacques required it for its exhibits. Jacques was using them as a platform to conduct international research on its previous whereabouts.

After all, a shooting had been committed in Spain when first buying the statue. Then distributing occurrences had followed the trail of the statue when the shopkeeper disappeared...

 But just as importantly, the Museum needed adequate insurance coverage reports and indemnification from any possible illegal activity related...This, the donor was required to do.

In addition, there was Tim Legardier who, with this request for further investigation, triggered an examination as to its authenticity and legitimate proprietorship since its disappearance during WWII. To say nothing of the diamond he showed up with. Did he mean it as payment? If he did, then they had decided to donate it to the Museum. However, a full explanation would have to be submitted with that donation.

Further, the matter of the DA's inquiry about the legacy Will and Testament might have ties to the events of the shipment in 1942. That might solve a cold case murder, which had no statute of limitations. Was there any connection? Barbara and Amanda went over it a dozen times.

Then there was the matter of Trevor's company and its litigation: What was going on? Allegations of fraud by the Insurance company due to loss of cargo at sea by a carrier? How had that issue suddenly surfaced? Wasn't the ship sunk? Where did that come from, thy wanted to know.

Still, there was something else in the air. It was the unmasking of a possible assailant who managed to avoid detection shortly after the war for crimes of theft, if not fraud as a financial broker first in London then in New York. The awful question remaining was the possibility that the beneficiaries might not only have profited then, but might be still operating today as the SEC was thinking...

More than once, they wondered how they had landed themselves in this situation. Or rather, how it had landed on their lap... The trouble was, the matter was expanding with unending possibilities. The space around them grew with opportunities and new leads. The blackboard was spreading. Images were now pasted to the wall, stickers on the furniture...

"My God" muttered Amanda.

"More coffee... " added Barbara.

Fortunately, the Study could be locked up with a key. That much could be assured in Amanda's apartment. Occasional visitors, housekeepers, special delivery drivers, servicemen, dog-walking friends and even Concierge management could show up unannounced.

No. They had to be discrete.

Nobody knew what they were doing. It was a clandestine operation of investigation. If perhaps from their days of disciplined and professional work as a Research Firm in Washington DC operating under tight security as government contractors...They required the assurance of confidential databases for analysis and classified intelligence. Officially, those days were over. But the analytical regimen and discriminatory skills were still there. Never was their need greater than to solve these issues...

The more they thought about it, the more they realized that this was not just about litigation or competition. It was about a crime rooted in the past, laced with evil, and with a legacy that remained masked.

This they had to solve. Before someone got hurt.

* * *

London.

Trevor was in the basement. He had a security officer at his side. Upstairs was a team of attending lawyers and accountants.

A building of this kind in London had seen its share of weather through the decades. It had emerged from an agrarian economy to forge industrialized factories; from gas light to electric and from wood fires to coal heat. The streets had changed from horse carriages to railroads and telegraph linking towns and markets. It had housed the painful transitions from patrician hierarchy to centralized labor houses. And it had survived the downturns of economy even as its architecture inspired the Victorian age of conspicuous consumption. .

Above all, its open-vaulted spaces valued the worth of individuals who worked here. And it had survived the wars. Such was the building when it was first built, before it lapsed into dereliction.

Trevor McDonnell bought it and restored it to its former gory. Today, it stood reflecting chrome, brass glass. wood and stone decorative arts and ornamentation - an icon of the city and the bank that used it...

The basement was well lit.

Glossy colored hallways, flanked by solid white wainscot. Parallel walkways provided for access to a row of bank-vault doors.

Temperature air-controlled precipitators ventilated partitions. Recessed lighting diffused illumination for subdued and natural thresholds, music audible from above grade-level. Sprinklers shone brightly at intervals along the ceiling. It was the access to bank vaults.

The windowless subterranean tunneling was a repository. Access restrictions between sections and partitions were computer-driven. Security admission enabled for few individuals, some requiring fingerprints and retina-recognitions only. Trevor McDonnell was one of them.

Once inside the innermost hallway, separate quarters attended each vault-room as a waiting area. Secured by reinforced concrete with sensitive monitors, the vault-chambers held some of England's most precious assets. Art work, statues, gold bullion, platinum, diamonds, mineral and man-made valuables lined the walls of some chambers.

Trevor was interested in one chamber stacked with papers. He gave his set of keys to his security officer who waited outside. Trevor worked alone in his chamber.

Documents and paperwork had been held for safekeeping by this bank for generations, some of it legacy and some of it viable. Mostly, they were Bank Notes and Bonds. One stack contained bonds of £100,000 bought by companies for gold deposits in 1942. This, he noted.

By the time he walked out and signed off, he had viewed most of his bank's collateral, issued against bonds or currency from the Central Bank. His signature was vital, and his certification was needed to meet the compliance requirements of his Bank.

His actions were itemized by his security officer, verifying ever step with a signature and time/stamp entry.

Next, Trevor inspected a room at the end of the hallway. He counted the stack of large 50-Lbs packets, and again asked the Security officer to verify. He entered it for a closer inspection. These were his own holdings.

As expected, he closed the door behind him and the vault keypad turned red. Twenty minutes later, he emerged with a look of satisfaction on his face.

 "Room 48 is accounted for" he said.

Their business complete, all security systems were re-sealed, and the progressed toward the elevators to upper floors.

In his mind Trevor was certain of one thing. There had been no miscalculation as alleged. His books were clean, his records accurate. Whatever litigation was out there would be challenged to the fullest extent of the law.

This, he asserted to his lawyers sitting upstairs in his offices. Both the recording secretary of the meeting, and the security officer who accompanied him affixed his name as witness to that statement.

The inventory was Certified and registered, their annual meeting adjourned.

x x x

New York

"Right" said Barbara, notebook in hand. "What have we got, so far?"

"So. We've got a statue that was picked up in Spain, found to be valuable, and donated to the Museum here in New York..." said Amanda, sitting on the floor and surrounded by papers.

Barbara moved to the laptop and documented the entry, adding "The museum accepted the statue and decided to put it up for a centerpiece exhibit for its fundraising campaign..."

"Do they plan to sell it off?" asked Amanda, relying on Barbara as her office manager to administer their Gift to the Museum.

"No! Not according to the director with whom I spoke. They just want to use it for promotion purposes, and to keep it under their management for now. Truth is, they don't know it's full value. It could be a work of art that is worth millions. They want to know, for sure, before losing it to a happy bidder at an Auction!"

"Uhah.."

"So far then all they had on file was their Antiquities Dealer's valuation on the International markets...what's his name?"

"Jacques de Toulaine. He has Galleries in France, Brussels and Rome..." said Amanda. "They know their stuff. And they have the financing behind them. So if he says its worth something, then its worth something."

"Do you trust him?"

"Yes. He's an old friend..."

"But we need an *American Insurance Certification*, right?" pressed Barbara.

"Right"

"And what about a American *Appraiser's Report*?" continued Barbara, delivering a string of strokes at her keyboard.

"Well. That's the problem. There's an issue..."

"O.k."

"Well, it's in the hands of an Underwriter who is required to report any unknown or illegal antiquities, if he finds it without provenance or catalogue history. That's what he's done. And that's why it's taking a bit of time."

"To whom is the Appraiser submitting his report?"

"Well, that's the thing. He's reported the matter to the SEC..."

"The *SEC*?" repeated Barbara.

"It's related to an investor's Asset that was supposedly listed on a manifest of a ship carrying precious items to the United States during the war..." Barbara remained silent.

"...But *not* received" finished Amanda. "They're unsure if it's the same piece or not..."

"And what will their Finding be?"

"It's hard to say what they'll decide... That depends what the Treasury can find in its Assayers Records of that time" said Amanda. "They recorded all they received."

"So what did it say?"

Amanda moved, shrugging a falling silk mane off her face and she lifted herself from the floor. She found a chair in the corner and collapsed in it. "That depends on your man"

"What man?" puzzled Barbara.

"Tim Legardier. The one who approached the museum about the statue. They sent him to you, remember?"

"Right, him!"

"He claims that his father, Thomas Legardier, was a London broker who invested for a German client called D..."

"Oh...Him with the diamond for hire!"

"To do his research.." Amanda finished.

"Yes. But we aren't doing his research. We're doing this for the Museum" she paused and thought. "So..." proceeded Barbara, now on the Laptop "He said his father's client, "Mr. D" claimed to be the son of a man who owned the statue?"

"Right. Mr. Kline" responded Amanda.

"So...err. The father, during the war was in business. And his son the client Mr. D"

"Right. Recently" said Amanda.

"But Tim wanted to know more...He said his father, Thomas Legardier, contacted the SEC. He asked about an asset supposedly listed on a Ledger during the war in New York."

"That makes sense. Mr. Thomas Legardier – your friend's dad, was told by Mr. D the statue belonged to *his* father. That is, before Mr. D's father suddenly went missing. It was during the war. He also said that his father had a partner. The business partner turned up in the United States shortly after the war..."

"He stole the statue from Mr. D's father?"

"No. The statue is never mentioned. But there was a Ledger account number, which Mr. D knew about."

Barbara looked down. "And that's when the trouble began at the SEC, right?"

"Yes. Trevor got a call from the Museum, and he called the SEC. Apparently, they found that the Account in question was found vacant, and never supplied."

"Which is where they found the ship's manifest listed in the Ledger. Right?"

"Right" repeated Amanda.

"And the ship's manifest itemized assets that were shipped to the United States for safekeeping..."

"Yes"

"The Manifest included a list of stuff, including a *drawing* - a sketch only - of the statue..." said Barbara running her eyes down a list of items from a copy of a document that the DA had given to them the day before. "Err...It lists 50-Lbs Packets, Gold Bullion, Jewelry Pieces, Precious metals, manufactured pieces etc.. Magnification pedestals, instrumentations, tool-bits and sharpening agents for cutting precious stones, etc.. So, it's a supply list for a shop's workbench, basically."

"Right"

 "Yes. And with the New York bank vault empty – the owner of the Account is a cold case ...subject to a Bank Fraud Alert Bulletin issued by the SEC and Department of Justice!" said Amanda.

"The Alert Bulletin was filed, citing stolen property. An image of the Ledger cover was included" recited Barbara.

Amanda nodded. "The   image... on the Ledger actually showed the name and address of a Construction company operating in New York during the war..."

"And that was picked up by the NY Detective in the District Attorney's Office who recognized the name of the Construction Company?" asked Barbara.

"The same construction company address and name was cited in their cold case at the DA's office involving a Last Will and Testament..." said Amanda. Barbara, returning to the keyboard to keep the facts straight, adding "Geeze, this is complicated!"

"It's connected" said Amanda. "'Without any Statute of Limitation on Murder cases, the file is *not* a Cold Case, just Unsolved."

"What's the connection, again?" said Barbara struggling at the key board.

"The matter was sent to the D.A.'s office by the Orphan's Court. The Orphan's Court was unable to file a Last Will and Testament, or retire a case, without prior Judicial decision or approval to execute the Last Will and Testament."

"Got it!" repeated Barbara. "So...*Damn* this keyboard!"

"It involved the Last Will and Testament of a woman saying that her husband had been murdered while working for a Construction company in 1942. She cited the name of construction company name. The same company cited on the Cover of the Ledger... It came up on the data files of the Alert Bulletin."

Barbara's fingers at the keypad froze. She looked at Amanda "Why would the woman wait all these years before coming forward?"

Amanda picked up the Factsheet that Karen McCullock had given them. "Because...she was threatened maybe? But that's just a guess..."

"A good guess!" said Barbara, thinking aloud "Why not wait until your own life is over to expose a husband's killer? *Tell* the Court about the crime in your Last Will and Testament...I think that's plausible."

"Once that Bulletin Alert went out, the novelty was fresh in people's minds. Especially for those who read police blotters news for entertainment!" said Amanda.

"Ha! And here we walk in with a statue to donate; a diamond to add...and the Museum starts wondering about us!" chuckled Barbara. "No wonder the Museum called me in!"

Outside, the sun came out.

They took a coffee break and went out to walk the dogs.

"...And what was the bank fraud about? An old empty account?" asked Barbara, unlacing two dog leashes. What does the SEC find?"

"Misrepresentation of Assets - and using them as collateral for borrowing large sums of money, for one charge. By showing the Ledgers 'authenticated and stamped,' who needed to lay eyes on the collateral assets? They just weren't there physically, evidently..."

Barbara stared at her, her mind clearly in places long ago in play.

Amanda handed her a fresh cup of coffee.

By early afternoon they were surrounded by a sea of notes, papers, pin-ups and files in the Study. What remained stubbornly unresolved was the core foundational question.

"So, who is this German 'family partner' who came to the United States and opened this bank vault box with a Ledger but *not* the goods?" said Barbara, finally.

"His identify remains elusive!"

"We don't really know which items were claimed. Maybe they were *taken out*? It's just empty. As in, without record," said Barbara, adding "Hey! ...So, why not ask the man who sold you the statue?"

Amanda looked up. That was a fair question, but one that actually put a frown on her face. Foolishly, she had asked her son Tray to approach the shopkeeper. She should have known better...

"The police found him dead!" said Amanda, tiredly. Her thoughts swept back to Tray.

He was the last person to see the shopkeeper alive.

And the last person to image the Workshop's documentation. Accounts that belonged to the shopkeeper...

* * *

Amanda spent the morning alone.

She was about to switch on the lights of her office but instead reached for the windows and drew back the curtains. A blast of sunlight flooded the room.

It had become a den of chaos.

She took a big breath.

Today, Barbara was not coming in because she had a doctor's appointment. That, plus a list of necessary chores to get done. Amanda didn't mind.

Without Barbara, there was opportunity to catch up on housekeeping. Amanda needed to freshen up the place. But it wasn't long before she re-entered the office.

Amanda focused on sorting through their findings. She organized. She tossed papers. She decided on false leads; poor assumptions and disappointments... You had to start eliminating things, she decided. Barbara kept everything. Cluttered everything. There was no space to think...

Frankly, she did not have the kind of eidetic memory that Barbara displayed, nor did Amanda like working in clutter.

She circled the room, clarity and deductions coming to her thoughts. Uninhibited, she had free range and delved now with depth of analysis...

For some reason, these days, she'd needed calmer surroundings and subdued lighting - Conducive to deeper investigative reflection, as she put it. Uninterrupted, she could find insight and reasoning embedded within simple facts. It was just her style.

Had she always been so conflicted and distracted?

She and Barbara had worked together before.

Perhaps that had accounted for their complementary abilities years ago. They accomplished much with some success in Washington DC.

Certainly, theirs had been the business to go to for difficult cases, and though they no longer worked professionally, this was a task they were now deeply invested in.

Regardless, she needed to clear the decks for some other matters.

She made tea. She made a list. Shopping, there was shopping to do. Gifts; clothes, provisions... She needed fresh seasonal clothes. She needed to visit the vet with dogs for their check-ups...

There was a ski trip to plan for! Surely Tray would need a ski-suit of some kind?

Then, if she could get a confirmation, a possible trip to the UK to follow Trevor? Still no word. And there it was... the lingering anxiety.

Christ!

She decided to focus on the provisions of the Law. Someone had clearly gone to a lot of trouble *knowing* of that provision. *Why?* How many years had it been? Why not come forward earlier?

Fear. But from *what*, exactly?

She checked their databases online. Subscribed, they had access to much archival and research information from source databases.

She played with the topic of Art History. Period Art. Personal Collections. Special Auctions...

Finished products were easily viewed in catalogues for commercial display, or when sold at Auction. However she found very little on artists' biographies. Of course, Jacques would have gone over all this, as would his various contacts and network of Appraisers across Europe. Still, she was glad she took the time make her own search online.

Finally she decided to visit the library herself to make a list of leads that would be helpful to look up. Especially downtown.

New York certainly had its history of fabulous private collections - and famous collectors! There were some private museums she should visit related to WWII. One was the National Archives at Hyde Park.

She was glad to be getting dressed. She needed to get out of the house. She checked her watch. Ten minutes and then she'd go!

Just one quick view online to check her email and she'd quit, she decided. There was an email from Derek Salaman .

"A journalist from the New Times (Mike Sparton) wants to publish a feature about the fundraising event and its donors. He asked to interview some the houseguests who came to the cocktail party. I gave him your name, if that's ok? He has questions about you and about the Statue...If that's alright?"

"Sure!" responded Amanda. "Any time early next week for lunch, if that suits him... By then I should know something about the Statue. (Going to Hype Park, tomorrow)

Glad to help!"

Best, Amanda Wells."

* * *

It was rainy outside. The sun came out periodically to glisten window streaks with silver threads, but inside the great Library, joy was found in pages and laptops for those sitting over them in quiet wonder.

Whereas most of Amanda's time was reviewing books found in nooks and crannies for possible leads, there was only one image that caught her attention. Ironically, it was in a Tourism magazine featuring President Franklin Roosevelt and his wife Eleonore at their home. The article was written in 1942, a Spring edition of the magazine, and it looked granular, if well preserved.

Amanda examined the picture. The couple were seated at their garden, she knitting, and he, reading. Behind them was shrubbery and bucolic blue mountains that surround the Hudson river. Further in the image, behind their bench, Amanda spotted a feature of white granite stoneware resting on a slate parterre at the river's edge. Too distant to be identifiable, it might have been something with recognizable characteristics. Amanda couldn't decide. Besides, it was partially concealed by bushes and barely a suggestive outline.

Yet, it had a certain grace. Such stuff was everywhere at that time, almost everybody had some kind of garden sculpture in their gardens. Back then, it was *de rigeur*. Hardly a work of art known for its artistic integrity or commemorative notoriety!

She had to get back.

For a day that was supposed to be free of tasks, she was remarkably busy that evening. Mail packages had stacked high with the concierge. Messages on her cell phone were left from just about everyone. Tray called.

"Hi Mom. Call me when you get a chance. I need to speak with you!"
Barbara called. Sonja called. Sandra called.
Sandra! She was in Sweden, with Eric, she said. They were having a wonderful time.
Amanda sensed that she was being prepared for possible news about a serious liaison there. And for Sandra, Amanda had all the time in the world to talk...
She looked down at her desk phone.
Still no word from Trevor.
Amanda fixed herself a light supper, watched the news, listened to Barbara's message about tomorrow's plans and texted her that she was off to Hyde Park in the morning for research.
Later in her bedroom, Amanda switched on the lampstand and stretched out on her *chaise longe*. She picked up her personal note book.
It was habitually her quiet time, a place to contemplate on matters, trips or events. She found holiday images of Trevor and her - standing together in Spain. The place where she had first laid eyes on the statue. In fact, if Trevor were not holding the thing, a bullet might have penetrated his shoulder...
She got up abruptly and went down to her laptop. All those images were saved. She brought them up and examined them closely. Images of the street; the river, night lanterns...The stone bridge where Trevor had pulled her tightly against his body...
She had taken images of the shop where she bought the statue: Two photos were taken indoors. One, an interior gallery shot, his wares and items on display. Evidently, the shop had so delighted her with its textile scarfs; filigree silver icons, embroidered bags,

local pottery, brassware and collectibles...that she had asked to take a picture! She smiled. The shopkeeper gave her permission to do. His shop was full. Items draped from overhead beams; lined the shelves, and filled all spaces. Even the shelve with the statue on it, which she bought...

Her eyes lingered over the details. And there was the statue. Beside it was a ship's model, doubtless carved by a shipwright and rendered in full with its ship's jolly-boat in tow, its little gunwale painted in blue and gold. How could she ever forget that wonderful day, she wondered, passing her fingers over the image.

But she had a reason for examining the picture on her laptop. Digital files opened and closed at her command.

She found it. The digital images sent to her by Tray were downloaded together in one separate file. She opened the file and zoomed in for magnification.

There again, the shopkeeper had obliged Tray to take images of the Ledger in which the statue was first listed. Evidently, the Ledger was long neglected, of no further use. Being old and unattended, the pages of the Ledger opened like empty tombs. And Tray had captured the pages of the Ledger as images!

Amanda examined each page and entry. A few pages of tiny handwritten notes – perhaps inventories, supplies and tools. Liner notations filled the pages now yellow with dust and age.

Orders of dye, grain, seed, beans and oils... From the few words of modern Spanish that she knew, Amanda could see inventories of deliveries of wood, wax, paint, even some mention of ivory. Boxes, bags,

piles and weights were listed, often with little more than faintly penciled ditto marks, and even less to show of any items shipped, received or sent.
Money? What money?
'*50 libras de paquetes – Sin Parar?*
 It was a hodge-podge of loosely drawn thoughts, written by an old shopkeeper...
She sighed. In all probability they were kitchen provisions, perhaps never even fulfilled in those early days of the modern world. It was a semi-imperial lazy colonial culture, back then. The sun was gracious to rural villages in that part of the world where ancient stone towns, olive trees and fishermen swarmed down by the warm wind off the blue sea. Who needed much more?
Amanda was tired. Tired of the unanswered, tired of shadow punching at ghosts.

x x x

Chapter 9

August, 1942

The *Rebel* was an American freighter on her way to Fall River, Massachusetts. A vessel of 4,600 tons of the Barber Line, she cruised up the Atlantic and was scheduled to stop in Trinidad.

She had been at sea since mid-June, having stopped intermittently along the coast of colonial West Africa. First at Takoradi, then along the Gold Coast, her holds laden with tin, copper, palm oil, liquid rubber and cocoa beans. She had a crew of forty five men, including ten officers of the United States Navy.

 In addition to her routine cargo, the ship also carried a secret cache of gold known only to the Captain. For this reason, the Captain made a decision to stop at Gibraltar before crossing the Atlantic, a sea infested with German U-boats.

What caused him to demure, however were the telltale signs of his rigging.

At the Straits of Gibraltar a differential had occurred in the weather. Usually in winter, this was unusual. The crew greeted the Levanter warmth with glee. The air had been stable, and the spread in the Atlantic between England and Spain seemed without incident or report... But the clouds, locally, were unusually low. Fog curled off the coasts. Other than tropical feelings, there was no cause for alarm for the Watchman.

Still, the Captain was wary. He noted that the characteristic banner cloud, flag shaped and normally seen atop the rock of Gibraltar, was absent. *"No flag sighting"* It was entered in the ship's log.

The Levanter cloud might stretch for a mile or so to the west. That meant that the wind speeds were below Bft 5. If a tad or two over that wind-speed, and the Rock of Gibraltar was known to create eddies and turbulences, often resulting in violent squalls and gusts, stronger even than the prevailing winds. It made for unpredictable sailing at this strange juncture between two continents.

No Westerly Poniente winds were evident since they usually caused residual choppiness from receding Mistral winds. Neither could he find signs of decreasing pressure or rising temperature.

The Captain was familiar with his naval history, and while this was a modern ship in a modern world, it was well documented that in the 17th century this very storm characteristic had taken down the entire Royal Navy Fleet, including its entire Treasury, followed by the monarchy of King William of England.

The Captain made a decision. He stayed off shore until nightfall. The pressure did not rise. Now he was certain that this was a hurricane brewing. Just before dawn, he spotted a fisherman's sailing vessel off his stern through his binoculars. He knew the signal. He had been 'waved off.' He understood, and he knew the reason. He also knew that he was under observation.

Within an hour, he approached Gibraltar, suggesting that he going to anchorage. He stayed within the channel where it was in the interest of all nations to keep open the waters - free of obstruction from any vessel sinking. Surely none would go through the Straights and venture into the Atlantic sea in such a storm.

The *Rebel* appeared to hesitate, then it surged through the Straights and sailed out to the Atlantic.

Rather than bearing westward, he headed north toward the United Kingdom. He remained just offshore to sail beyond the range of battery fire from the coastal gun placements. But he knew that no defense plane would fly, and no ship would give chase in this mounting weather.

He skirted the coast of England, and with the storm surging, he made his next decision. He took the vessel up to the Northward passage and crossed the northern Atlantic. It was a risk he had to take.

The destruction of American supply lines to the Allies was taking its toll. Daily, reports of American ships lost at sea carrying arms to the European were mounting. They were sunk by German U-boat torpedo attack.

He determined to elude the German U boats. He knew they would not be at sea under these conditions. It was too hazardous, even beneath the surface. That was their reserve when engaging in attack, certainly. Otherwise, they relied greatly on surface combatant sailing cargo...

The skipper made directly for Halifax, Canada. The *Rebel* carried enough fuel for that eventuality.

Below decks his was filled with 50 lb packets from Africa. It was a calculated risk, and he used the storm to avoid detection by the enemy. But the crossing had caused some damage to the hull. She was listing and taking on more water than the pumps could handle. It slowed her down.

By the time he reached Fall River, Massachusetts, he knew the ship needed repairs. He sent word to his US Naval Command that he had docked without incident.

The Skipper received a reply almost immediately. His orders were to sail directly to New York.

By the time *The Rebel* set out to sea again, the storm was abating in the northern hemisphere. It had shifted.

Further south, at the US Naval Air Station near San Juan, Puerto Rico, a Lieutenant in command of VP-31 gave the order to fly a squadron of naval aviators. His mission was to fly PBY's in search of submarines. Moreover, his command served as escort squadron for southern convoys of ships leaving South America for England. His instructions were to remain on High Alert.

The storm had intensified in the Caribbean, now a fast moving major hurricane, and it's destination was uncertain.

Flying was hazardous at best, the charge of ships afloat in the vicinity were surveyed. Oil derricks and petroleum refineries dominated the coastline of Trinidad's configuration, from *Serpent's Mouth* at the southernmost reach to *Dragon's Mouth* at the northern end.

At the Port-of-Spain harbor depot, ships were also loading petroleum at Point Fortin and Point-a-Pierre, all of them laden with oil destined for foundries, fuel depots, transportation stations and installations across Europe.

The Lieutenant was nervous, he peered out of his binoculars. Storms did strange things to ships to make them change direction, he knew. Especially in these waters where just beneath the surface, Jerry U-boats searched for ships to sink.

He was also aware of a Convey held at port by the storm.

A V-class destroyer *HMS Vancouver* had arrived at Norfolk Virginia, having escorted the *HMS Queen Elizabeth* from Freetown, Sierra Leone on the west coast of Africa.

 The *HMS Vancouver* had honorably delivered over 3000 troops from Dunkirk two years earlier. But later s assigned to the Convoy Escort Force based at Freetown. Now, along with other destroyers, her task was to ensure the safe passage of troopships and battle ships attempting to cross the Atlantic from Canada and the USA.

A U-boat was cited just off the coast, and the squadron of aviators were called up to investigate.

The Lieutenant thought it an easy run and back, ahead of the storm. But this call came out of Norfolk, Virginia, and he'd have to deploy special aircraft for a longer range, some 450 miles north.

His messages came in rapidly. Firstly, a report that the ship *Huran* was down, a tanker. German U-boat U67 was known for her accuracy in sinking ships. Once she got a bearing in her sights, there was little that averted two short range torpedoes.

The next call gave the coordinates.

"Longitude ten degrees, fifty north; latitutde fifty four degrees even."

The Lieutenant started to calculate the sighted positioning, he repeated the numbers from clenched teeth, recognizing the spot. A deep horror gripped him.

U-Boat 67 was going to Norfolk to destroy half the US Navy

He sent up everything he could.

The U-Boat was searching for the entrance channel. But as the storm gathered, the waters receded along the continental shelf, and the submarine pulled away from the American shallow coastline.

The U-boat changed bearings due northward, and within several hours, positioned itself off New York in deeper waters.

The *Rebel,* before reaching New York, had come into the sights of the U-boat. Easily, it fell victim to torpedo attack.

The *Rebel* sank with all hands.

x x x

Amanda toured the gardens at Hyde Park, the home of former President Roosevelt and his wife Eleonore. Located along the banks of the Hudson river, all sections of the estate and gardens were open to the public as a Park Museum. The grounds were groomed, all access paved and secured; and its library a national archive for the collections. .

As a Presidential Library managed by the National Archives and Records Administration, it housed original documents and papers both private and public. Franklin D. Roosevelt had served as President of the United States for four consecutive terms of office at the White House in Washington DC. He and his Cabinet had managed to navigate the country through tortuous years in American history, especially WWII.

Under supervision of tight security, Amanda gained entry into the Library by filling out the paperwork and passing the scrutiny necessary to access valuable collections.

As the day wore on, she was astonished at the intensity of a war that became the purview of the President at that time. In this collection were documents of epic battles, victories and defeats. It engulfed almost every continent, leaving over 70 million people dead.

With the help of an archivist, Amanda viewed the world that had surrounded Roosevelt during his terms of office. Most remarkably, she knew, Roosevelt accomplished his work as a man disabled by polio and confined to a wheelchair.

In addition to the archives Amanda found a reading library of attending published works about the events that followed. Amongst them scholarship and journals related to policy changes. The New Deal. Public Health. Monetary Policy. Thus, Amanda had both the benefit of private documents and published analysis about his decisions.

It was a prodigious library. Chief amongst those topics were some of the desperate measures that Roosevelt had to be taken during his tenure. Or, as one senior official said 'desperate measures for desperate times'...

One was the abolition of the Gold standard as a monetary system, world wide. It a daring move, and a necessary act of financing the war.

Historically, the gold standard was a monetary system where any normal financial unit of account, or value, was based on a 'fixed' quantity of gold valuation. Three types of gold were known. Specie, bullion, and exchange.

Gold specie, Amanda read, meant all monetary units associated with circulating gold coins.

Gold bullion was all monetary value held in gold bullion by the authorities, and sold on demand to banks at a fixed price in exchange for circulating currency.

The Gold Exchange standard was the Government's guarantee of value, based on it's gold reserves.

Roosevelt changed all that. Since the Depression of the 1920s, when adherence to the gold standard prevented the Federal Reserve from expanding the money supply to stimulate the economy, or to fund insolvent banks, or to fund government deficits that could "prime the pump" for expansion, the gold standard monetary system was considered too restrictive.

However, during World War II, the gold standard was kept without domestic convertibility. The role of gold was severely constrained: Now, all nations currencies were fixed in terms of the dollar.

As a result, many nations sent their gold supply to the United States for safekeeping, the Archivist told Amanda. At the very least, it was kept out of the hands of the enemy! Most of it was delivered by ship, he explained. Other commodities followed. But there was also another reason that gold was shipped to America. It was to pay for the war, to finance the armaments - wartime equipment, airplanes, tanks and combat ships that the Americans were sending to Europe as an Allied effort to fight Nazi-Germany.

Amongst those lists, were ships which sank when attacked by enemy submarine torpedo U-boats.

Amanda's eyes fluttered down the names of the ships. The lists told of cargo loss, lives perished at sea, supply and deliveries from America prevented from reaching Allies.

By each name, its country of origin was shown with little flags, their colors filling the lists in pages, and their tons of cargo listed in ways that showed how vulnerable the Allies were...

One little flag caught Amanda's eye. It had colors beside it that she recognized. She could not discern what it was, exactly. But she asked the Archivist to pull the file that would hold its particulars.

Shortly thereafter, Amanda knew, Russia entered the war on the side of the Allies. They, along with British and Americans troops at their side, came to the fronts of battle. Russia paid heavily in troops and men, even as she emerged from the war with a socialist government under Stalin. Clearly, Roosevelt knew him well.

Amanda left at 4 pm. Her thoughts were a jumble and her heart heavy. Yet, it was said to lead to a 'golden century,' as Winston Churchill put it when he met with Roosevelt aboard the *HMS Prince of Wales* off Nova Scotia. The pictures of that Conference were vivid. Its decks, filled with seamen, showed Heads of State aboard to strategize and prevail in this war.

Newly built by the British, the *HMS Prince of Wales* battleship was the pride and joy of the Royal Navy, and clearly, the newspaper picture of Roosevelt seated besides Churchill and his ministers was an encouraging sight of might and invincibility. Yet, barely eight months after the event, the *HMS Prince of Wales* was sunk with all hands.

It wasn't until Amanda was half way home that she recognized why it was that in the list of ships The *Rebel* stood out. *She had seen its colors!*

Painted along the gunwales of a Jolly-boat in tow, it carried those colors in the ship's model displayed in a Spanish tourist shop. *The Rebel*, in fact, was not a sailboat after all.

She was a merchant ship of the sea, fitted for duty.

And the carpenter had carved a model of her.

She had been a supply ship sunk by the enemy in enemy channels because she was carrying valuable cargo.

x x x

Derek Salaman got a call on his cell phone. He'd just been chatting with his brother in Miami...

The call was not long.

"It's Stephen. You told me to call. The file was pulled and reviewed..."

"Who...?"

"The researcher was someone named Amanda Wells."

"Got it. Thanks!"

The Archivist hung up and proceeded with his duties. It was closing time, anyway. He knew there would be money in his account by morning.

He got into his car, and drove home to Connecticut from Hyde Park.

* * *

Amanda was pleased to have the weekend to herself. She would reflect on the files now captured in her laptop computer, images of documents taken when researching at Hyde Park.

Amanda was curious about something else.

When at Hyde Park, she spotted something that she saw in the New York Library, showing the President and his wife sitting in their garden with a granite figure in the background.

At Hyde Park, in the personal papers collection, Amanda found a file of correspondence between the President and an artist. A sculptor. She didn't have time to linger, but she quickly took photographs of the pages.

It didn't surprise her really. Amanda understood. It took her no time to read through Roosevelt's matters about his house and gardens. Especially his interest in his garden statuary. She stood back, contemplating the similarities. The granite figure was remarkably like the smaller statue that she and Trevor had purchased in Spain. In fact, she was almost certain of it!

Further, she found considerable correspondence between the artist and the President. This, during a time of war? Who would have guessed, she thought. Why?

The answer came soon enough. He was corresponding with a recognized American artist. Certainly, the President could have had his pick of European work, but he wanted an American sculptor, depicting the same kind of grace and beauty that his garden ornamentation offered, he explained. It gave him solace, he told the sculptor in correspondence, because he found such expression in its face. It moved him, it was a moment that quieted the mind and soothed the soul...

His words put a smile on Amanda's face. She touched the words, as if in utter sympathy with his anxious state of mind.

Yet, surprisingly, from his personal account, the President had commissioned another statue, a second statue!

Now at home, she thought about it.

The sculptor's letters left her puzzled, if not annoyed. What artist would *argue* with his patron? Especially if the patron was the President of the United States?

What on earth was going on here?

Evidently, the sculptor was straying from his mission. He was an angry man. He wanted to artistic license to deliver what *he* thought was something more righteous. Something to be reflected in his artwork that expressed something of the circumstance in which they lived: This was a day of anger and activism for those who felt strongly about the war! Why were the laborers of America not compensated. He cared little for battlefronts.. and moral justice, he admonished...

He would do his art as he saw fit, he declared. He believed in the Labor Movement, a movement that did not agree with this war in Europe. *Let other people sink with their own problems...*

Amanda's heart fell with every letter that passed between them. How lonely a place it must have been for a President to be surrounded by people all day, and to be prosecuting a war around the world, and yet not find the solace from a work of art that meant something to him...

Amanda felt angry at the Artist. How dare he infuse the commission of art with politics and pain and guilt at a time like this, she thought.

Her cell phone buzzed like a fire alarm. Barbara.

"Hia!" she said. "How are you doing?"

"I'm err...going through material I got at Hyde Park..." she managed to say.

"Guess what?" continued Barbara "I've arranged for us to meet with a daughter of Mrs Green tomorrow afternoon. She lives in Brooklyn. 3 oclock..."

It took Amanda by surprise, but she agreed. She had quite forgotten what the Assistant District Attorney had asked them to do.

"Sure!"

"I'll meet you at Starbucks, 1.30 pm. And we'll take a ride together?"

"Right"

"Ok" said Barbara, adding "... Err, you ok?"

"Yes!" answered Amanda, if a little too sharply.

"Tomorrow then" finished Barbara, ending the call.

She gathered up the paperwork for the night, and began to shut down the images. But something caught her eye that she had not noticed before.

Roosevelt wrote, in another letter to a friend dated later in the year, that he had sent a picture of the statue to an artist in Europe.

The artist made a sketch of the statue...

* * *

Karen McCullock opened the file. She had reviewed it once before, but again she read through the details. Not because she felt obligated, but because she recognized the name on the signed affidavit that disputed the alleged claim by the defendant.

The diseased had submitted a Deposition with a declaration amounting to a possible homicide.
The woman, a New York resident called Mrs. Green, referred to her husband's death. He had died, she claimed, after operating a large shipment of material in his construction business. She knew he was murdered, she said, and could prove it.
Karen understood the crime of murder had no statute of limitations. The passage of time made no difference to prosecute a murderer. But proving a cold case was not easy.
She returned to the evidence.
He was a cement mixer. It was during the war. He had lifted solid material into his cement mixer to be camouflaged. The material was steel, or metal, used for ship construction at the Naval shipbuilding yards. The work was to elude notice by enemy spies, they had told him.
The process was repeated for several nights. He was to deliver the camouflaged steel bars to a construction site. The shipyard was supposed to come to pick them up.
Shortly after the last run, the statement said, he was killed, and his body never recovered.
The wife suspected foul play. A building was erected over the site where he had delivered the material. She felt that the Shipyard never recovered the

material. She visited the site often over the years. She kept a list her husband's jobs. His job instructions had been saved by her husband, a work-contract of sorts, signed by the construction project manager. Now, in her Last Will and Testament, she enclosed the list, and revealed the name.

Mrs Green suspected something was wrong. Her husband was killed because he knew something. He claimed that a cargo had been stolen from a shipment of cargo during the war.

A hand-scribbled note above the transcription said:

"The site of a construction project waiting to pour cement allowed him in the darkness of the night to upend trucks into its hollowed structural pillars, then he in-filled with cement. There, the metal would wait, even until after the war when he could reclaim it as a contractor. This, he could arrange as the bond-holding contractor, and he would re-construct the columns of the building.

As they all sat in her office, Karen discussed the matter with Amanda and Barbara. She told them this was the reason that they were called in.

"So, as you can see" she said "I need more information. Ideally, I need to find a body!"

A message came in and interrupted them. Karen was needed downstairs in court.

"So, *whatever* you can find for me, anything close to the sources as possible would be a help. Remember, my challenge will be to show relevance through the passage of time, which has a way of clouding the issue..."

"Here!" bellowed Barbara, seated beside the driver. She pointed and looked up from her navigation device. "There is it is...down there. Turn!"

They parked not far from a site once marked as the Navy Yard. It was now a sprawling site fenced off and deteriorated by years of neglect.

Two blocks away they found the house.

They had debated whether to take a cab or drive, and they were pleased with their choice.

"I never did quite understand what the ADA wanted us to find..." muttered Barbara.

"Evidence. And credibility" affirmed Amanda.

"What we have to do to prove her case for her..." said Barbara.

They walked up to the entrance of a house, a structure aging, yet position in a row of upgraded homes that had increased in value

 "No. Just the facts. So let's ask..." said Amanda, ringing the doorbell.

"Please do come in!" said the woman in her late fifties. "I'm glad I can be of help. We prepared a little something for you, my daughter and I..."

Their afternoon visit was quite anticipated. Prepared on a sideboard was a buffet with coffee, tea, cookies and cake.

They chatted. A world of stories passing through the years of a city like New York filled the hour. Dorothea told of her parents and her family, especially her mother, Mrs. Green.

They owned the house, she told them. But a developer had recently approached them, now that her mother was dead, and they hadn't decided what to do.

Barbara was the one doing the talking. She related easily, she was saying. Many had left the city after the war, others still living in New York had become outdated, surrounded by a new culture of edgy activism and angry politics. Most had found a simpler life on the margins, like Dorothea who worked as a bookkeeper.

A young girl came down the stairs and stood by the door.

"My daughter, Phebe" said Dorothea.

The girl smiled, then entered the kitchen. She did not engage. She waited. Hers was a world away. She attended a school where students wore leather clothing and shackles for jewelry.

"So. Yes. I asked her, I did.. Ma, I said, why you doing this?" said Dorothea.

"To avenge your father!" she told me.

Dorothea thought a moment. "I swear, the lawyer charged her five hundred dollars for that statement...She wanted it all on paper!"

"So, what exactly did you mother think happened?"

"Well...Let me see. She said my Dad worked on this construction worksite during the War. He had to unload cargo from the ships at the docks, then pour cement. There was much going on at that time. New York was ...People everywhere. Life going on, you know... But a mess of things happening. Still, bars, clubs. Newspapers. Lights-out at night...that's what she said, my mother..."

"Where was your father working, do you know?"

"At Consolidated. He owned his own cement mixer! And it was trashed years later after he was gone..."

"He told my mother he worked for a man called Herman. He unloaded his goods at night, and stored them in his warehouse. He had told her that he thought it was ingots he was unloading in his cement mixer, so as to coat them in cement..."

They waited. Thoughts of such a world in turmoil left them silent.

Dorothea got up and brought over a plate of sliced cake.

"Then one day, he never returned from one of the sites he was working on" she continued.

The young girl appeared from the kitchen with a jacket on, clearly ready to go. She gave her mother a look of furious impatience.

Dorothea stood and talked to her daughter. They were "leaving soon" she whispered.

On the drive home they said little.

It had been a long afternoon with Mrs. Green. They were entertained with pictures. They took notes, asking questions, consulting documents and looking at family mementoes.

A lifetime of family existence had unfolded before them. Less privileged than most perhaps, but the Greens had lived a life full of colorful events, stories, and laughter. A world away, it seemed.

Finally, Amanda pulled over and paused, the engine still running. Neither spoke.

They were to pick up where they left off in the morning at 8 A.M. That was the plan. They had work to do if they were to piece together connections that would be of help to Karen, especially as she asked them to do...

But something had altered, and they drifted forward, lost in thought.

By the time they crossed the bridge the sun was disappearing into the night and they drove along the parkway.

How to explain the situation to Karen, they wondered. Clearly, they were on the right track.

Amanda was supposed to drop off Barbara. Instead, she said "Shall we stop for food?"

She pulled into a space at the Blue Restaurant. The rustic décor on the harbor suited them well. It was as if they were in a world gone by...

After the daughter Phebe had left, Dorothea stood up to retrieve a family heirloom that she wanted to show them. Something her father had given to her mother, she explained.

There it sat, as she unfolded a dark velvet napkin. A brilliant blue diamond...

Amanda ordered creamy Tomato and Basil soup. Barbara ordered clams and artichoke.

"So what do you think of her?" asked Amanda finally.

"Well, the daughter is a teenager in High School, frustrated. She lives daily in a conflicted world where family is the enemy. What's *not* to understand?" said Barbara.

"Are you prejudiced?"

"Who cares? I'm not politically correct, if that's what you mean..."

"Public coercion has many names. I get it. But if that's your opinion..."

"See. It's more than my opinion. It's a fact. Why? Because it comes at a cost. A human cost. A cost in new Foreclosures. Immigration invasion. Unemployment. Disrespect for our parents. For their jobs, their contribution to society...To us, even. Yeah, it's my opinion. Damn right it is!"

"We embrace the future with courage and hope, Barbara."

Barbara didn't respond, and Amanda knew she'd said enough. "How are the muscles?" she asked.

"Well... it's easy for you to say" said Barbara, pushing the food around her plate. "You're in the kind of financial world that doesn't see all this. But for the rest of us, there's always a price to pay..." blurted Barbara, her face distraught. "Who gets a thinking job if you're over 50 in America? Huh?"

"that bad, eh?"

"What, the jobs...?"

"The muscles."

They paused. Finally Barbara raised her napkin to her lips. "Hey, I'm sorry! You don't deserve that outburst. You've been the champion of things that matter...It's what I admire about you Amanda!"

The waitress returned.

"How about we share the *Twin Lobster Tails*?" asked Amanda. "Or would you prefer a steak?"

"No. That's good!" said Barbara, looking up at the waitress. "Two plates, please!" She grinned. "Any bread rolls?"

Amanda ordered a bottle of California white wine to be followed by coffee and desert.

The sun set on a slow-moving waterfront.

Inside, it was warm. Overhead beams and early stonework took on a home effect that enveloped them.

 "What do you make of Mrs Green's account of her mother?" Amanda asked.

"I think she's a world away. Quite lost in this vicious economy. I mean, where does she fit in exactly?"

"But that diamond..."

"Definitely. It's the same batch from the piece that Tim Legardier produced for *our* services - which we're giving to the Museum, of course. It's the same cut, size and color of gemstone. No question!"

"Do you feel certain?"

"I do."

"I agree" nodded Amanda. "So if that's evidence of the same source of gemstones, is there any connection?"

Barbara shrugged.

"Well in that case, I suggest we keep things simple. For now at least. Let's make our report to the DA's office showing only what we've discovered so far. Plus a copy of this image..." said Amanda producing her cell phone with the image of a diamond in the hand of Mrs. Green.

"Right!"

"I'll have it written up by Monday morning. When is she expecting us?"

"Tuesday."

"Ok. No specifics. No analysis. No speculation and no Legardiere visit!" said Amanda. "Why advertise our findings with an email?"

"Right. It'll be all over the Internet within 2 days!" agreed Barbara. "So much for online privacy...I mean, that's another thing I don't like about big tech, did I mention?..."

Amanda held up her hand. *Enough!*

They paid the check.

"Are we still shopping tomorrow? I need some clothes, please..." asked Barbara.

Amanda nodded.

Barbara always paid for her own clothes. But she loved having Amanda around, regardless.

x x x

Chapter 10

Karen McCullock poured sugar into her morning coffee when Paul Talbot knocked on her office door jamb.

"You're not going to believe this..." he began, lowering his bulk into the seat across from her desk.

"Hmm...I hate it when you come in here with a you're-not-going-to-believe-this...story. What's up?"

He tossed the file onto her desk and sat there looking disgruntled, his tie loose, and his clothes rumpled.

"Long night?"

"The police called me at 9 pm. I've been up all night trying to 'reframe the question,' let's say."

"Here..." said Karen, placing a paper cup of hot coffee his way. "Drink this, give me the paperwork, and get some rest..." Talbot was one her best detectives.

"Not so fast" he said. "Word got out to Nick's office. The police commissioner wants an immediate Response to deliver at his Press Conference. How it got out, I don't know. But I'm giving you fair warning that they want this one done on short order. It's not pretty. It's bad publicity..."

"OK" she said. "So tell me about it... What happened?"

"It began with a pipe bursting on 53rd Street yesterday..."

Karen took her place at her desk.

"At first they thought it might be a gas leak. But it was a water main. They called in the District Maintenance Management office, then the Utility company and they started digging for repairs. They hit a power line, and the street was shut down. No injuries reported, just delays and inconvenience..."

"Oh God!" chuckled Karen

"Then...turns out they unearthed some brickwork from an older foundation of a building that was demolished in the early 70s. There, in the rubble, were the remains of a body."

Talbot sipped his coffee, a serene expression of gratitude crossed his face. Karen waited.

"They called the Medical Examiner's office, and nearly had it all delivered away by dark. Except that a couple of neighborhood kids got a drift of the story and played with the street covering, a temporary metal plate that covered the opening in the road. They opened it up, someone got hurt and an ambulance finally got there in the early hours..."

"So what is the official complaint?"

"The skull remains had been immured in the foundation brickwork, and some silver fragments turned out to be chains. This, the kids discovered, and now it's a matter of public knowledge that a crime was uncovered in a neighborhood that is unsafe..."

"Forensics?"

"The medical examiner won't get to his findings until tomorrow. The press conference is scheduled for 10 am. The city commissioner wants to explain

that the 'time frame' of the incident is far distant from today's situation, and that the street will be repaired in a safe and responsible manner...And that the neighborhood is safe!"
"Any means of identification with the body?"
"None"
Karen was already opening the file and dialing the medical examiner's office. "What I'll be needing..." she said "is...at the very least, a date of death..."
"Right."
She put down the phone and looked at him directly, her thoughts forming a plan. "There's no way around this but to tell the truth and explain that this event happened decades ago. That's for starters..."
"Right" said Talbot.
"*Not* what this city needs just now..." she added, dialing a Contact direct for the DA's office. "We've had our share of disaster, God knows..."
He nodded, knowing what she meant. It was always the same when something so public occurred. The specter of 9/11 was never distant from the authorities of New York City, old wounds or not.
Karen was kept on Hold, and silently she mouthed "get some rest...you did a good job staying up..." She turned suddenly. "Hello? Yes..thanks! I'd like to meet with both Denis and Peters, asap, please!"
Talbot was leaving when Karen's administrative assistant popped her head around the door "Police Commissioner is calling you on Line Two, waiting..."

* * *

"What do you think?" asked Barbara, spinning on her platform boots, weaved tights and bell drop dress.

"Err…" began Amanda.

"It's sharp. It's edgy and it's the coloring that goes with her hair highlights" said the attendant, a short girl in pigtails, apparently from Yugoslavia.

Barbara peered at Amanda straight. No need or words. OK. She got it. She'd gone a little too far over the top.

"Right then. How about this?" she said, pulling a sweater and pants from the dressing room.

"For… an evening soiree?" asked Amanda.

Barbara's eyes narrowed with annoyance. "Fine!"

They walked out with only the boots.

"What do people wear at Museum Galas, like?" muttered Barbara as they crossed the street and entered a corner café.

Amanda didn't answer. This was a performance, she knew. Barbara could dress very well when she wanted to. This was messaging time. A time of annoyance, evidently.

"What?" insisted Barbara, her chin out in challenge.

"Well. You dressed very nicely in Washington…"

"Oh, that thing. Well, Trevor was with us, and for that I dressed up!"

Amanda balanced her coffee on the small table, hesitating.

"So, you heard from him?" asked Barbara.

Amanda looked out the window.

"I see" said Barbara. "So, you're gonna sit here like a victim and stay calm, is that it?"

"What do you expect me to do?"

"Raise hell... Fight for your life! For his life...or for everyone else, for that matter."
"Oh? Play activist just because the world isn't going my way?"
"Exactly!"
"I'm not the screamer type"
"No. But you're hurting. And more importantly, somebody might get hurt if we don't dig deeper and get this right. Something is terribly wrong with all this. We've got to find out what it is..."
Barbara's cell phone rang. "*Hey...* That's great news! Thanks. I'll tell her..." she said, looking straight at Amanda.
"Well..." grinned Barbara. "That was the museum informing us that they have an insurance company willing to underwrite the statue for the exhibit! So we're in the clear, for starters..."
Amanda had to smile at her long-time business associate. Always efficient. Always able to get results.
"That's great news!" said Amanda.
"Yeah. It is. Especially since they delivered the message to me today, directly."
They bought more clothes. With a nod here, and a *Yes* there, Amanda ended up directing all Barbara's purchases. The choices were a tad more conservative, but versatile, and not always that expensive. Even a haircut followed. Later, with a nice sheen on her bangs, Barbara looked ten years younger, and not as hard.
"I'll say this for you - since I'm the one doing all the talking today, you *do* have better taste than I" said Barbara. "Now how about you?"

The last thing in the world that Amanda felt like doing was shopping for herself. However, to please her friend, she did pick a scarf off a peg in a small garden boutique.

"You going on a cruise with *that* thing?" asked Barbara.

Amanda laughed. "No, not really. It just reminds me of Miami, all those pink flamingos..."

"I'll say!" giggled Barbara licking on an ice cream cone. "So, when is your Trevor-Anthony coming back?"

"Tray, for short..."

"Tray, then."

A looked of apprehension filled Amanda's eyes.

"So. *That's* what's worrying you!"

Amanda looked away. They walked.

The cab dropped off Amanda first, stopping at the foot of her building. Barbara added "Anyway...We got good news today: The Museum is happy with the provenance of the statue. It's insured!"

Amanda waved back.

Upstairs, Amanda received a hearty greeting from both dogs. She unpacked her shopping bag, filled their water supply and leashed them both for a quick walk around the block.

Amanda showered. She had fixed herself a light meal with a short glass of chardonnay. She retreated to the lounge and switched on the evening news.

Since when did museums make personal calls about getting an item *insured*, she wondered.

And on a *Saturday?*

Surely business hours were Monday to Friday.

Why today?

Why call Barbara directly on her private cell phone and not leave a message at her business number...? Usually those kinds of administrative proclamations came officially by mail, on formal stationary with the museum disclosure and certifications etc.
Otherwise, a quick call by an Administrator could be made if applicable to other matters.
What was going on here?
These were not volunteers. These were paid professionals with strict organizational procedures and authorizations who worked within the framework of normal policy.
No. Something was amiss.
Especially regarding an item of inventory listed in their catalogue. An item of some worth and value?
She walked into her Study and sat at her desk.
 On her phone was a message from the District Attorney's office.

> *"Hi. Call me! I can't make the meeting*
> *Tuesday. But this is important. So, err, mind*
> *if I ask you to bump up your schedule and*
> *come in Monday? Actually....Call me. And, if*
> *you can just come in Monday morning. Paul*
> *will be here..."*

x x x

They were met in the lobby by Detective Talbot.
"This way ladies!" he gestured.
They followed him through several offices.
Clearly, there was no rest here. In this building, they were serving a big city with activity calling in at every hour of the clock. Conversations were ongoing at every nook and cranny of office space.
"...It makes no difference if he does have diplomatic immunity...We still have the right to meet with him and ask him questions about the incident..."
Talbot waved.
"The Judge wants us to do what?...Wait...But that's privileged source-information that the journalist won't give up!"
Talbot finally led them to a quieter area. He indicated the table and closed the door.
Out came a folder. He placed it on the table.

"Ms McCullock is downstairs in Court this morning. She asked me to see you. I wanted to ask you a few more questions, if that's alright?"
"Sure" said Barbara.
He looked up. "So, you work for the McDonnells as their private secretary from time to time?" .
"Yes. I used to work for them full time in Washington. That was a few years ago."
Talbot nodded. "You say that a man contacted you about the donation that was made to the Museum by the McDonnells?"
"Yes."
"...which is being valued at some price, I'm told. Is that correct?"
Barbara looked at Amanda.

"It holds value as a work of art in rarity and artistry"
said Amanda.
"Which...you err...bought in Europe. Is that right?"
"Yes."
"Is it insured?"
"Yes."
"For how much, if I may ask?..."
"At the moment, $3 million dollars" said Amanda.
"You have the paperwork. As does the Museum!"
Talbot inspected the document.
"Is there a problem detective? Ms McCullock asked
that we come in this morning?"
"No. No problem. Just asking, is all..."
He looked up.
"Who is this Assessor, Jacques de...Jacques de"
"Toulaine. He's an Antiquities Dealer in France"
responded Amanda. "We're waiting on an evaluation
by a certified US specialist or broker who can
appraise the piece also."
Talbut turned to Barbara. "You told Ms. McCullock
that you were approached by Mr. Tim Legardier who
recognized the sculpture? Did he give you any
details as to where he knew about the piece?"
"No. In fact, he asked us to research it further..." she
answered.
Amanda cast a fierce warning look to Barbara. They
had agreed not to divulge the details of his offer to
pay them with a diamond for research services. That
would be disclosed in due course.
Barbara understood.
The room fell silent.
Amanda felt uneasy suddenly.

"Detective, this visit is voluntary. However, if there are any further questions, perhaps we should ask our attorney to be with us?"

He smiled.

"The thing is Mrs McDonnell, we know that the Museum suspects a diamond was offered to you for your research work. Ms. McCullock is downstairs meeting with the SEC and their attorneys. They have some interest in the source of that diamond. In fact, as we speak, we have a search warrant to inspect your apartment..."

"*What*?" blurted Barbara standing up.

"We shall retrieve all your paperwork and research, as it relates..." finished Talbot.

Amanda placed a retraining hand on Barbara's arm. She turned, her voice calm.

"Detective, you invited us down here on false pretenses. So that you could search our apartment?..."

Talbot got up. "May I bring you ladies something to drink? Coffee? Soda?"

He left.

They sat in silence. Speechless. Turmoil filled their thoughts, Barbara's face was pale with anger.

Search Warrant?

Amanda felt outraged. A simple request would have been adequate. She would have cooperated. She felt that her privacy had been violated.

When Talbot returned she said "Was this...*necessary* detective?"

"I'm afraid so Mrs. McDonnell."

"But I don't understand...Why you would need to ..."

"I'll explain," he said, adjusting his seat.

"And I do think you might want to consult with your attorney. The thing is, we've just uncovered a body whose remains show that the victim had swallowed *this* prior to his demise..."

He opened a digital image and placed it on the table. Barbara and Amanda gazed at a Petri dish containing a small item, untarnished by age or dirt.

At first, it was hard to distinguish. But it soon became evident. It rested solitarily, a diamond. And it looked almost identical to the one Mrs. Green had showed them.

Neither Barbara nor Amanda uttered a word.

"Frankly, we're puzzled" continued Talbot. "We have no answers for the SEC. And your statue is attracting attention Mrs. McDonnell. We'd like to know why..."

"I need to speak to Ms. McCullock" said Amanda firmly. "We were about to submit our report on our interview with Mrs. Green..."

It took several calls, and it did cause some disruption, but Karen McCullock come to the phone. "I'm sorry Amanda. It came to a head very suddenly.."

Amanda interrupted. "We're trying to find the identify of the man who killed her husband in 1942 - as cited in the Last Will of Mrs. Green. As *you asked us* to do!"

"Go on!"

"We met with her daughter, and we asked her questions. She did *not* know who it was that her mother was referring to..." Amanda paused. "Now, please tell us. What is all this about?"

"I understand your frustration. But there are just too many coincidences right now. Mind I call you back in a day or two?"

"Excuse me Karen. But you are searching my apartment. You are seizing all my records and research papers" said Amanda. "I'd like to know what grounds you have to do so. What *'probable cause'* do you have to qualify for a search warrant to inspect my premises?"

"I'll explain later..." said Karen. "The probable cause came from the diamond showing up at the Museum! It was connected to an enquiry made about your statue. We needed to follow up..."

"You could have just *asked* us..." said Amanda.

There was a pause in the conversation.

Then a thought occurred to Amanda.

"Who is conducting the search?" she asked.

"An attorney's firm is doing that part of the investigation for the SEC. Bill Wickowsky, he's doing pro-bono work. He's on the staff of Salaman brothers..."

They left the building. Neither uttered a word.

Nothing had been disclosed about the diamond that was held by Mrs. Green, daughter of the diseased.

Nor was there anything written in their Notes - now being searched and collected.

As they walked they were both thinking the same thing: There would be found nothing that revealed incriminating evidence. Nor any trail of suspicions. That much they had learned from their years of working as Researchers for the government under strict security provision. It was an old procedure used as precaution against prying eyes and unfriendly competitors. Work habits died hard. Every day they had practiced caution and care with their work papers.

"I need coffee..." husked Barbara, out in the street.
"Let's go!"
One thing became clear.
Somebody wanted their information.

x x x

Amanda decided it was time to retire Barbara.

The less she knew, the less danger she'd be in. And quite definitely, some serious probing was underway with regards to their research.

However, short of firing her outright, there was little she could do to mitigate its impact on Barbara.

Regardless, she had had to negotiate. For at least a month, Barbara agreed to remain in the dark, as she put it. That is, outside the realm of Amanda's investigation, and she was not even to communicate with her much.

Well. That was the agreement.

That didn't mean that Barbara didn't persist.

She called periodically. She pushed. She complained. She cared, she said. And she was counting the days of their deal. It was small comfort for Amanda who could reveal nothing. She had to duck her calls, and ignored her messages, unanswered. In fact, it was an effort that almost became annoying. Still, Barbara was Barbara.

Amanda worked alone. This gave her the opportunity to take off in any direction she wished. And it wasn't long after her chat with Karen McCullock that she returned to Hyde Park to read more of Roosevelt's papers.

There had been something lurking at the back of her mind. Something else that was fomenting...another commodity of interest for some reason which, if anything, related more to Trevor's professional banking exposure than to her own quest...

One set of papers, originally classified as Top Secret, were scribbled over and "declassified" only recently under the Freedom of Information Act.

On a sheet with black ribbon ink, typed by a stenographer in bold Courier font, the initials of the President were circled.

Dated 1941, the document was *CIA Intelligence Memorandum No. 154.* It was a report on diamond supply and production. Phrases were cut out, or redacted.

"...Industrial diamonds have become increasingly essential to mass production in modern industry. The small size and light weight of the diamonds...[add to the complications of shielding this commodity ...] and make it very difficult to control their shipment. Our greatest demand is in the manufacture of war material. Principal sources of supply are largely areas in Africa, and later, Russia, our ally. Our requirements are 5 million carats per year - roughly one half of the total world output.

The United States - because of its highly mechanized industry, would be particularly affected by any interruption in the supply of industrial diamonds. The product and sale of industrial diamonds are largely controlled by the West, but the location of most of the African diamond-producing areas makes them strategically vulnerable..."

Amanda felt the intensity of the moment as it must have been in the hands of the President trying to win a world war in which Americans were fighting from ships, planes, tanks, and battlefields across Europe and Asia.

"Industrial diamonds are classified by use as tool stones, die stones, crushing bort, and diamond powder. Tool stones include industrial diamonds used in drill-bits utilized by the mining, petroleum, and heavy construction industries; in boring and

turning tools, where the diamond is mounted on a suitable vice and used to produce finished edges of one-thousandth-of-an-inch tolerance; and in dressing and truing tools, in which the diamond is used to turn other types of abrasive wheels and to give a high finish to automotive and aircraft parts. Die stones, or diamond wire drawing dies, are pierced sound stones of ¼ carat which are used to draw wire uniformly to extremely fine sizes. Crushing bort, which is graded to size and embedded or bonded with metal or resin, is utilized in making diamond drill-bits and other diamond abrasive wheels. They are used to sharpen drilling tools, and the diamond power is fragmented bort, crushed to micron size and used to finish carbide dies, jewel bearings, glass lenses and other glass instrumentation and mechanical products."

Amanda looked up, recalling something. Someone had said that the war of Europe was won as much by machine tool-makers as by guns and ammunition!

"supply is obtained largely from Belgium, the Netherlands and Switzerland. However other outlets have been found in Mediterranean countries which reship them across Europe.

We are in serious need of supply..."

* * *

Amanda folded clothes.

It had been a long time since she'd done the laundry. Usually, it was done by their housekeeper. With Trevor gone and the apartment empty, she decided to clean out the furthest reaches of closed bedrooms.

They'd had visitors all year. Friends coming to New York from overseas. Family. Business associates, and some of Tray's college friends...

It was time to check all the guest rooms.

Of course Carla did a good job of cleaning up. But she found items sometimes left behind and pushed back - tucked away in unused spaces like upper shelving and recessed drawers.

Amanda held a dust rod and hand vacuum, plus a damp cloth for swiping surfaces in dark corners. Not that she expected to find anything in closets where blankets and extra pillows were tossed for children visiting.

She finished one room, shut the door and moved to the next.

There she discovered a discarded garment; someone's hair brush; one make-up compact and a pair of mismatched socks. At the wall plug was left an electronic charger ...

She had to smile. As urban as their lives had become these days, how could she forget those summer balmy days at their seaside beach-house? There was always a "community" drawer for extra Tee shirts, swimming trunks, flip-flops or sunglasses for anyone to use!

In the bathrooms would be extra towels; Sunblock and sand-mats for house guests.

...To say nothing of a fridge full of water bottles, snacks, salads and citrus fruit.

 Nor could she forget those warm dark starlit nights on the house-porches, just off a beach campfire where they grilled steak over charcoal; ate watermelon and drank beer into the night...

Those bucolic days began with bathrobes and coffee on the house-decks where the surf could be heard crashing on a beach for a new day, followed by a day of swim suits and sand showers outdoors... More than once she had conducted professional business over the phone with New York wearing little else but a bikini and flip-flops!

Still, for a city apartment, they were kept pretty busy with house-guests. She had gathered an armful of seasonal towels and covers to toss into the laundry, and she folded them carefully by color or by room designation or by stack for ironing...

Carla would in on Monday, besides. The place was quiet.

She paused, Trevor on her mind...

A sense of desertion threatened to overwhelm her. But she knew him. He did little without a reason. He was a purposeful man, someone who did things with meaning.

Keeping her in the dark was with determination, she decided. It was his way of assuring her safety, she knew. But from what?

Why?

More importantly, how long was this going to go on? Another closet. No laundry needed here. Just general stuff. Seasonal changes, refreshing of color selections, personal items to stow away...

Next, she'd cull from their wardrobe a compilation for cyclical dry-cleaning to be sent out...

She emptied the pockets of Trevor's casual-wear trousers. A couple of receipts were stuffed into his pockets. One receipt listed coffee (2), croissant (1) scone (1). She was about to toss them when she recalled that order. She looked at them, and noticed the date. It was the day he left. Just... *hours* before he left!

In fact, precisely the events before they came up the elevators and when he... received his call. She sat on the edge of the bed.

The other was an ATM receipt where he withdrew cash. It was a larger withdrawal than usual, but not sufficient to alarm Amanda.

She stopped, both receipts in her hand, trying to recreate the events of that hurried morning when he walked in, and almost without warning immediately started packing.

A cab was waiting...she remembered.

She inspected the receipts carefully. They were plain, printed in ink which was not too clear. Large papery accounts for their purchases, and they were crumpled. Of course his hands were full...the dogs, coffee, the newspaper tucked under his arm. The Concierge had called him over for a message...

And she, she had gone up ahead with the dogs, if she remembered correctly. The elevator doors closed and he was... at the Concierge's desk.

Nothing but papery signs of crumbling and coffee stains!

She thought about it. What *triggered* his reactions? How did all that happen so fast? When had he called for a cab? Why hadn't he packed more thoroughly if

he expected to go? The only thing of value he grabbed - besides a backpack with superficial stuff tossed in - was his laptop and extra cell phone.
He had intelligence.
Little else remained in his office, come to think of it. In fact, why had he even changed his trousers?
She flattened out both receipts. He must have handled them both, just hours before, and they were still in his hands... So he must have stuffed them swiftly into his pockets, when?
Especially the one receipts upon which he set his coffee cup. It left a partial coffee stain. Yes. He'd been carrying his cup when they left the coffee shop. In fact, he still carried his cup when he entered the building and when he was in the Lobby. She remembered that he was still nibbling the end of his stirring stick, a little wooden coffee stirring-stick found in most coffee tables. He was casual. Having fun...A Sunday stroll in the park with the dogs hardly warranted ceremonial behavior, after all. He was relaxed.
Yet something had happened between the moment she left him in the Lobby, and his reappearance in the apartment, as if something - or someone - had informed him of something that set him in motion to vacate. What had happened? *Why the rush?*
She sat staring at the receipt when she realized it was not a perfectly formed coffee cup stain. The ring of the base of the cup was oddly shaped. She sat up. Had he dipped his wooden stirring stick into the coffee and dripped on the receipt? Almost like a pen, had he made a *shape* purposefully... It looked like a bird. A bird? A bird with two clear wings?

If that was made by design, he'd tried to express something. What was the bird? The bird was...was...what?

She got up and walked around, the sun creeping across the room through soft gauze curtains.

The only bird she saw recently was on stationary. Stationary that held the emblem of an institution... Like the stationary that showed a golden eagle in herald position. It splayed like a logo of the university...

The University? *Trevor-Antony?*

Was it about *him?*

If so, Trevor had left her a message using the coffee in his hand. The receipt was also in his hand with the coffee stirrer. He'd drawn the shape on the back of the receipt...A receipt left in trousers which she would find.

She thought about it. Something had propelled Trevor into action because he'd received something alarming that threatened their son Tray?

Then again, she could be viewing the stain as nothing more than a stupid Rorschach test!

x x x

Italy

Today was the day. Dimitri must make his impression.

Either he belonged in this marketplace or he didn't and he needed to establish his credibility. He selected his stock, and he placed his game plan.

He posted a promise that he'd make a big gain. Nobody responded.

The large cap active fund managers had recently trimmed their relative weight in the technology stocks to 1.18 times the broader market, down from 1.23 last month. Yet he noticed that the *Banco di Bandino* launched an Exchange traded fund aiming to triple the return on 10 stocks, including the FANG stocks. He checked them each one: Facebook. Amazon. Netflix Inc. Google, and parent Alphabet. They were all winners, and why had investors shied away just last month?

There was no catalyst that alarmed Stock Traders, he decided.

Traders seemed to find it a sure bet every time. Yet perhaps that was the problem. The herd mentality or "Crowd trade" in technology stocks had become a situation where all investors shared the same opinion: Too much of a sure bet. No danger. No deflation. No risk and no competition. They had all made the Nasdac Composite Index surge 7,532.

So, how to isolate one from the herd, then start a stampede? That was his mission.

He knew they were composed of Pension funds. One of its biggest pension funds was the Teacher's Union.

If they pulled out, others would follow. Especially since the teacher of today depended increasingly on education-enabled Tech company Apps. And now Dimitri did notice one thing, an opinion of his own.
Neither were the technology companies complaining about the business given them by education, nor did they worry about selling intellectual property globally. Nobody was watching.
He searched for another fund to tickle.
One investor with a big footprint held a basket of sovereign state government retirement funds. Any Traders looking for a catalyst would be given the jitters if they spotted such heavyweights shifting position.
Dimitri planted a post that travelled its way up to the surface and was picked up a News circuit engaged in activist and disruption opportunities.
'Teacher's Union threatens to disrupt the investment-base by pulling out'
He turned to the State government and found a feed to its major source of revenue: A Dam project, producing hydro-electric power into at least two states and one major industrial city was located at a major high technology center in Austria. He found its Engineering Management Offices, and infiltrated one of any number of unsecured emails.
Then he posted a rumor that there was a reported malfunction in its calibration cages, a problem of concern to Boards of Safety and Compliance Regulation.
He placed his bets, and waited to see what would happen.
He sat back.

The information filtered to the surface and across the Internet. By the time such allegations could be refuted, the damage would be done, he knew...
Sure enough, while the information didn't penetrate the mainstream media feeds, it did find its way into the database monitoring factors: This was the place where large investment Traders searched for any hint of failure or risk assessment. ..
Little happened at first. But slowly the stock wavered a tad. Then a steady decline showed up in one tech, and a second just slightly faltered. By the end of the week, most had lost value. Two in particular depreciated noticeably. Then the sound of investors running for the door was clearly evident. Their stock was tumbling.
It was another week before they bounced back. But he made ten million dollars US in his trade.
Dimitri posted again. He had made his mark. He sat back and folded his hands on his chest with a smile. Now he had credentials. A chip in the game of gaming. His credibility was worth gold.
And he bought himself a car. A Ford.

* * *

Miami, Florida

They'd been swimming and playing volley-ball all day, and now they looked at *Le Massif de Malderock Mountain.*

Boasting unending snow cover, and posted as the highest vertical drop east of the Canada Rockies, it was a "UNESCO biosphere Reserve" said Pete, reading from the brochure.

"Here..." said Laura handing Guy the Sunblock "...get my lower back?"

Clustered under an umbrella, the group was prone on beach towels or on beach chairs.

Rubbing the sand off both hands, Guy squeezed sunblock from the container and spread it down Laura's back.

"Yeah! ...And listen to this" added Pete *'Founded by Daniel Gaulthier, developer of the phenomenon known as Cirque de Soliel, the 5 acre ski resort found little of artifice in the such spectacular surroundings of natural beauty and glacial wonder.'"*

They might chose the site for its location, for its access and its amenities. Resort activities and options were plenty. The decision was getting raucous. It was their office winter vacation trip...

Finally Guy looked up. "Where's the bar?"

"There's a Tiki Bar over on the deck, but they don't open until the kids' beach camp has closed. Beach rules..." said Laura.

A child wearing swimming trunks down to his knees and an inflated life-vest was being admonished by his mother. His sister was wailing with sand in her eyes.

Under the umbrella, the beach party looked on with pained annoyance.

"I say we take a vote" said Miriam.

They turned to their vacation planning, and the girls chatted about what ski clothes to pack. And there was more. Ice skating, town shopping, hot tubs, tobogganing and huskie rides through forests and glens...it sounded good.

Still, the guys liked the vertical slopes for skiing. Plus snowboarding and nightlife. It came as a surprise, in the end, that the final tie breaker came because of its view of the river from the mountain, and its proximity to regions of the past - the unknown and the undiscovered. Such as a possible settlement of Viking landings, made centuries ago. Or fishermen and seamen from the warmer climes... perhaps navigators from Spain, explorers of the Empires? So it was decided. And that was the plan.

The day-camp mother marched her children to the car, opened the rear gate and handed both kids a bottle of cold water. They chugged, quelling all issues. Finally, they left.

"Yeah... The bar!" said Guy.

Some stayed late, others returned to the Rental House off Key Largo. It was a long weekend for the beach party from Miami. All expenses paid, an office perk.

* * *

Under the sea was a marvel for Trevor-Anthony McDonnell.

Carp swam around him in a live silver otherworld barely parting for humans following schools of blue, silver white and glassy fish undulated in magnified shapes, flowing through the aquamarine waters of the Florida Reef. As large as they were, they swam like chimeras without gravity.

They had picked the reef for scuba diving. Underwater marine life in the Florida Reefs boasted 1400 species of marine plants and animals, 40 different species of corals, and 500 species of fish.

While some fish appeared large, the hardbottom glimmered with algae, sea fans and stony corals protruding from limestone rock. Mysterious and hidden, shimmering in aquamarine waters were Smooth Starlet coral; Mustard Hill Coral; Golf-ball and Elliptical Star coral.

Swimming deeper they discovered Common Brain coral, anemones, mollusks, crabs, spiny lobsters, sea-stars, sea cucumbers, tunicates and a other varieties of colorful fish.

Tray had never seen such an array of tropical vibrance. He flashed his underwater camera at a snapper and a grouper, both camera-shy. He saw tang, ocean surgeon and in the distance perhaps it was a long fish -a barracuda? This, he would brag on his computer where he could download the images. He swam.

That evening, at a campfire beach party alive with night lights and music, Tray felt uncomfortable. An incident had occurred that marred the day.

It happened just before they surfaced. The matter dimmed as the hours passed, and he felt relieved that it went unnoticed.

One girl was absent from the party, Kalua, an Intern from Asia. Granddaughter to the Founder of a Japanese company that had over the years invested heavily with the Americans, she wanted to learn English and was majoring in international banking law as a student.

It happened maybe 45 minutes into the dive, with less than 20 minutes reserve air in their breathing tanks. Mark Ruttenberg had swerved away from the crowd of swimmers, taking with him Kalua. They disappeared behind an outcrop, and Mark give them a Thumbs-Up sign, signifying that all was well and they were having a little fun...

With approximately 5 minutes of airtime on their Regulators, Tray looked back to search for them. Mark had disappeared, but Kalua was still clutching onto the coral reef, afraid to break free and swim up. Tray approached. He pointed to the surface, signifying time to swim up. He saw her face. Etched with distress behind the goggles, she had a fear in her eyes that showed she understood the minutes left on her Regulator.

Tray came closer and she crouched further behind the outcrop of coral. He paused. Then he swam to her and saw the cause for her distress. The bottom panties of her bikini swimsuit had gone missing. She was ashamed to surface, the minutes passing.

Tray closed in and looked into her mask squarely. This was no time for inhibitions. He quickly took off his own swimming trunks, indicated that she put them on and swim up. She understood.

Air bubbles following, she swam up and surfaced at the boat.

Tray rose to the surface and swam to the rear of the boat. He flipped off his face mask and called to Hannah to toss him a beach towel. She handed it to him at the swim ladder, and he wrapped the towel around his waist before rising out of the water, soaking and dripping.

Onboard he spotted Kalua darting down to the cabins, his swimming trunks tucked up around her legs like hoisted culottes as swim gear. Nobody noticed a thing.

Tray spotted Mark at the rear of the boat, a beer in his hand, chatting with the crowd.

* * *

It was a long weekend, and Tray got a drive with two of the girls leaving the weekend party early. One had an exam she had to study for; the other meeting her boyfriend flying into Miami International Airport. Tray, being an office Intern himself, cited a need to catch up on work piled on his desk.

They teased him mercilessly on the drive back, but dropped him off at his apartment Sunday night.

Truth was, he was glad to get away. And to a large extent, he had spoken in earnest: There *was* much on his desk that seemed complex. At best, it was tedious. Worse, it was dated stuff long ago finished business.

Perhaps that had a lot to do with his assigned Mentor, Mark Ruttenberg dredging up every last unsolved risk-assessment report he could for a fresh review. Especially those that had resulted in non-performing loans for the company. He enjoyed watching Tray cope.

Mark Ruttenberg was turning out to be an ass. Why he chose to turn the screws on Tray, he couldn't figure out. Every opportunity to show him up as an incompetent and underperforming Intern was Mark's mission.

It was clear that Tray posed a threat to Mark. For what reason he could not quite determine. But with the help of Sophie, who had given him templates from similar cold cases, he worked his way through the case files.

Finally, there was one other chore that brought him home early, though he omitted to mention it openly. One which he had scrolled over a dozen times and postponed. It was a request from his mother.

She had wanted a brief report on the Ledgers which he had imaged when in Spain. He had promised to get to it, and in fact, he had started to do so on two occasions. But on both occasions it soon became clear that he'd need to do some research.

These were banks and accounts long since closed or forgotten. He'd have to check through their sovereign charters, and such historical records were usually available only through authorized repositories reached by access portals online by large financial and fiduciary institutions. In some cases, academic libraries. But for this particular case, only business institutions with international data bases.

He'd use the computers at the office, he decided.

* * *

Chapter 11

The office was quiet. Today was still a bank holiday. Yet he was in.

It took Tray all day, but he had achieved a solid *Table of Events* that represented spreadsheets of the Ledger. His mother would be impressed.

Without much thought he had imaged the lot – and at great speed, flipping through pages of the Ledger, and finding that somehow it would all come together to tell a story at some later date: The Shopkeeper had given him the Ledger to read, and with permission to take notes and photographs, he responded to Tray and his effort to discover more for his mother and the statue that she had bought from his shop. Tray showed him a photograph of his mother holding the statue.

The Shopkeeper looked at him somberly, and retreated to the recesses of his shop, emerging with a large Ledger.

"Por Favor..." he said, "por L'istoria! Estate bono.... Accommodate!" Tray took a picture of him clutching his Ledger, and thanked him.

He had been left alone in the back room, the shopkeeper emerging from time to time with sweet cakes and fresh lemonades. It was almost as if the

Shopkeeper *wanted* him to image the entire record of the Ledger...

Now scrolling through the pages which he had downloaded onto his computer, he could view them more closely. He had labeled them, page by page, and he saved them.

The photographic record was complete, stored on one digital file of many thumbnail data images, all readable as high-resolution pages.

At first it was an accounting of chronological sequences. But he renamed each one by page-number and date of accounts.

 Before long he could discern the inky pen and annotations of each entry. Transactions appeared to be clearly annotated, and sequential.

Here was the Inventory of activity showing the flow and supply of raw materials entering the workshop. First as a commodity, then as a finished product.

The workshop, in fact, seemed to take on the substance of a local ballet class -one expert vendor surrounded by workmen and apprentice workers.

Another manufacture required other workmen and artisans. There was sand, gravel and cement delivery, evidently for pottery making. Fuel showed up as logwood, charcoal and even components to mix with metals for foundry work.

All sources of delivery were itemized, along with their payment in Lira and other cash: Some exchanges were made as barter, and labor was generally lumped in with the finished price of the product. Presumably a bonus of sorts.

Other added expenses seemed to be unexplained...Especially as they occurred on a regular scheduled date of each month, perhaps a payment, or a 'Protection bribe' of some kind. But there was clearly sufficient to run a business, if not entirely lucrative, a business model ample enough for a local family and his workers to live by.

What Tray could not figure out was the type of product, and ordering, or client that matched it. Sometimes, the product and the labor expended was less than clear. Other than the money which was transacted for something finished and entered in the book, Tray remained puzzled. The schedule and the pick-up was annotated with some measure of regularity. But client names remained elusive.

There were recurring names. Antonio. Theresa. Sabastino. Maria. Lupino. Each warranted a designated mark by a sum of money, often with a semblance of a signature next to it, or perhaps a receipt for payment marked on the Ledger itself. Certainly the pages were faded, finger-stained and smudged, if somewhat illegible because of the dirty hands of workmen and the use of their charcoal pencils. But it was all there.

On his laptop he was able to amplify details under magnification, and he could read them. Clearly, it was legitimate, and represented sufficiency of credibility.

There was, he noticed, attached to the end of the Ledger a 'pocket' for cashed checks.

They belonged to a Bank in Spain which had long ago since closed its operations. He checked the International Banking Community Archive file which told him their date of closure; former location and archive repository. He sent out an enquiry to the Archive, asking for bank verification on certain closed accounts in their records. This, he knew, would take some weeks.

One other check found in the Ledger showed a second bank in the UK, or receipt rather, for a War Bond issued by the Bank of England. He sent another enquiry request for information on that source in their Archive department, which he knew would also take time.

Fortunately, his office, the Firm where he worked, had the data access to many of the world's banking historical archives.

Being unclassified, they were frequently accessed for scholarship or judicial review in modern times. Some archives held their records on data of old stock trades; former bonds or retired coupon-receipts, such as the Railway Bonds of the 19th century.

He looked up at the clock. This was not exactly sanctioned work at his office, he knew. But he was an Intern, he was supposed to be learning things, too. So he was not exactly outside his realm of learning...

Worse case, any good library at a University business school would presumably have similar database access as part of their academic subscriptions. This information was old, unclassified material. Law schools, he knew, would also have access to such archives since law studies relied frequently on databases to analyses precedent litigation related to regulations, banking compliance and valuations.

Still, even if it was a Sunday, he did feel obliged to report his half-hour Internet search log-in time. He was using office computers on company premises. He emailed Sophie, his office manager, with a quick explanation and a brief description of his two

Archive requests - made for private research. He offered to have any related Fee attached to his paycheck, if necessary.

Finally, he turned to the office pile of work on his desk. He picked up the files, inserted his print-out sheets showing a different risk assessment model that might have altered their evaluations, added his typed analytical report, then took the files into Mark Ruttenberg's office where he placed them on his desk.

Finished.

He returned to own desk, sent an email notification to Mark saying that the work was completed. Then he switched off his terminal, drained his soda, grabbed his back-pack and checked out with his signature at the Central Log-In Desk in the lobby.

He had saved everything on a stick.

Tray left the building in his car parked underground, and returned to his apartment.

At home he took a quick dip in the pool, ordered a sandwich, then returned to his Laptop where digital images downloaded to a file.

By the last ten pages of the Ledger, Tray saw a world on his computer. A collection of photographs - an eclectic account of who was going where, doing what, with whom and why.

The obligation made to his mother was now a task of intrigue. As his forensic re-creation took on a life of its own, the story seemed taking shape under his hand was thriving with real people, posing with their items and accomplishing works, their smiling faces, family gatherings and favorite habits was a world full of vibrance.

Angelina. Antonio. Sabastino. Some photographs had been kept between the pages of the Ledger. He imaged them too.

Straw hats, ribbons and muslin was for the girls; vintage cravats, culottes, bandanas and suspenders on men – enjoying relationships and outings.

The assembly feasted together, laughing and eating and drinking at tables with lavish platters stacked with food; colorful flowers and fruits. What drew them to the shade of gardens under warm Iberian skies? Children, pets, priests and guests came and went. Boating, fish and a blue sea at their feet showed up in all photos. Everywhere there appeared a bucolic sense of harmony and peace.

This - all of this, he would send to his mother. He copied it all for her as an attachment, He hit SEND. She would know, for certain, about the shop from which she bought her statue.

There was time, he decided, for a swim before dinner.

Not too far distant, a long ultra-filter telescopic camera spun off multiple shutter frames at every move he made.

Tray was photographed in his trunks seated by the pool.

* * *

Amsterdam

Trevor strolled. But he wanted haste. He had a bad taste in his mouth. He had for weeks...
He did not particularly like walking through the Dutch Museum in Amsterdam. He did it to spot anyone following him. Two faces reappeared with pernicious regularity, and he strolled most of the morning. Finally he paused for coffee.
Housed at the Paulus Potterstraat between the Rijksmuseum and the VanGogh Museum, the Diamond Museum was created by Coster Diamonds - a venerated Amsterdam-based diamond polishing and trading firm with a 200 year history.
Tours of the factory were scheduled, and the exhibit showed how diamonds were geologically created..
He pressed the large button on the wall for an English language film. Only one man followed him into the seating theater.
The history of Amsterdam -as one of the most important diamond centers began in the 17th century. Jews, chased from catholic countries in the South of Europe, were allowed to settle in Amsterdam with the rise of Reform Protestantism. And though barred from the Guilds of Craftsmen of trades, diamond polishing was one of the occupations open to Jewish people.
Colonized by the Dutch, the last discoveries of diamond rock formations in South Africa increased the influence of Amsterdam as the diamond center of the world.
"Whereas the polishing of diamonds has been largely transferred to Asia, Amsterdam remains – along with

Antwerp, London New and Johannesburg, one of the most important cities for diamond trade."
Trevor strayed. He walked outside. He passed through the Square to the large Rijksmuseum and strolled around the pond, already being prepared for the next season's skating tradition.

He moved back northwest through the Van Gogh Museum and the Stedelijk Museum. Then to the House of Bols Cocktail & Genever and back to Coster Diamonds.

He aimed for the southwestern border of the Museum Square, toward Van Baerlestraat Street and walked passed the American Consulate. He entered, and waited in the lobby. He had asked to see the Administration Officer of the Consulate Section.

She came. She was a tall American with blond hair, emanating a calm sense of professional purpose. Hers was a world made jumpy by unpredictable events and international incidents. Calm was good.

Trevor asked her about any Port-of-Entry records in their Archives dating back to WWII.

She smiled and knew the answer. Such records were dated Intelligence matters following the war, she told him. Those records would have long been shipped to the United States following the liberation of the Netherlands. This was a nation that had been occupied by the enemy during the war, she reminded him, and suffered casualties in commercial losses both at home and overseas across its colonial Empire.

He listened, and he understood. Such resources were perhaps of interest to all parties concerned, he asked.

"I can tell you this, "she said "In an attempt to save as much of the existing diamond stocks as possible from the Germans, the 500 dealers in Amsterdam transferred their diamonds to Antwerp."
He nodded.
"The British government agreed to an organization known as the Correspondence Office for the Diamond Industry, set up to register the diamonds and keep them secure for the duration of the war. Thanks to that organization large quantities of diamonds were returned to their owners after the city was liberated, and the Industry was preserved. In fact, she explained, the Antwerp diamond industry also got off to a promising start after the war was ended."
They chatted, and he thanked her profusely, telling her that he was here for research. He gave her his card.
Later in the day Trevor returned to his hotel accommodations – the satisfied tourist sightseer for the day, as he told them at the Front Desk.
For dinner, Trevor McDonnell went down to the Dinning Room and ordered a substantial meal. After coffee and desert he retired early to his room.
He knew he was being surveilled.
His lights went out at ten.

Trevor was in the "City of Diamonds" for a reason. e Information might reveal a trail of money illegally cited in the United Kingdom following the war.
His bank, at that time, had historically been the repository of its stock and supply. It had put up the money as Guarantee for safety of delivered stock.

The room had a stocked bar. He walked over and poured himself a drink, then sat in the dark and gazed out at the night sky of the city – a city whose background he knew from the tales of his father...

At one time the center to the commercial world, Amsterdam held the position key to the diamond trade for over two centuries: Owners of overseas mining interests in Africa, Australia, Brazil...As shipper of unlimited supplies of raw material around the globe it distributed diamonds to be cut and polished by craftsmen, jewelers, laborers and other supply chain manufacturers.

That is, until news in the 1800s that its Brazilian pits were exhausted. For the merchant trades, this almost spelled disaster. But the Dutch discovery in 1867 of the Kimberley mine in South Africa began a new century of prosperity, with Amsterdam again supplying nearly 10,000 active polishers.

Still, a voracious consumption by expanding domestic economies proved challenging for Holland. As the Industrial Revolution increased demand, a decline ensued.

Plus there was competition. Luring Amsterdam's traders with lower tax regimes, cheaper labor and less aggressive Unions, they moved to Belgium. As a result, by the 1920s it was Antwerp of Belgium that led the diamond markets and not Amsterdam of Holland.

Trevor sipped his drink.

By then the world had changed. *Art Nouveau* styled works in diamonds flourished. Domestic mercantilism, wage earner's disposable income and increasing wealth in the industrialized nations displaying decorative splendor. Jewelers and goldsmiths performed artistic creations and design; workshops became renown across Europe and America. Gemstones worn everywhere were conspicuous signs of wealth and success.

Trevor knew what happened next.

The invasion of Holland by the German Armies of WWII inflicted a devastating blow. The Dutch industry failed and the Jewish workforce fled, or were deported.

By 1945 at the end of the war, the number of people involved in the diamond business in Holland was less than one thousand.

The morning was under grey cover. Trevor was not deterred by rain and he prepared to conclude his business today.

He was being watched, he knew. Downstairs at breakfast he ate, then in normal fashion left the hotel lobby with his umbrella.

But his thoughts were far away.

These days diamonds were processed in anonymous industrial sheds in the outskirts of Surat, or rapidly-sprawling towns in East Asia. One in a chain global economy that traded in commodities; out-soured by the West, and tracked by management of tech giants.

Trevor took a tram.

He got off at the historical *Bourse*, once a Trading house or stock exchange. His family bank had no doubt done business here in the last century. Today's Bourse, he knew, was in modern headquarters some seven kilometers south of Old Amsterdam.

No longer a tourist, he walked to meet with someone in particular about a specific transaction.

"You ask a difficult question." said Mr. Gustaff, an elderly scholar attached to the Diamond Factory Archival Library. "Friends of the History of the Jewish Diamond cutters?..."

Trevor knew he was opening old wounds, and the man was loath to enter into that kind of conversation. He hesitated. Finally he said "There is a man...Someone I know, who can tell you more. This is his name. I will call him and tell him of your arrival" adding "In 1866 the Kimberley deposits were part of the De Beers Consolidated Mines Ltd.," He peered at Trevor "This massive influx of rough stones was instrumental in contributing to the city's statues of Antwerp, you know..." He looked up and smiled.

Calm was good.

Trevor nodded "Yes. Please go on!"

"The depression of the 1930s hit the diamond trade hard. In 1939 many Jewish businessmen fled the country and went to the United States, Portugal or England. Those that remained...continued to meet and to do business. Some getting their supplies from..."

"From Belgium Congo?"

"Precisely!"

Again they smiled.

Calm was good.

"May I suggest the Factory Tour of the cutting and manufacturing of diamonds? You seem interested."

"Yes. Thank you!"

They shook.

The tour was conducted by a Guide of college age who spoke good English.

"In the cut of the diamond, only those of the 4Cs where human skills and creativity actually play a role, are given particular attention in Amsterdam. Companies have invested a great amount of resources and expertise into developing innovative shapes – all of which have been patented – and in training top-level polishers..."

A hand shot up. "What's a 4Cs?"

"All major Dutch brands propose their own signature cuts, surpassing traditional products in terms of shape and number of facets. The Gassan 121, the Coster Royal 201, the Royal Asscher cut, are among the most exclusive cuts available on the market.."

Trevor found a delightful café in the open square, and ordered Lunch.

He would meet with his man. It was arranged.

* * *

It had been a week since Tray put files on Mark's desk.

Mark Ruttenberg, he knew, was hunting for excuses to disparage his work. At any rate, not a word had come back, and Tray was anxious that the files had gone unaccounted for since he had them. He would check with Mark Ruttenberg, he decided.

He was about to do so and stood up from his desk. Mark approached him with one hand in the air, and the other holding a file for everyone to see.

"Everybody.." he called out "gather around for some news from upstairs!"

They came, puzzled. Even Sophie was surprised.

"I have an announcement to make about our young Intern!" shouted Mark. But for the happy look on Mark's face Tray felt he was called up for public humiliation.

"Mr. Tray McDonnell has just landed us one the Firm's *biggest*.... clients!" said Mark.

Tray wondered if he was just being capricious.

To those standing around, Mark had just uttered mystical words. *Someone had brought on a new client for business!*

They moved closer, and Mark had to repeat the hallowed words before someone started to applaud. Even Sophie was grinning.

"Apparently, Mr. Tray convinced a potential client to invest with us! And invest he did... He brought in an account for us to manage at over $50 million dollars annually. Congratulations Tray!"

Tray hated the way he played with his name. Somehow it sounded disparaging. But he smiled graciously, if clueless still.

Tray was wracking his brain as to what had just happened. He made routine phone calls to prospective clients over the phone – it was his daily obligation. But he very much doubted than any one of them took his recommendation seriously, even if they had made the enquiry.

Evidently one did. The prospective client had asked tough questions which, ordinarily, would have deferred to someone of authority. Tray looked up the data himself and answered the client directly with real figures and facts over the phone.

"Err..." he said, stepping up, his face fairly glowing with a red flush.

"Speak Up! I say..." said Mark, deepening his embarrassment.

"Thank you" said Tray, still in the dark. It would probably have helped if Mark had taken him aside and talked to him first. But no. Mark was all about splashy actions and attention-getting...

"Apparently, that client contacted Mr. Bellows our CFO and told him why he chose to place an account with our company!" proceeded Mark. "Tray, your future here is guaranteed! If you choose to stay, once your term is over, this will be *your* Account to manage. Congratulations!"

"Wow!..." said someone "Tray, spread some of that gold dust over here, will you?""

"Yeah... Here too!"

"Well done!" whispered Sophie

"Congratulations Trev..."

Finally Mark resumed his role of MC "I suggest a party for our Tray. Friday night at the Mexican Coastline Bar, to celebrate?"

"Oh yeah!" they all agreed. "You're on!"

Mark walked him back to his office. "Well. Well. Well. Seems like you've made quite an impression with the Front Office upstairs. How shall I put it, you got the golden ring?"
Tray chucked.
"What's funny?"
"Actually, I'm totally surprised. I didn't think..."
"Ah!.Well...Sometimes around here it doesn't pay to think...So. Friday night then?"
 "Thanks!" Tray turned to go. "Oh, I was wondering. Did you find those files I left on your desk last weekend?"
Mark's eyes passed to his sideboard. "Hell yes! There're over there! Did you forget one?"
"No. I just wanted to check that you received them, that's all."
Mark looked at him with deep examination, as if wondering what it was that had propelled this man to gain the attention of the Upper offices.
"Oh! No need for any of that stuff anymore. You're in! See you Friday." he said, dismissing him like a school boy.
Tray returned to his station and spent the rest of the day answering queries and e-mail.
Sophie came around later and smiled at him. It was time to wrap up for the day.
They walked towards the elevator, chatting.
It wasn't until the button was pressed that Sophie said quietly "Be careful. This is a treacherous playground..."
Tray looked at her and was about to speak when the elevator doors opened.

x x x

"Yes, I knew the man Krautz" said Frederick Barnheim, 72 years old and wearing silver bifocal eyewear and a starched white shirt with a stylish cravat.

"Rather, my family did. He was known to my father, and I heard stories about them as a boy. He was a diamond cutter like no other, if I recall. That's what I understood from family conversations when they gathered around the dinner table, you know..."

Trevor grinned, adding a nod of understanding.

To re-pictured those childhood memories with a softness in his eyes, Barnehim said "He was quite a leader in the community, many worked for him and his projects. He had many skills attached to his shop. Painters. Sculptors. Iron workers. Filigree and decorative artists. Beyond the scope of just diamonds, you understand.. But this Krautz, he had such business going because he produced such good work, and he helped to employ others for their works also...."

 "I see you have a strong sense of family recollection" said Trevor.

"We do!" chuckled Barnheim. "That we do..." He leaned on his walnut cane and moved to a Welsh cabinet from where he pulled a locked box. "We have photographs..." he added "In spite of all those events, we never stopped to cherish happiness and those moments of enjoyment. That too was part of our Jewish tradition..." He paused. "Yes. As I recall, what he had was a special talent. I do know that Krautz was known for the way he cut his diamonds. There was only one man who cut diamonds that way." He pushed the box aside and reached for a paper and pencil and wrote. He gave it to Trevor at the table.

"You see...diamonds as a decorative adornment evolved. As you know, naturally excavated diamonds gleamed with natural beauty, and they were historically venerated as precious gems and items of wealth and magnificence....Especially in India. But when they became popular, new cuts, new shapes and designs started to emerge."

Barnheim looked up to imagine how he should explain things. "In their history, I believe it was in 1375,   one of the very first designs appeared—the *Point Cut*. Like so..." he drew a diagram.

"Yes"

"This design demonstrated the natural contour of the diamond.."

"So, the *Point Cut's* predecessors were like the accepted well-shaped diamonds. Any diamonds that came in the rough, if jagged, uneven, were not even considered attention worthy. Why? Because there were no cutting 'Masters' who could shape it into a particular design. That is, until we designed new looks and shapes..."

Trevor nodded.

 "So. What began in India as a venerated gemstone shifted in popularity to Europe by the 18th century and ended up in Brazil. Thus, even though the diamond was an article of rarity from the natural environment,   it became famous in all the world when it was 'cut' to emulate a natural item of beauty in the raw..."

He drew lines across the block shape and developed a prism and facet that resembled gemstone jewels.

Trevor smiled. "Can you tell the origin of a diamond from its cut?"

"Well, as you know, the modern fashion trade of cut diamonds was derived from mines in Africa, where a diamond discovery was made in 1866..." He paused. "This man Krautz was known for using rough diamonds out of Africa to cut into finished and polished gemstones. He rarely left a square base, if I remember. He had a tradition of cutting and grinding the corners to make them round by smaller cuts. Only to those he knew, he gave gifts. My family had one of his cuts. They were with a signature..."

"..signature?"

"Well. it was his way, and this was a big secret, if I'm remembering....I believe...err...yes. I believe it was that he *never* left the corners to be sharp. ..Like so! When you saw that, you knew it was his work. But his gemstones shone like no other!"

"You believe he was unique?"

Barnheim smiled. "It gave his work *meaning*, if you understand what I mean. That is to say, he said the world should be more forgiving of its sharp edges. That was his *philosophy*... Only later, in the end, he left one corner sharp. Yes, that is what was said about him. One corner of a rough cut was sharp-angled and without soft curve..."

Trevor looked at him.

"Perhaps it meant it as a mark of Protest, perhaps...*Who knows?*"

"Betrayal?"

Neither spoke.

Finally Bernheim a stack from the box and uncovered it. "Here, I have pictures...Ah yes! He was in Spain, see? His diamonds came always from

Africa to Spain. They used blue diamonds for the supply line...Here he is with his partner, in Spain. He had a shopkeeper he worked with, a family going back...ancient times." He waved his hand.

"Here, with his wife and son when they lived in Antwerp, and here, his business friends..."

"Thank you for showing me these!" said Trevor.

"I hope I have been helpful to you, Mr. McDonnell."

"Absolutely! And...there is something more, yes. If you wouldn't mind?" He fished out an envelope. "May I ask if you could inspect this?"

The folded packet lay on the table between them. Both men knew what it was. A sampler's packet.

"I have kept these in my vault for a long time, waiting for their rightful owner. I need to know if these were part of the batch that your man worked with at that time..." said Trevor.

Bernheim raised his eyeglasses and rested back on his chair. "You are an honest man" he said simply.

"I'm a banker with a reputation to protect!"

They smiled.

Finally Bernheim nodded. "I have a friend, the son of an expert who is well trained in the trade. I shall ask him here. Tomorrow. You should ask for his opinion, if that's alright? He is the expert."

"Yes"

"Come back tomorrow at 7 oclock. You shall have your answer Mr. McDonnell"

"Thank you."

* * *

Tray, as he was now occasionally called by the crowd at his office, received a package. Sophie had informed him to go down to the Front Desk.

The delivery was made directly to his building, since all mail was scanned for dangerous substances.

Neither was this labelled a security risk for delivery couriers, nor did it have any sensitive confidential or proprietary company material. Still, an elaborate mail packaging software program that tracked internal pick-ups on plasma screens displayed at various floors.

It had been a policy of the company to keep outsiders in the waiting areas of the Lobby. Nobody, and no package was allowed into the building. Security. Evidently, this was a special delivery that had passed all manner of check-points for reasons of recognition by the company and access.

He opened the package at his desk. It was a square box, stuffed at the edges with packaging material.

Under the wrapping a product package was wrapped with a blue ribbon, and a card stapled to it.

Tray recognized the company name of the Firm on the stamped packaging that sent it. The company that sent it belonged to Kalua's father.

Kalua, who had not returned to the office as an Intern since the weekend of play in the Keys, had sent him a card with a gold embossed print.

It had a graphic design, customized. Dust-like grains of sand trailed at the bottom left corner, plus a tiny star-fish and a pair of tiny diver's goggles. Only one word was on the card, no signature.

'Thank you.'

He opened the product box and found a full-sized scuba diver's mask. There was no need for words, and clearly, Kalua had returned to her homeland.
Tray had sent her an email message on her office mail address, which had not yet been cancelled from the staff directly.
"You're welcome"
Adding,
"I'll have it donated to the children's swimming camp with your name.
Best, Tray"
She would understand.
If there was one thing that ran against company policy in Miami was that any employees should accept gifts. Perceived as bribes, such gestures denied fiduciary responsibility at a company where large fortunes were daily placed on stock exchanges.
This, Tray knew that Kalua would appreciate.
He looked over his shoulder, back towards the office of Mark Ruttenberg.
 The office was empty. It would remain private.

* * *

New York

Amanda was at her laptop all night, in an hour it would be dawn. Tray had sent her a lot of information, and it was a puzzle.

Not since Amanda attended college had she engaged in analytical studies, let alone quantitative comparative theory. Certainly IT had since come a long way to aid forensic science in evaluations, testing and databases. They provided digital solutions and high probability statistics.

But here her efforts were low-tech, and she decided to rely on hand notes from a document which had been sent to her, entering the information on a spread sheet. She reviewed it.

It would take days to piece together, perhaps the less obvious foundational texts would shed light on later developments. That was often the case with research. Cataloguing for accuracy and verification was the chief aim. Then came the layering of probabilities. The interaction of historical events to support certain facts and evidence would help piece together the puzzle of what happened..

Shipments of the shopkeeper's Ledgers were itemized. His commissions to create works compiled a picture of what happened in those fateful days of the war.

What she had were three sections: The first a listing of all that was entered in the Ledger in a true and clear spreadsheet.

The second listed items that needed answers within the entries.

The third defined possibilities and assumptions that best fit the information. Unsolved, the Ledgers looked like doodles without a legend.

Many times during the night, her desk light shone brightly on an image that made her smile. This was like a magical world of re-creation. It was a human story of values and wonders...

What might have been misconstrued as idle sketching and pencil markings were real work-orders performed in the shop.

Raw materials, metal and gold filigree work; sculpture, jewelry designs in gemstones...some beautifully depicted. No affectations of artistry here, just remarkable sketches equal and worth of any celebrated museum exhibit...all stayed in the warp and woof of artisan's culture.

Some sketches were actual portraits of people, renditions of likeness for artistry within lockets, or to be inlaid for woodworking and marquetry. Each were as meticulously depicted as any other, those drawings made by charcoal or in free-hand, and they began to show a pattern of markings.

Other sketches were actually Rubbings off heraldry icons to be used on replication of metalwork and foundry-works – sometimes hammered upon an anvil, or worked by hand-held pounding mallets.

Brasswork suggested bells - a technology and expertise closely held for their secrets of campanology. Strength, pitch tones, aesthetics and impact in bell-ringing.

The shop's fuel supply was also annotated. Coal. Wood. Sand. Marble. Granite. Milling stones. Notations denoted labor hours, persons. Foundry Ironworkers were especially listed.

Amanda identified 'Instruction guideline sketching' often to show design, patterns, templates, processes and even work locations. That is, if she understood the markings.   Amanda found herself pondering many times at this work shop capacity.

Amanda felt tired. Yet with the body of work sent to her by Tray, she must solve the clues left hanging at the margins of the pages, often sideways annotations with possible names, dates, work progress and targets. Especially the movement of shipments, deliveries, pick-ups and money transactions.
Now her spreadsheets began to take shape. Soon, a clearer picture had emerged.
Her first priority was to list from the Ledgers *Accounts*: Orders. Delivery dates, their stock supply. And with some precision, she traced a time line, history of supplies and provisions needed for each. Finally, the finished product was delivered.
She unlocked a code that appeared to identify the clients, often giving the point of origin - or type of supply needed... and the specific shipper to be used for that particular order.
Actually, she had accomplished a great deal of identification from the data on her spreadsheets.
Finally she got up to o stretch her legs went to the kitchen feeling absolutely ravenous. She made coffee. Daylight was turning shaded street lights into a blue grey foggy day. Drizzling, and lazy clouds were drifting off with a morning breeze.
The thought of going to bed was enticing. But the dogs found her, and she decided that a good run with the dogs after a hearty breakfast would clear away fatigue. The long dark night was over. She took

a big breath. She felt like she was getting somewhere...

Still, as the day wore on, the questions that faced her next were perhaps less clear. Specifically, how did the material listed on the spreadsheet bear any influence on the facts known that they had accumulated in this investigation?

Was there any connection to people identified in the Ledger who came to America at the time? Some orders were clearly marked *"Americano."* Some even *"officio"* if with nationality of origin including Spain, England, France and several Frankfurt. These annotations Amanda had been able to identify from a pattern of the hand that jotted down the notes, if inconsistently...But occasionally the author wrote out the full country of order. Other times, just the abbreviation.

Next: Source of raw materials, specifically the diamonds. What was there a source? How were the shipments shown, and from where? None were actually written out.

Amanda identified three different sources, and two different destinations: Belgian Congo, Brazil and Johannesburg were clear source-points. Antwerp and Frankfurt were destinations - usually the same locations as other workshops doing specific work.

She paused. What if there was a supply chain in manufacturing? Maybe not all items were made by the same person, or place?

The record showed increasing interruptions. Especially as they approached 1939. Clearly, they were affected by the invasion of Poland in WWII.

Amanda noticed an accelerated delivery schedule for shipments of diamonds from the Belgian Congo came into Spain. But they were abruptly halted in 1942.

After that, she noticed orders from Frankfurt and Antwerp taking on more new names, *"Officiale"* as the ledger listed them. But new. Odd...

Then, workers started to thin out. Fuel supply for the workshop ended...

Amanda was delighted when she found an order for a statue. A photograph could have been hers...

The name of the source who ordered it was not given. But he was an American. When did the owner pay for it? The ledger showed no claim or payment. Just a fee amount, paid early in the transaction.

The phone rang. "Hi Barbara"

* * *

The usual banter followed. Barbara could talk. Amanda got up and walked around with her phone at her ear, reaching the front room and across a space newly bathed in sunlight from tall windows. She peered down at street traffic thirteen floors below.

Barbara was questioning about work, making a less-than veiled attempt at asking if she should come over.

Amanda was tempted. But the last thing she needed was a Barbara dredging up the past, asking loud questions and inviting open enquiry that drew attention into Trevor's absence.

Clearly, while this wasn't exactly a hostage-taking, the silence by Trevor suggested acute discretion, if not outright danger. Keeping Amanda in the dark was her shelter, she knew... Barbara would never understand.

"I'm doing O.K..." said Amanda. "Actually, I'm going over stuff that Tray sent me from Miami. When I have something, perhaps we could go to the DA's office together and show her? There may be a connection with some real evidence of what happened to her deceased cold case..."

Barbara wanted to know more.

"Well. There are a couple odd things, disparate items collected, if you will. One is a possible enquiry ..."

Amanda was about to say "about a shipment." Instead she said "an object..."

"About a diamond, perhaps?" pressed Barbara.

"Perhaps. I don't know. Other than he noted some request."

"the other...?"

"The other is an old copy of a message that was kept. It was sent by the British Government regarding a cargo supply that was expected on a delivery date..."
"Bill of Lading?"
"No. The ship was the *Nova Bella*. That's all it says"
"Anything else?"
"Another ...coincidence is the visit by a possible friend who appears frequently during WWII. Kurtz. It's usually marked by K, but I know it as Kurtz. He shows up in marked pictures of family gatherings..."
"Oh, I understand."
"Basically there's a dramatic cut-off. Just ends, with blank pages..."
"Oh, I understand."
"I mean, there's a shipment out of Morocco but no receipt. Then a savage pencil line striking out that delivery, or an arrow. The date was June 1942."
"So, when can I come over to type it all up?" asked Barbara
Amanda paused. The very question that she had hoped to avoid. No. Barbara had been dismissed from the project since Trevor was gone.

 "So, I'll be over tomorrow! Now get yourself cleaned up, get some rest. I know how you work. Eat! I'll be there early. Oh, and I almost forgot. The reasons I called..."
"is what?"
"Karen McCullock does in fact want us to meet with her Thursday morning, if possible. She called and made the appointment. She and the Detective have picked up new information. We'll be armed to answer their questions with the work you've done.

And we can hand it all over to her!. Anyway, seeing as its pertinent to their investigation..."
"That's fine, if the two are connected..." said Amanda glancing at her spreadsheet and wondering how on earth the business of the workshop could be connected to the diseased Last Will and Testament... Still, Amanda did feel relieved that she was not alone. She knew the Shopkeeper was found dead shortly after her son photographed his Ledger. Yes, she hand been anxious. Barbara seemed to have a sixth sense about arriving as Relief Party.
Except for one thing. Amanda paused, her mind exhausted, if not muddled.
She made a copy of her Spreadsheet on an electronic device and inserted it into Trevor's encrypted computer.
She didn't know where he was, or what he was up to. But one thing she did know. He did have access to his computer, remotely.

* * *

Chapter 12

Miami.

The party began with a meal at the sprawling outdoor restaurant, *Mexican Coastline Grill &Tap.*
Here to celebrate their Intern's new client, the sounds of the samba soon took over the event.
Miami was a beautiful city at night, the air redolent with sea breeze and local blossom, festive lights along sidewalks, creeping wisteria, and the aroma of foods with music was intoxicating.
The guys ate robustly - mostly beer and pizza. The girls liked Crown Millers fizzing with lime. Especially with tacos dripping, saucy and juicy. And if fingers and drooling were dabbed with table napkins, they lapsed with episodic giggling.
Laughter grew. With all tables full, they seemed to have swarmed the place. If the Restaurant Manager smiled at this office crowd, he also saw the more quiet family cars pull away from his place. This was not the night out for children, many of them Latino. Within two hours, he knew, this crowed would vacate the restaurant and vaporize into the soft and decorative street lights of Miami's nightlife.
Tray loved it. Visiting student that he was, he felt safe, even as the pulse of the city coursed through the night.

Some of the girls had marguerites, the guys were still on beer. What Tray could not understand was how informal the evening party was: No change of dress from office to evening-wear for the dinner out? They just all showed up as they were. No pithy comments, no speech. No MC for an announcement of the event. Just a '*Hey! You'all are cool...*'
It occurred to him that perhaps the party was actually a staged excuse to get everybody out for a dinner. Or drunk, now that he saw the flow of alcohol.
Mark Ruttenberg wasn't there. The deeper into the night the party went, the less clear the event became. Many from the office just dissipated into the night.
As the crowd thinned, he turned to search for Mark Ruttenberg, the host who still had not arrived? Perhaps he should say thanks for arranging the event.
He shot off a Text message of thanks...
"No problem" came back the text from Mark. "The party is yours!" Adding "...as is the check! Ha! Ha!"
The waiter came over with the tab. Tray paid it with his credit card: $291.00.
 A few of the girls waved him a thanks as they left, and the rest, gone.
Tray drained his beer, still thirsty somehow, and he loosed his tie in the warm air. He got up to leave. A girl came over, someone from the next office, she said.
She was a blond, sharp shoulders and hair loose, like his tie. It was Friday, she announced, still wearing her office ensemble. Clearly she'd had a Sangria or two. She asked if he had ever danced in Miami. The

Flamingo? Oh? They could go to a Club she told him, 'for night dancing to Latino music!'
Tray smiled, not yet knowing her name or which office she worked in...
 "Why not visit the deeper parts of the city?" she asked, pulling him off his stool. "I know a place..."
They danced. He drank.
She promised him sweet moves as he stood and watched her gyrate to the rhumba. Her eyes held him "Is a dream *Si?*... To move with the music?"
His mind felt dull, his mouth dry. He drank his beer and they danced, swaying to the rhythm and then kissed.
Something sweet passed into his mouth, both of them swaying. He ordered whiskey.
Careful now... he heard her once say, in tease. Careful it was - he in her breasts and she yielding with more kissing and hands passing over his body.
Then she was gone.

He found himself alone, and parched. Dawn traced a horizon of the sea, he was in Miami Beach.
The keys to his car were gone, his pockets empty. But his wallet was with him...
His feet were in sand, he was barefoot. Between two beach buildings, white walls of structures converging in an alley, he stood, stiffly.
The venue seemed like fiction, his head the only reality. It hurt, throbbed, and he could barely see, his vision blurred. Yes. He understood. He'd been partying, and he realized he had a hungover. A night of whimsy, perhaps. So supremely empowered, it was, moving organically to the beat of the drums...

He entered a morning breakfast café and took a seat. Food, coffee and sobriety were clearly his aim now. That was what he wanted. He wanted to straighten out before returning to his place. He was almost embarrassed when the waitress poured coffee. She smiled courteously. He said he was an English student visiting Miami.

He knew only one thing. He wanted to do it again. That is, if he could find that girl...Who was she? From which unit in his office?

He ate, he drank and cradled his head. Then in less than half an hour, another cup of coffee, adding pancakes. Finally he left, his legs still stiff.

He would reach his Apartment building, grab his gear and proceed with his Saturday morning jog down to the boulevard and back. That was his routine.

He'd swim. To shake the fog that collecting on his brain. *Thirsty.* He drank from a water supply, started to make his way across the street. He bought Lemonade from a food truck.

The drink turned his stomach, he needed to throw-up. He stumbled back to the Café, the waitress recognized him. He headed for the bathrooms and vomited.

He went back out into the street, his head whirling and his mouth dry. He hailed a cab and gave his address. He read it from a card in his wallet. He was left on the curb, and he entered the lobby. He reached the elevators and pushed the button. But he had spun off, heading for the Foyer's Rest Rooms. He felt his heart pounding, his pulse racing. He sank to the ground.

Rarely was the facility used, he was alone. Few used the Rest Rooms in the Foyer of the building. Except perhaps janitors, odd personnel, waiting guests who had needed entry access.

He wanted to drift off, and he waited, fighting for air, his eyes closing. His head ached, he struggled to rise, but his limbs were heavy. He wanted air.

What was happening? Why was he so...something was wrong!

He felt dry. Parched. His mind was telling him to get up...his arms heavy as lead.

He filled his lungs with air, his tongue swollen and bitter, he wanted air. He could barely breath.

He hefted himself up.

The Concierge Desk was busy. Visitors, families signing in and children clinging to parents. Luggage was arriving, and room service pushed past. They never noticed.

He leaned against the wall and followed the cold granite curvature that led to the elevator, He pressed the button and up he went. He reached his floor, fumbled down the wide halls with brass numbers and found his apartment door, leaning against the jamb.

He was gasping for breath, his eyes straining and his face swollen. He pulled from his wallet his keycard and jammed it into the door lock. The card failed to trigger green access, it bent, being brutally plunged back into the slot. He tried again. Again. Again.

Finally, the tiny light turned green, and he lurched into his apartment, throwing up on the floor.

He stumbled to the bathroom, thirsting. His chest was burning, his limbs useless. He slumped, succumbing to darkness.

Karen McCullock was behind her desk wearing an off-white silk blouse and pale green scarf. She and Dave Talbot both looked at the file.
For a man bordering on retirement, Dave was remarkably agile, thought Amanda, and she came to appreciate why it was that the Assistant District Attorney chose him as her lead detective.
A copy of the Coroner's Report was on the table where Amanda and Barbara were seated.
"As you can see, a forensic examination suggests that the cause of death was not necessarily asphyxiation, but rather dehydration" said Talbot.
"Furthermore, the medical examiner said that while dental evidence shows a touch of malnutrition for some years prior to his demise, trauma was not the cause of death. He had been debilitated and was trapped before he died" added Karen.
An image was put on the table. It showed a decomposed body. "I'm sorry to have to expose you to this but I thought it important since you have a lead on the motive behind this crime..."
"So, you do call it a crime!" chimed Barbara.
"Well yes!" said Karen "I have to admit I was skeptical about a Last Will and Testament that suggested foul play. But there was no evidence. And those many years of silence had lapsed. Why not come forward, if that was a suspicion in the family?" she added.
"Now we have reason to believe this was Mr. Green" said Talbot.
Barbara looked at Amanda, shifting forward on her seat. "We met with his daughter. Yes, I'm sure Mr Talbot will also want to visit with her... But we got

the distinct impression that Mrs. Green had been warned off from reporting her suspicions when she lived. In death however, why not tell the truth? – I mean, after so many years…That's what her daughter said"

"There is no statute of limitations on murder" said Karen. "We did have a record of a Missing Person report made by his wife at the time."

"Evidently a search had been made by the local Precinct office. But it came to nothing. A cold case" said Talbot.

They sat, a room filled with sadness, and nobody spoke. Before them lay the image of the remains of a man long ago perished.

"The Coroner says, in his report, that the body was well preserved only because it was severely dehydrated at the time of death. That implies he may have known or seen his assailant. Possibly he even knew why he was being attacked" said Talbot. "If it wasn't an accident, then it was murder."

"The fact that we discovered a diamond with his remains…" he looked apologetic " - I'm sorry ladies, not a nice topic, I know…"

"Go on" admonished Karen

"Well, it suggests that he swallowed the diamond on purpose."

They glared at him, imagining the specter of the wretched man at his death

"What does that tell us?" said Talbot.

Karen spoke. "Usually, it's a willful last act made for a reason of desperation."

"Like a…a message or something?" asked Barbara.

"Precisely" said Karen, clearly having discussed the matter beforehand.

"Well...I don't know" muttered Barbara, her mind sorting through anything the daughter might have said.

Amanda got it immediately. "The diamond will identify the killer. The diamond is pretty unique!"

Karen looked at Amanda, nodding. "It's a blue diamond. Very rare in indeed, as you pointed out."

"Oh God..." groaned Amanda. She looked at Barbara "And there's one circulating for the Museum today...right?"

"Right. With my name on it, according to the Museum..." said Barbara. "Hey...I didn't know the guy, Legardier. He just showed up. I promise..."

Amanda looked at Karen "But even if the perpetrator is identified - as a cold case, he has long ago died himself. So how would any prosecution be relevant?"

"It's relevant legally. If we examine this legacy and find that a perpetrator's estate profited in any way, then we have cause to follow the trail and retrieve damages. Especially if the bounty was subsequently used for gain or profit by any other beneficiary. They would be liable. Especially if they have knowledge of its origins, or are cognizant of the circumstances without coming forward. In this case, with antecedent criminal intentions..."

"So it's not about war profiteering?" asked Barbara

Dave spoke. "If those funds were used to defraud, misrepresent or damage anyone else. Then we have a serious case."

"Again, if it is proved that it resulted in any *other* transaction or gains based or misrepresentation..." added Karen "It's about providing evidence and accountability!" She rose from her desk and glanced at her phone. She was needed downstairs.

Talbot nodded. "If its big money, then we call in the Security and Exchange Commission."
Amanda stood up.
"We have no knowledge. But we can discover the connection, if you'll give us a chance?" she said.
"That's why we called you in. Give us the Perpetrator, ladies" finished Talbot.

* * *

They took the rail out of the city to Bayview where Barbara lived. From Bayview, Barbara was driving Amanda's car which was parked at a station depot in New Jersey. Now that they'd completed their meeting downtown, Amanda had plans to join her family for the weekend in the Hamptons where there was a home.

"For a Morris Minor..." teased Amanda "there's lots of room in here..."

There was less traffic than usual and the conversation turned to the meeting.

"What I don't get..." said Barbara "is how they seem to assume that we're *implicated* somehow. I mean, I didn't have a clue who Legardier was before he entered our lives with his story. Then to ask us to do research for him which he wants to pay for with a *diamond* for crying out loud? How strange is that?"

"The whole business about the diamonds is unusual. I know it goes back to the 40s, and I understand that shipping aid to the Allies was significant for the war effort. Canada helped"

"They did?"

"Ships stopped in Halifax first because of the shipping waters...In fact, Trevor's family helped with banking during that period. He told me that's when they had their bank in Toronto..."

"Right" said Barbara. "The guy, the victim, he worked at the shipyards of New York. Mrs Green mentioned, I think. But I don't see any connection..."

"Umm..."

"What?"

"Well, I was just wondering about the comment about the Security and Exchange Commission. Is that what she said? Who was the attorney representing *them*?"

"I dunno. No. Wait. Bill Wakowski? Out of Salaman Firm?"

"Perhaps, if they got wind that diamonds were mentioned. I'm wondering if that's why they're challenging the claim of a cargo loss from a ship sinking..."

"Either the ship sank or it did not!" exclaimed Barbara.

Amanda looked out the window, her thoughts went back to the night before when she decided to clear out her desk drawers. In the bottom drawer she found a file labelled. It was supposed to be a file for papers on Tray's University. She had flipped it open and found not the paperwork of her son's enrollment, as expected, but a litigation case citing Trevor's company in 1945, and its false claim about a cargo loss and insurance claim. What was that all about? The ship's name was absent. But it did say the ship stopped in Halifax.

"So err...Sorry to interrupt your thoughts, but what would you like me to do next?" asked Barbara. The car was parked.

Amanda hesitated a moment, then said "Could you call Rebecca up in Halifax. You remember her, right?" Barbara nodded.

"She's retired now from working at Trevor's bank in Toronto. She lives in Halifax with her husband. Could you set up a call with her and brief her about the case we're looking at. She'd have some thoughts about where the archives of his bank business are stored. Even though it was Trevor's father's business at that time - and long before Rebecca worked there. But I'd like to ask her a few questions... For when I get back next week? I'd love to catch up on news, too. Would you mind?"

"Not at all" said Barbara. "I've been your Administrative manager for what...over 16 years? Rebecca Manheim was the CFO to Trevor's bank up there. I'll be glad to set up a call for you...When you get back?"

Amanda was about to get out of the car when a call lit up on her cell phone.

"Mrs. McDonnell?"

"Yes?" Amanda's hand gestured for quietness to better hear her caller.

"My name is Sophie Gonzales. I work with your son Tray at the Miami offices of Salaman and Salaman ..."

"Yes Ms Gonzales. How are you?"

"Mrs. McDonnell, your son was taken to the hospital in an ambulance this morning, around 9 a.m. I thought I should call you right away since he listed you as his Next-of-Kin as Emergency Contact. "

Amanda's face paled.

 "He is in the Intensive Care Unit receiving treatment."

"My God...What happened?"

"He is being treated for possible heart failure... "

"Surely you are mistaken...?"

"He is not conscious. You may wish to come and be with him..."

"Of course...I'll catch the earliest flight out of New York. Thank you for..."

"Mrs. McDonnell. There is something you should know. There is a police officer in attendance, in case he survives..."
"What do you mean?" She listened.
Barbara waited, her fingers gripping the wheel.
Amanda turned to her, stunned. "Tray is in the hospital..."
"Huh?"
"Drug overdose"

* * *

Tray survived.

It took three days to sort out the details. Amanda's only focus was an inward relief that her son had survived. That's all that mattered.

Sophie met her at the hospital. They stayed and talked.

Tray came around and opened his eyes.

They kept him under observation all night in CU. Amanda spent the night in the lounge outside.

Tray came fully awake the next day, and he smiled at his mother.

There were more questions than answers. By then, an attorney had appeared to help Amanda. Sophia reappeared for a morning visit.

Tray was stable. He breathed on his own and started to sip water and sit up. By the time he ate his first food, Amanda felt that she could relax.

Her intention was to stay at a hotel. But by the end of the story, she found it best to be moving in with her son at his apartment which had an extra guest bedroom.

The matter was settled at the Concierge Desk. There, Amanda discovered that the reason for Tray's rescue and recovery was because of early distress detection and immediate treatment.

The clerk at the Concierge Desk of the Building noticed the repeated lighting-up of the Apartment Key Access. Someone from management was sent up and found the Key Access card jammed into the door, and the electronic card had stuck in its magnetic-position. The door, technically, was still open. The Manger entered and found Tray. He called Emergency services.

Tray could remember none of it happening, and the fragments that he did recall shed no light on how he ingested drugs. Still, as he gained his strength, his deeper concern was how to move on.

It was agreed, finally, that he would complete his term of appointment as an Intern with the company until Christmas. Only six weeks left. For that period, Amanda would stay in Miami as family. He'd start the new year back in the UK.

It took little persuasion for law enforcement to find that Tray was not a user. His record was clean, his premises searched, and his tests negative. He had moments of recollection, and he could have perhaps found a reason to file a case for illegal activity perpetrated against him, especially recognizing those who might have placed him in harm's way. But he chose not to file charges. And he was cleared, himself, of any charges of willfully ingesting illegal substances.

Amanda stayed. Partly as his parental supervisor, and partly for his protection and recovery. She spent most of her time on the veranda when he was at work. Or, she retired to her room early with her computer for the evenings. This way, she could stay in touch with developments in New York.

Still, Tray worried her.

His sunny disposition held shadows. She helped him through it by keeping him engaged and chatting...

It was hard to find evil in the overflow of well-wishers for her son. Amanda watched carefully, and she noticed the details.

Tray was much subdued by the event. His enthusiasm for Miami had waned. Except for visits from friends like Sophie, he cared little about joining the crowd, even as they lavished him with sympathy and attention.

Plus, he fatigued easily. But he did return to work.

He put out a lot of energy achieving his tasks. Outwardly, he seemed ok. But in the evenings he was happy to relax at home. He would watch TV, or exercise in the Gym downstairs. Occasionally he swam in the Olympic pool, or he walked outdoors to the Beach Park and back. Twice, he played tennis with his neighbor, but just for a game or two.

It was Amanda who urged him to go out. This episode should not leave it's mark, she told him.

She found ways to mix up his routine - a change of scenery, she insisted. Once, she surprised him with a Tux for a formal night out at the Opera! *Tosca* was in town. On another occasion they drove up to Cape Canaveral for a rocket launch. Another weekend was a football game.

When finally the term of her stay approached, he pleaded for the ski trip. Actually, as Amanda discovered, there was no dissuading him. In a way, she was glad.

Amanda had her reservations. His safety and health had been severely compromised. Keeping her suspicions to herself, she felt that someone might try again to do harm.

Drug distribution was pernicious. Especially in this city. Not that any other city was immune from the epidemic in America. But the problem had been allowed to flourish under the influence of social media to the great cost benefit of big technology companies whose users online translated into accounts. There was few filters on social issues made popular by liberalizing laws on drugs and crime.

As to Tray, he had been targeted. The question was why? By whom? What was the motive, let alone evidence? There must have been a plan. This she had failed to figure out.

Amanda arranged for security wherever she could - not by being intrusive, but by taking simple safety precautions whenever possible. More than once she pleaded for a need on her part to feel 'safer' at a family restaurant. On some occasions, she knew, she had arranged for a detective.

Tray turned down the idea of security.

Amanda asked about a local investigation. Who was the woman that had taken him out all night dancing?.. Obviously she had induced a drug overdose, especially since the substance was laced with deadly effects that caused heart failure. A mother could only advise. And politely.

Was it her fault, she wondered. Amanda had always believed in giving her children responsibility. As a result, they each held a high measure of independence. Tray was a young adult. He was imbued with a strong sense of right and wrong. This decision of security, she knew, could only be made by him.

Amanda harbored doubts about the investigation. It was slow. In fact, she had spent much of her time communicating with others on the local drug enforcement procedures. Not only was there much to learn, but much to discover if she was to rule out deliberate intent to harm.

With only a couple weeks left in Miami, Tray focused on the ski trip to *Le Massif de Malderock*

Mountain. As he put it, this was his final trip with the office crowd before saying Farewell to his Internship in America!
Amanda understood.

 Amanda was fixing breakfast.
"You know Mum, I shall be seen as fat when I return to school next Spring? Boiled eggs are no contest for these sausages and toast-things!"
Amanda laughed. "French toast and sausages are the best in America!"
"Umm" his mouth full. Then, "gotta go!" He flew through the house collecting tie, jacket and briefcase, then answered a call from his ride waiting downstairs.
She smiled. His recovery had been satisfactory. Amanda took her cup of coffee and settled on the veranda. An endless view of the sea lay at her disposal.
Beneath, a city stirred with robustness. Business. Traffic. Tourists. Shipping. An eclectic mix of culture was everywhere tracking. Miami was a major port facility to the United States, a distributor of goods coming in from all over the world - supplier of food to countless Caribbean islands and resorts and the ports were always full of ships loading and unloading...
Amanda took in the warm breeze, and she had to admit that the climate was welcomed. This was one of those mornings when she sat here wondering to herself - even whispering a small prayer of thanks for her son's life.
Thank God he was discovered in time for emergency response to medical treatment.

At the same time, Amanda knew that many were not so fortunate. The Opioid epidemic was worse than most people understood. In the decade of liberal progressive drug enforcement policies that had been relaxed, the Mexican drug trade and foreign nations had taken its toll on too many: The statistics were staggering. More young Americans had died to Opioid over-dosage than all those lost during the entire Vietnam war.

Amanda had her suspicions. Especially after a strange encounter that occurred about a week after she arrived. It was a delivery made at the door by a young woman - a beautiful girl of Latino coloring. She had a package for Tray, she said. Then she was gone.

A basket of fruit was left. Only later did they discover a flat plastic pouch filled with white powder. Amanda reported it immediately.

Two police officers responded. One hispanic, the other an African American. The purpose of the delivery, the young black officer informed her, was to develop a drug habit by the recipient.

"Not for *this* recipient!" retorted Amanda.

"Yes Ma'am. Lucky for your son that he has family who cares..." he grinned.

"Thank you officer" she said courteously, "kind of you to say so."

Later that week, the matter was still being discussed with Tray. *Who was the girl?*

Tray was reluctant at first, telling his mother that this was his own battle to fight. But quietly, she insisted on knowing more.

Especially when he admitted that the girl at the door with the basket of fruit could well have been the same with whom he had danced and partied all night...

But there was more that Tray wanted to say.

It came out later, as they sat on the veranda, talking long into the night, mother and son. Amanda had fixed herself an evening glass of apple juice with a twist of lime, stirred with a cinnamon stick. Tray had a beer.

Tray asked about his father. Where was he? What was he doing? What made him leave New York so suddenly? Amanda told him.

Tray's grandfather, who ran the company - shipped cargo to and from the United States during WWII. Troop transport, food, munitions to the Allies. It was a difficult period. They lost ships. Family and friends and crewmen perished - all doing their best for the war effort.

Tray listened.

Then one ship sank from enemy torpedoes, the cargo was claimed as a loss by the Carrier.

In the case levelled against his father it is alleged that new evidence shows that cargo claimed as perished was *not* lost at sea. It was carrying a delivery of precious metals and a commodity for the war effort, which the owners stole and kept...

"That's ridiculous!" blurted Tray. "Dad would never do that!"

"Of course not. And remember, this was *his* father, your grandfather As you know, the company was operating as a bank at that time. It had obligations as well. Fiduciary trust and allegiance to its sovereign government..."

Amanda sipped her drink. "I don't know where he is, Tray. But I'd say he's in London facing the charges and disproving the case. The prosecution has filed in the United States, and the burden of proof is on the defense, which he is preparing to do."
"But he hasn't been in touch..." said Tray.
Amanda told him of her case in New York. Clearly, the two might be related, she explained. Adding "There was much I have to get back to. Much to solve, and much to explain about the museum statue and its provenance. Evidently, it has tripped some deeper suspicion of malfeasance somewhere. Possibly connected to a shipment during WWII" she said.
"And possibly a cold case murder?" said Tray.
Amanda sighed. "It's best we all take precautions, that's all. That's what I feel Dad is asking us to do." She looked at him and smiled, their porch lantern dim.
They looked out into the darkness.
Finally Tray jumped up "How about a hot cup of coffee Mum?"
She was about to say no, that she was ready to retire for the night. But it was Tray who spoke. "The thing is..." he said, "I found something strange, at work here. It's this man Mark Ruttenberg. I feel that he's been told to keep an eye on me. Clearly, he doesn't like me. But I have this feeling that he has intention to do me harm..."
"Have you told anyone?"
"Don't have to. Everybody in the office knows he's a piece of work..."
"You don't think that he had anything to do with your incident, do you?"

Tray didn't answer. He looked out across the night view of a city rimmed with street lights.

"You know that information that I sent you about the Ledger...?"

"Yes. We poured over it to find answers to any tracing of an original perpetrator related to a murder cold case..."

Tray chuckled. He knew of Barbara and her work-drive.

"Well. I used the office computer. Someone accessed my information, I know it. And... I received a threat. *Leave this alone, or someone will get hurt.*"

Amanda was stunned. "Who ...?"

"I don't know. Probably that Mark Ruttenberg. But then, I discovered it came from New York's office. The only email code in the office I could connect it to a man called Wickowski."

"Wick...?" repeated Amanda, the words dying on her lips.

"I have no idea."

"Look Tray. Just be careful on this Mountain ski trip will you? I'll have to talk to Barbara. We'll get to the bottom of this..." Amanda got up.

"Okay Mum. 'Night"

* * *

Chapter 13

Amanda's cell phone buzzed.

"Rebecca!...How are you?"

There was warmth in the conversation that followed. "...How can I forget your kind hospitality when I come up for Trevor's Annual Meeting?"

They chuckled and remembered it well. If it weren't for the CFO of Trevor's company in Montreal Canada, Amanda would have felt overwhelmed in her representation on the board.

Especially that briefing at a quiet Conference table where Rebecca Meinheim coached her for a presentation on the Bank's Executive Summary. While much of the material was the bank's Annual Report. Highlights and summary certifications were needed. Rebecca helped explain it all, especially those solid figures for investors, and the sound balance sheet for government compliance...

How could Amanda forget that week of events...

Trevor had asked her stand in for him because he deployed for duty in service to the Royal Navy for a mission. She was in Washington DC at that time, working on her own Research Firm. Their children were young...

It had been a formidable gathering of the world's bankers. Rebecca had taken Amanda out for dinners while she was staying at the Conference Hotel.

Rebecca briefed her about other bank attendees and about what to expect at the Annual Meeting.

They had laughed about what to wear, where to sit, and what time to rendezvous...Yes, Rebecca Meinheim had been an extremely able Executive Financial Officer, and a good friend.

Not that it had been an easy start to their relationship. Engaging with business colleagues was one thing, but discussing business with the wife of the CEO and to put on her stage for a keynote speech was quite another. "Your husband's bank is not without recognition" Rebecca had remarked, and from there they had developed a trust.

No wonder Trevor relied on Manheim. At that time, it was a huge risk sending a wife to stand in your place: The Conference that year was held in the Hotel of a building with a long history of the world's money exchanges. He was risking his credibility.

The building may have been modern - food courts, multi-tenanted floor lobbies; large spaces of the old stock exchange.

Center of banking and finance displayed Canada's biggest banks including the CIBC; Bank of Montreal; Bank of Nova Scotia; Royal Bank of Canada and Toronto Dominion Bank.

Plus, the venerated history founded by Trevor's family, Sterling Bank had its place there...

Amanda had to walk in his place across glossy Foyers filled with competitors, industry interests, investors and representatives - a procession of energy icons like Cameco Corporation, Canadian Natural Resources Ltd., Canadian Oil Sands Trust, EnCana Corporation, Huskey Energy Inc, Imperial Oil Ltd, and Nexen Inc.

The Annual Conference was filled with large-enterprise industries with exposure to drilling, mining, offshore capital projects, pipelines, tankers, storage, systems engineering companies and shipping carriers.

A dazzling display of companies, hiring thousands of people and investing billions for the world's energy prospects – all of them cognizant of Trevor's portfolio and his company background in underwriting; insuring and financing a post-modern world of energy production.

Amanda was delivering a key speech for Trevor.

Neither was this a forgiving corporate culture, nor idle in affairs of world energy policy. And while Trevor's brand name was well known, Amanda was an unknown. Thus, it was Rebecca who walked her through it without so much as a shadow of hesitation – ever shielding and enhancing the corporate presentation with professional grace and brilliance. Rebecca, and her team of legal agents for the Annual Meeting.

"Yes. I would love to come up to Halifax" said Amanda.

x x x

Dimitri had a client.

Why bother to infiltrate affairs of state, or police, or politics? He had hacked his ticket into the world of finance. Economic warfare, he decided, was at the heart of it all anyway.

And now he had his client. Something he liked. Imagine. The laborer who slept in the kennel had a New York Client. How he liked free market capitalism!

Now he had to be careful. He could talk. But his accent and inexperience might be obvious. No. He would communicate like a man in business. He studied the emails of men in business...

The client's name was arbitrated by a third party, a trader who spotted the gains that Dimitri had achieved. He made a compliment, and Dimitri was pleased.

Of course he had his Username AGEAN.

The client was not committed, just a prospect. So he needed a way to show savvy into the world of trade into Asian markets for profits in America.

Dimitri found traffic from CFIUS. He read it carefully to understand what it meant. Committee on Foreign Investment in the United States. It reviewed foreign acquisitions by US companies for potential national security risks.

The company under review was in Singapore, a chipmaker which failed to declare its US domicility under US Trade protections policy.

Before, nobody cared. Nobody feared. And if one nuclear submarines failed to operate because of a foreign manufacturer was delivery faulty chips, who cared? Or, who won?

But here, the shareholder's meeting had been cancelled by the government. And suddenly Dimitri entered a post, saying that its assets of '$110 billion could be taken in a hostile takeover.'

The lawyers were outraged. Many on Capital Hill came to the rescue, mainly politicians from the party that favored globalism and hated the military because it took money from their socialist agendas. The company itself filed for protection in America, and summitted to re-domicile under new laws. But the Singapore Court disagreed, wanting the chipmaker on Chinese soil.

Dimitri's client wanted to know if there was anything in the intelligence about how the CFIUS demand to re-domicile might affect the price of an acquisition. It was a legitimate request.

But it came through an illegitimate channel. Dimitri's world. It was asking for inside dark intelligence.

Dimitri infiltrated internal communications. What he found delighted him.

He reported that a decision had been made internally by the Singapore Company. They had no intention of complying with CFIUS. There would be no relocation or re-domicility to America. The company was not for sale. The money by a new acquisition was not wanted. They were digging in. They had the technology. Dangerous technology. The Americans would capitulate...

By itself, the information was non-eventful, even expected. But for an investor it was explosive stuff. The Trader directed his investors elsewhere, with thanks. Dimity gained immeasurably in the estimation of this client.

Of course the Trader would not divulge the name of his client. There would be more business.
But that was easy enough to discover. Before long, Dimity and the Trader's client would be doing business together, Dimitri felt sure.

x x x

Trevor McDonnell informed his office that he was not flying back immediately.

His staff in London wondered. Was this advisable, they had asked him. As a leading banker travelling in Europe - and without a secure line, they had been concerned about him. He had been gone a week. He insisted.... to enjoy some more Paris time alone. He some friends to visit, he told them.

He went to Holland. He was glad he did. And when it was all over, he did take the train back to Paris. It gave him time to think.

In Paris, while his arrangements amounted to little more than snacks at coffee shops, he had little baggage to worry about. He would indeed be on a train from Paris to London by nightfall. This, Jacques knew - but only Jacques.

All arrangements had been preplanned.

The train returning from Holland passed vast landscapes of crop under cultivation, or cattle management. Cities came into sight, gleaming with public and modern enterprise. The train moved on.

Trevor imagined what it must have looked like during the war – muddy fields ravaged by tanks, rain and the dying. Yes, Europe had been rebuilt, but it had come at a price.

Yes. Evil had been vanquished. But the demons that possessed it lurked ever near the surface of civilization, he knew.

Trevor was worried, his mind returning to the matter at hand.

Amanda was in the States, his son in Miami...both of them inextricably involved with the Salaman group.

He himself was in a very vulnerable position, and he had no doubts whatsoever that his family would be damaged with impunity if his suspicions proved correct. Trevor had to be careful.

The Salaman's Investment Bank was not what it purported to be. It had misreprented its worth, betrayed its fiduciary obligation and cheated its investors with false assertion and subterfuge. The government was steps away from finding compliance issues. It was now under pressure to find assets and show financial growth where it had none to show. It was a place that drove business to dangerous places and deeper into the wood.

If Sam Salaman was getting desperate, Derek his brother was a man with a poor head for finance and an ego. That he was the CFO was worrisome. Such combinations could be deadly, he knew.

The company and its affiliated network across the globe was tenuous, he knew. The finances were shaky, the full extent of their reach alarming. They were entering communications, tech and public dissemination areas where they could exert influence and shape government policy with public opinion.

Trevor had plenty of time to think. He made enquiries. Certainly, the case against him was fraught with false allegation. But he was still unsure about the extent of their operations, if it bordered on crime... the motive behind their actions.

"Better to know your enemy..." advised Clive, his council preparing to defend their position when they talked.

He looked at picturesque clouds.

Not only had the Prosecution managed to implicate his company in a frivolous law suit, but they embraced his family – Now the District Attorney of

New York was threatening them with Amanda's professional help on a related matter.

Worse. Tray had been put in danger.

He would have to be very careful indeed. He was certain that he was being surveilled.

Better that his staff think that he was meeting with a client in Paris, than to know the full purpose of his visit to Holland.

The information he carried was damaging. It would implicate the Prosecution in a nefarious matter related to war crimes in any international court, let alone in the United States where the company was domiciled.

Trevor knew that his own company had operated with honesty and integrity. Of that he was certain. Once it disembroiled itself from such damaging accusations, there would be redemption.

But it hurt their credibility and professional standing. Their defense would have to be robust.

Clive told him this in London. Their legal battle would have to reach back into history to defend their integrity, and then go on the offensive to cite the Prosecution in *their* actions over the last several decades - especially following WWII.

Moreover, new intelligence was coming to light.

Alpha, he discovered, was Salaman's father...

His two sons had built an empire on his profiteering, spying, betrayal and damage to innocent victims. His case would be heard in London, since he wasn't sure if he could trust political prosecutors in the United States. Their influence and infiltration at the Department of Justice was troubling...

 His thoughts went back to Amsterdam.

"There is no question," said Mr. Stultz after a long and careful examination. "This is of that collection!"

Mr. Stultz had been consulted as an expert to examine the diamond sample package.

The moment was intense. .

He pushed back his chair after he spoke. The diamond lay on the white damask tablecloth, a shining gemstone. He had looked at his grey-bearded Uncle, the room redolent with memories.

Trevor had visited his Uncle and was invited back to meet with Mr. Stultz. They had dinner, roast chicken and peas served by Mr. Lavine's housekeeper. Now, over torte and coffee, they conferred on the gemstone.

Schultz was an authorized diamond cutter now shipping to the United States under license. The question of identifying whether *this* diamond belonged to a particular batch known to have circulated during the war was put before him. Those brand of diamonds were legendary.

"Yes. I'm almost certain" he said again. "This... this is the original batch – the blue tint of diamonds from the of the original order that came from a certain mine in Africa. They are rare!"

"How certain are you?" asked Trevor.

"Almost 99% certain" said Schultz without hesitation.

"You need to trust him" said his Uncle, looking directly at Trevor.

They sat in silence, the table warm with truth and sincerity. Trevor was still, the verdict of identification sinking in.

He took a deep breath. Now he owed them his own truth.

"I have six packages Lbs50 in the vault of my bank. They are not lost. They have been authenticated and certified as grade diamonds. But I did not know their origin. They have been there since 1946."

"There were ten packages of 50 Lbs," said Schultz slowly, his eyes fixed on Trevor.

"Yes." Trevor cleared his throat and his fished from his briefcase a file with a document. "This is a copy of the New York Assayer's Office records. They acknowledge receipt of four packages in 1942." Adding, "they safely arrived in Halifax, as expected..."

"We wondered, Ah, yes!." said the Uncle. "We wondered if they ever arrived in the United States."

"The ship that delivered them to Halifax was one of our Fleet. It was subsequently torpedoed off Long Island. But it had already delivered its cargo into the Bank of Montreal. If you say that this is the same batch, then we have every package accounted for!"

Schultz and his Uncle smiled slowly.

There was little to add. Their silence attested to the suffering and betrayals that had occurred during that time. Their culture had seen great loses at the hands of the enemy.

It was the Uncle who broke the silence. "I may be an old man, but I say we have cognac!"

They laughed, chortling over modern times, families and the economy...

The evening ended with Stultz agreeing to submit a petition for a Certificate of Appraisal on the diamond sample. It would be used as evidence in the case against them, and Trevor was assured.

Trevor thanked them.

A spy had betrayed them to the enemy during the war for his own gain, thinking to retrieve the cargo for himself. But the ship was sunk.

However, not until *after* it made its delivery: True, the ship that sank did *not* carry the cargo as alleged by the prosecution in the suit filed. The cargo, rather, had already been unloaded in Halifax before leaving for New York...at the time of its sinking.

"It seems that someone is bluffing..." said the Uncle. "He must be hiding something!"

"I know what it is" said Trevor, referring to the Salaman brothers. "They...and their father before them, remained angry that they never got their hands on that shipment of diamonds."

"In any event, I will write my report. These samples, if they are from your vault, are unique" said Schultz. "I will send you a copy of the Report, with the certification and authorized seal of our company as Registered in Amsterdam. Then the matter will be re-examined, notarized and certified by the board of diamond trade. After that, you'll have your official Authentication certificate. I'll have it sent to Paris by Courier."

Schultz took a breath. "There will be no doubt, once it's certified: We will know exactly what mine and vein these diamonds came from. We know how much was yielded, and where they were delivered... I shall need to come to London to see consistency in the stock you have, of course. But if they are the same, they are unique, and they are identifiable. No question."

"Good, yes? But ..."said the Uncle clearing his throat. "The trouble is, how do we connect them to the *Alpha* spy?" said the Uncle.

"I'm not sure…" said Trevor. "At this point, it's just an allegation. There is no proof of direct tampering. Nor is there evidence of direct implication."

"Wait!" said the Uncle. He rose from his chair, and leaning on his cane, reached for the box on top of the buffet dresser. It opened like a dusty attic suitcase. He pulled out a larger manila envelope. He sorted through a number of hand-written pages. "This letter…it was sent to me from Spain. They were planning to ship the delivery to us to start work on a number of items. But he said the shopkeeper's supply had been compromised. And the shipment never arrived!"

"how can we prove anything from that letter, Uncle?" asked Schultz.

"He cites the packet number as they appeared when they were sealed at the mine before leaving Africa. They were in the Belgian Congo…"

"Can I have a copy of that letter?" asked Trevor.

"Yes."

Trevor imaged the letter on his digital camera. Schultz offered to send a cleaner copy in the pouch with the report to Paris.

"I believe the packets in the vault have the same serial numbers!" said Trevor.

"Well, at the least the batch you have in your vault are accounted for, now!" said the Uncle

"Yes. Thanks to you!" said Trevor, raising his glass.

"It will take a few days, you understand, to be officially registered, this report," said Schultz. "So, be patient, please!"

* * *

Chapter 14

The arguments in the court room were compelling. Viewcom, a large corporation of online video, wireless and TV was one step away from completing its merger.

The deal brokered by Salaman and Salaman was one of the biggest acquisitions made on US soil. According to the international news agency that reported the deal, anti-trust issues remained for the Department of Justice to argue.

The Judge was finding it difficult to harness such power under government regulation. Traffic, information, intelligence and control was doubling every twelve hours, he explained, how could a Congress even be expected to govern over a nation so beholden to one behemoth? What if it took on a political presence?

Too much power in a market filled with competitors able to perform the same service for less money was written in the laws of anti-trust protections. Such concentration was always a worry for Fair Trade.. It made for a monopoly, it enabled financing that crowded-out competitors. If the free market economy was to work, competition was requisite.

Besides, it was a particularly sensitive industry. Driven by high technology and potential of mass dispersion of information, like social media, posed a danger to constitutional representation. Worse, it exposed and exploited personal data on individual accounts. The government was concerned.

In their Briefs submitted to the court for Public Hearings, the two arguments came to bear: Did $85 Billion dollars paid for a deal of this size harm rivals? Especially those in television, communication, internet businesses and delivery systems...

"It's not that we should fail to embrace free markets, it's that we should embrace the spirit of healthy competition" the judge asserted.

This, Salaman & Salaman wanted resolved. By any means possible. This deal was already anticipated, and had to go through.

Dimitri got to work.

* * *

Amanda and Rebecca walked about. They strolled along the Waterfront together. "Over there is *Keith's Brewery*" said Rebecca

"It's beautiful up here!"

Rebecca Meinheim and her husband Roger had chosen to retire in Halifax Nova Scotia, and Amanda was a houseguest.

There were lots of memories to share about their years in Montreal.

Roger, as Rebecca explained, occasionally still engaged in government work as an attorney. "But I'm enjoying the life of a retiree. Audrey is close by, and her child is now 6. I'm spoiling my granddaughter with every excuse I can find!"

Amanda had to smile. She took in the scenery of the harbor. It was a sun-filled day on the Atlantic coast of Canada.

Boats and Buoys dotted the surface of a congested waterway. A large steamer, on its way to open sea honked deeply at any number of smaller vessels bobbing and dodging in its channel. Another fleet of tiny sailboats were set on winning their race, tacking in every direction to catch a breeze. Commercial fishing vessels, loaded with a sea catch for market, hovered and grunted for access to their piers.

At docksides, recreational fast-design power yachts displayed opulence in sleek chrome, glass portholes and girls in swimsuits.

Along the boardwalk people strolled and ate at the kiosks. University students in jeans mixed in with working professionals out for lunch from the business district.

Tourists, bicycle couriers, truck drivers and even police crowded. Cars edged around the highway tags from every state within Canada or United States. Delivery trucks unloaded crates and provisions for a vibrant nightlife of bars and restaurants.

"Lovely spot" said Amanda. "I can see why you chose to retire here. It's old, charming..." A girl in a bikini-on-wheels skated through them "...full of life!" she laughed.

They followed the water's edge. Rebecca told of the past. It was the world's second largest ice-free harbour. Museums, filled with their own narratives as the gateway into Canada told of those who settled.

"I want to take you to the Dartmouth side" said Rebecca, passing off their tickets and finding a seat on the Ferry. "There are locally-owned shops, galleries, cafés, restaurants, and pubs. And of course, the fabled donair, the offical food of Halifax..."

On the top deck of the Ferry Rebecca explained the events. She related the exposure that their bank had in WWII.

"It was in this very harbor that much of the cargo was delivered" she said.

Rebecca had done her digging. If anyone knew of the ledgers of Trevor's bank, it was Rebecca, his Chief Financial Officer in his Montreal Bank for 26 years.

"The steamship that had sailed into New York harbor in 1942 did carry cargo. But not the cargo expected by its manager, a man called Albert Kurtz."

Amanda listened.

"You have to understand that since World War I, the gold specie standard for money had ended in the United Kingdom. Treasury Notes replaced the circulation of gold sovereigns and gold was stacked in the vaults of central banks. The British Gold Standard Act 1925 introduced the gold bullion standard and simultaneously repealed the gold specie standard..."

The story of so many people caught up in so many struggles had never been far from her mind all through her career. Rebecca was glad to talk about it.

Amanda nodded.

"...But the idea did not work. In May 1931 a run on Austria's largest commercial bank caused it to fail. The run spread to Germany, where the central bank also collapsed. International financial assistance was too late, and in July 1931 Germany adopted exchange controls, followed by Austria..."

"Must have been desperate times..." murmured Amanda.

"I sometimes wonder if all this didn't lead up to WWII, though it's never defined..." mused Rebecca. "The Austrian/German experiences had consequences. Britain had budgetary and political difficulties. It undermined the Sterling British pound. By mid-July 1931, bank runs caused the Bank of England to lose much of its reserves – including your bank that Trevor's family owned then..."

Amanda touched her on the arm, a gesture of understanding for all those years of work.

"In America," continued Rebecca "the story was different. There was the Industrial Revolution, the great Depression, the new political landscape full of rhetoric and anger...So, the contraction of money supply resulted in *deflation*. Like so: When interest rates remained high the economy slowed. Right?" she gestured.

Amanda nodded.

"Recovery in the United States was slower than in Britain, in part due to Congressional reluctance to abandon the gold standard and float the U.S. currency as Britain had done. For those who traded as brokers and exchanged money and gold, the profits were lucrative. This manager of the ship, Kurtz, he *knew* about this. I suspect he was a player. He enjoyed the turmoil with wealth accumulated at his dealings..."

"Anyway... Congress passed the Gold Reserve Act on 30 January 1934 which nationalized all gold by ordering Federal Reserve banks to turn over all their supply to the U.S. Treasury..."

"By WWII," she continued "Roosevelt called in all the gold bullion, and most of Europe's supplies now crossing the Atlantic. By 1944, the gold standard was kept without domestic convertibility. The role of gold was severely constrained, as other countries' currencies were fixed in terms of the dollar... Are you with me?"

"It would pay for the war?" said Amanda, simply.

"It paid for much of the manufacture of supply and provisioning of the war...something no treasury on earth could do. However, some of it was a token of payment by the Russians and British for American Aid, as allies"

Amanda said "Let's take a break. I can see that its upsetting you. I do appreciate your background work..."

A loud crashing and entry was heard from the garage doorway.

Roger walked in wearing his bicycling gear. "Hello Ladies... Anyone want to use my bike?" he grinned. "I'm done!"

"You're sweaty" chuckled Rebecca.

Amanda waved.

They didn't talk again until after dinner at home. It was a meal replete with jokes and stories about their lives in Montreal.

Finally Roger said "You know...If it weren't for Trevor as a boss, I'm not sure Rebecca would have stayed with the bank. I don't think I would have wanted her there otherwise..."

"Yes, he was terrific. He let me run the place!"

Amanda and Rebecca chatted over the kitchen table. Rebecca returned to the events of the war, and the bank's role.

"Your bank sent shipments of precious metals to the United States. And it underwrote other Steamers who transported war material across the Atlantic. Ledgers kept in Montreal...showed a full accounting of its shipping to the Admiralty, with certified documentation. Many ships were sunk. There were spies...The company had to be careful."

"Shipments of precious metals and valuables ordered by Churchill were sent to Roosevelt for safekeeping and payments. Lend Lease was the program that paid for the consignments of arms and supply in the prosecution of war against the Axis powers of WWII. We carried those cargoes and brought them into Halifax, sometimes unloading here, sometimes reshipping to New York for the Asseyor's office.."

Amanda waited.

"There was other cargo onboard. Packets of diamonds. But it was not what arrived in New York. The manager in New York apparently found the cargo shipment short. He found only some other personal valuables on board. It was arranged that the Captain of the ship was to be paid for the lease of his ship and his services with a small payment of diamonds..

"But he was found short?"

Rebecca nodded. "Likely, he was killed for it. The dockside manager felt he had been duped. The ship had unloaded her cargo in Halifax, Canada. It is recorded that she unloaded five packets of 50 lbs of diamonds from Belgian Congo. Plus five tons of gold, and three tons of platinum. All of it under the management of the Admiralty and under the terms of Lend Lease by the US Treasury."

"The cargo that had been unloaded in the dark of night occurred like a fine tuned orchestrated operation. In stealth the cargo was crane-lifted in large roped crates and placed into waiting lorries, tarped over, and quickly driven off within two hours, total. It was known that spies had her in their sights..."

Rebecca sipped her coffee, then continued.

"The lorries drove into a hanger outside the city. From there they were reloaded. Once inside the vaults of the Halifax Repository, behind an Armory of military guards and barricades, the shipment was again counted, catalogued and entered into the record as having been received by the Treasurer's Office. Those were the precious cargo supplies delivered by your bank..."

"And the sinking?" asked Amanda, sadly.

"They discovered that the enemy had infiltrated the communication codes. Messages now sent were different coded. Including all banking traffic."
"Did the plan work?" asked Amanda.
"The plan worked. This was the second shipment. And though the spies eluded Federal Agents, they knew they had caused some havoc. The manager, Kurtz was furious. When he realized that he had been duped, he had to think fast."
"At least, it was though that the man Kurtz went also by the name "Alpha." He was either a spy, or he was profiteering from the supply of shipments. It was suspected he had inside information from the Germans. Regardless, he claimed he had 50 Lbs packages of genuine cargo. Diamonds from the Belgian Congo. Turns out...they had been the Kurtz-supply promised to the enemy. Then he realized that he had been double-crossed! He expected the full shipment, as his handler in the German army wanted. Or so he thought...."
"But the codes had been changed to thwart spies..." finished Amanda.
" "Evidently, he had rewarded the driver at his side with a small token gift, promising a second prize at the next shipment. But here was a predicament. He had been shorted. And now his driver knew too much.
 "What happened?" asked Amanda.
"Kurtz - a.k.a Alpha rewarded him alright. He gave the cement driver one diamond as a Keepsake for his troubles, and told him to wait at the next Pier. Then Kurtz disappeared into the night... "
"Two hours later, a dockworker approached the driver. The driver was hit on the head and tossed

into the cement mixer. He was poured out the spout and tossed down into the pit of a building foundation in New York City. It's uncertain how long it took him to die. But his body was never discovered."

"Did this Alpha every get captured?" asked Amanda.

"No. Never. He used his skills to make money in New York. His identity was changed, although some people had spotted him apparently. He never found out who betrayed him, either!"

The news was all over the New York Municipality Offices. The judge was found dead.

He had been staying for a couple nights at the Hyatt Hotel of downtown, Manhattan New York. He was last seen at the conference banquet where he sat with his staff to honor the Speaker.

A Press Release, the following day was issued from the Media center of the Department of Justice building. The New York Police Commissioner was at the microphones.

 "In a city like ours, where law enforcement and prosecution of the law takes precedence, we let down one of our." He looked up. "We find on matters that are both local and global. We protect and defend citizens who work here. We serve in our systems of operations, whether in cybercrime, or in court rooms, we examine infractions, we defend justice, and we care equally about our residents..."

"Was this a *crime*?" interrupted one reporter.

"Yes. It was a crime. At this time we have no details to offer, only to say that we do have a positive identification, and a team of investigators to examine the situation."

"It is possible this was an accident? Or was this foul play?"

"Murder is always foul play" admonished the Commissioner.

"Was he attending the *International Forum on Business for Crime Prevention*?"

"Yes"

"Is this an international incident relating to *espionage*?"

"Again. We will have all the answers at a later time."

"Was he a *target*?"

"Ladies and Gentlemen. I can say this, as a city leading in international banking and stock markets, we do acknowledge the need for policing against sophisticated crime and tactics of intimidation. It is taken especially badly by us that a US judge could not be protected in our city. This we will have to review in the coming months as we weigh the importance of safeguarding those in authority and those in leadership..."

"What was he working on?"

"As I said, we will keep you informed, and I promise we will have answers. Thank you all for your concern and your attention. I will let the Mayor and his staff answer any further questions..."

The Police Commissioner stormed out of the Media room accompanied by his council and his senior liaison officer. Behind him a security detail followed.

He saw Bill Myers the District Attorney standing in the hall. Karen McCullock and Detective Paul Talbot stood with him.

"Did I give them enough?..." asked the Commissioner without pausing.

"You did Sir" said Bill Myers.

"Then find out what the hell he was working on, will you?" he barked, the elevator door closing.

There was no need to ask. They knew.

The International Forum held in New York City had benefited greatly from interfacing with members of US law enforcement; their management and the legal authorities that handled issues of policing. Mostly, the topics of interest were about crime that crossed borders. But also they dealt with matters of industrial security, commercial fraud, cyber-crime, theft, information sharing and intellectual property policies.

Increasingly, information technologies relating to International Trade agreements and Industrial espionage was a section of criminal investigation requiring highly skilled levels of detection and monitoring.

While most infractions dealt with damaged property and assets, crime against people with tactical policy issues was now appearing. Even financial transaction managers and decision makers were targets. Fraud and financial accounting was a close second. But in a city where billions of dollars were traded and exchanged daily, any decision or perturbation that might impact such huge transactions had its vulnerabilities.

The Judge had just presided over a blockbuster antitrust trail and adjudicated in Court against a merger acquisition between an international news and media group and an internet technology company. The decision was viewed as critical to the future of both companies, citing possible rate increases by the monopoly to consumers because of the merger. Moreover, the outcome of the case would affect other pending vertical mergers in which different parts of a supply chain, rather than rivals in the same business, join together or collude for market share...including global pharmaceutical company mergers.

But the Judge had been adamant. "The acquisition would give the merged companies a new tool to slow down the development and growth of disruptive online competitors in the future..."

That kind of public knowledge about the trail was bad enough. But in the offices of the District Attorney, it was also known that one of the companies merging were receiving vast amounts of money in a financial transaction from overseas. The judiciary were left in a vulnerable position, and without protection.

Back in her office, Karen McCullock and Talbot were discussing the file for the Commissioner. Her office assistant Sarah walked in holding two containers of papers, two cups perched atop, plus files under her arm.
"Mr. Myers wants to see you, when you have a moment..." she said, putting a coffee on Karen's desk. "And this is for you Paul, ice-coffee!"
"That's why we hired you!" grinned Paul.
"Thanks" said Karen, leaving immediately for the upper floors of the building where her boss held court.
The phone rang. "Ms McCullock's office" said Talbot, answering.

Karen returned less than an hour later. "You'll never believe what came in from the Special Offices of the FBI..." she said.
"There was an email found on the Judge's encrypted laptop. Apparently, he received it from a server manager on the dark web a Personal Message about his decision on the merger. A warning threat against his life!"
"Oh?" said Talbot.

"The IP address…" said Karen "traced the source. Cyber-security experts discovered communications at approximately the time of the Judge's death."
She picked up her coffee and sipped.
"The IP address unmasked an operator called Dimitri. They found his portal and traced his contacts. One message - clearly a signal to move on a plan of assault, was given to him from someone in New York City. It was traced to the New York offices of Salaman Brothers!"
"You're joking, right?" said Talbot.
"Turns out, they were financing one of the companies in the multi-merger court case!"
"No way!" said Talbot. "How does that connect anything to anything…?"
"I'm not sure. We're a long way from proving anything in a court of law. But we'd better keep digging!"
"Damned straight!" said Talbot.

* * *

Washington DC

"We have a Match!" yelled out the Researcher, her voice trailing half way across the 7th floor of the building of National Archives and Records. She clapped her mouth in embarrassment.

She'd been assigned a Task Order by her supervisor, Mrs Geiski, and she had solved the problem. ..

Originating from the Federal Reserve Bank in New York, it had taken her two months to piece together results that would offer evidence of an account and its place of origin within the financial records of US Treasury – something that she would have to write up on in her Research Report.

From countless findings, searches, discoveries and archival records, Lisa Demworth's quest was to show the world that even Liberal Arts graduates had their uses on earth.

Her supervisor, Mrs Giesky sat at her desk, just inside an office with a glass front.

Lisa beamed. She gathered her pen and pad, and walked into the office as if ready to disclose the prize of the century. She closed the door to the office so that even if seen, they could not be overheard.

Research, by its very nature, was a combination of data, feedback loops and deductive reasoning. Often it was proprietary and selective intelligence. Almost always of worth and value in commercial terms, and key in decisions that shaped them. The trick was to know what was what.

Not all people had the ability to manage all three attributes. Some were excellent at finding stuff, others excellent at compiling relevant data feed back, but few had the talent for insight and thoughtful reasoning. This could swing the balance. Many a legal case had been lost or won over the ability to provide cogent evidence. And while information was at the heart of making decisions, being a good researcher meant everything in the world to those who valued it for what it was, an asset. Or, in the case of Lisa Deworth, a gift.

Many on Giesky's staff had spent hours tracking and examining boxes upon boxes of papers only to fulfil their work-day obligations and to collect a check at the end of the month. Few had the perspicuity to understand why something would be where it was...Such a trail was worth as much to the parties involved as it would be to any forensic scientist doing a post mortem examination to find a murderer.

"OK" began Lisa "Here's what I found, and how. The account was opened at a time when little was required from a depositor, other than cash. This was during the war. In this case, the Banker noted on the applicant's form that the depositor also opened a safe deposit box..."

"Right. So. We know what the contents of that box was...What we need is the identity of the depositor..."

"He listed his name as Alexander Stephanophos Klein. He said his mother was English, and he spoke English. On his application, he cited his brother, aged 34, as reference. He said his brother was a machinist in Hamburg, Germany. As his place of residence he listed a New York address. A room in a local hostel. He said he lived alone. No wife or children. He told the banker he wanted to make a deposit of diamonds."

"Go on!" said Giesky

"The German authorities confirm that they had they have no record of any Kline -(or Klein, as it is sometimes spelled)- who was a machinist in Hamburg Germany in 1942, aged 34" said Lisa. "But they sent us a list of those who might be a close match to that statistical paradigm. Of fifteen possibilities with names in a similar vein, spelling, sound or close approximation, only ten were under age 50. Of the ten, only six were machinists, and of the six, only two had brothers. One was named Kurtz. He spoke English, with an English mother."

Giesky tapped her desk with the tip of her pencil, weighing the possibilities of an assumption. Had Kline changed his name from Kurtz?

"The Hotel burned down..." continued Lisa, "I discovered that information in a newspaper article at the US Library of Congress. In the article, the fire marshal said that few residents survived. Only two people did, one a Mrs. Stewart from Scotland, another a Mr. Hudson from North Dakota..."

"Anything to corroborate that information?"

"I called their heirs. Only Mr Hudson's son was still living. He remembered the fire, and the anxiety of his father's distress at that event. He said he didn't recall much. His father said another man in the building survived, whom he knew. He did not respond to Kline. He said the name sounded something like the Greek alphabet. His father was proud to be his friend. He had money. That was rare, back then. He was from Germany. He said he had a brother or something..."

"Can he agree to a written statement?"

"I'll ask."

"So, what about the bank account?" pressed Giesky, already impressed with the precise nature of the finding so far.

"The Bank was taken over in 1957 and the records archived at Treasury. There was some correspondence from the Bank relating to a Mr. Kline, or Klein. His box would be closed, and its contents confiscated, they said. Apparently, they received complaints from customers who claimed they had bought Bonds from Mr. Kline. Kline cited the bank as having the assets to back those Bonds, with collateral to redeem their coupons. The case was handed to the authorities, back then. But the trail goes cold."

"What about the confiscated items of the bank box?"

"Well, the case was opened following a recent Enquiry made by a Trader in London. The SEC got the request to investigate - that is, before it found its way to us as a Task Order from Treasury. I spoke to the manager of that docket, and he told me that all they found was a Ledger of bookkeeping for a WWII Construction company. It's impounded as evidence by the Department of Justice in New York. Sorry, no diamonds!"

"Umm, too bad!" grimaced Giesky. "Well... We've done our part of the investigation. Find out who we should send our report to, will you? Well done Lisa. Good work!"

x x x

The Conference Room at the District Attorney's Floor was packed with lawyers.

Bill Salaman had been invited forward for questioning, and he had a retinue of legal council with him.

Outside, the media crowded for attention, asking questions and flashing images of the team that would defend the icon financial figure of some renown. Allegations against him and his Firm - a major investment bank, were full of rumor and conjecture and had rocked the financial districts.

Karen didn't expect to be party to all this. This had become a celebrated case in the press. Normally, those in higher positions of authority handled high profile prosecutions. She was, after all, an Assistant DA lawyer working for the city - one amongst many. But the District Attorney and the Police Commissioner had both decided that since she had been the one to handle the original cold case of the Testament of Mrs. Green, followed by the discovery of her husband's body, then she should be the Lead in this investigation. If necessary, she would prosecute the case if it went to trial.

By any measure, such an opportunity would enhance any career. For Karen, it was a matter of taking the unwanted cases and doing her job as best she could. But she had impressed her seniors with her diligence. She was asked to continue. They vowed their full support and the backing of the Department.

She decided to keep her staff and her lead detective Paul Talbot at her side.

But today, it was clear that she was outclassed.

The celebrated case was hitting the news circuits.

Amanda recognized the name on the news.

Further, Salaman had been removed from the Committee at the Museum, they informed her, and she alone would be sponsoring the statue at the Fundraising Exhibit in New York.

The indictment against the Firm was already affecting stock market in trades, especially the tech sector since the merger involved large capital investors. And whereas normally such events went unnoticed, here was clearly a public following. Especially on social media.

They arrived in a stream of limousines. Bill Wicowski was there - ostensibly representing the interests of the SEC, but as an Attorney for the Salaman Firm nonetheless.

Before entering the hallway, Karen spotted Bill and waved him aside.

Bill was dapper looking, a tie with parachutes and balloons, a silk suit equal to any in the legal pack, and a grin that exuded confidence. He made a statement saying that they would refute with impunity any claim of malfeasance on the part of his client, Bill Salaman and his Firm.

"Bill, we've been friends since law school" said Karen "I know you're good at gaming the system. But this conflict of interest ends today. I expect you to remove yourself from this enquiry, and to inform the SEC that you must recuse yourself from any further involvement. You're not in a position to advise the SEC about the Firm that retains you!"

"Karen, you're bluffing, right?"

"No Bill, I am not..."

"On what grounds?" he asked defiantly. "You're just an administrative tool in this building..."

"On the grounds that after today, it will be discovered that the Firm operated on fraudulent representation from its inception, and continued to practice illegal practices for years... Bill, your Firm is finished!"

He looked at her. Karen was doing him a favor as a friend, he realized.

"Tell your wife that you're leaving for Connecticut. Sell your BMW, your home, and get out while you can! There is no reason so far, to implicate you for any acts of collusion. But you will be tarnished by association if you stay..."

Bill would have spoken. But he remained silent.

Karen walked into the Conference room, followed by several legal assistants from the DA's office, Paul Talbot with her.

Bill Wicowski did not enter the room. Instead, he took a seat in the hallway bench, his briefcase dropped loosely on the floor. After a few minutes, he pulled out a cell phone and dialed his wife.

"Gentlemen," began Karen "we have asked Mr. Salaman here to answer questions and to provide information necessary for the government to consider. This is a voluntary and preliminary Hearing of Discovery...We shall later decide whether to prosecute in a court of law..."

"Damned right!" spluttered someone at the end of the table, smoothing his tie in indignantion. "Our discovery, rather!"

The day was long. Mostly, Karen was playing legal points before arriving at any nugget of truth. These lawyers were relentless.

Bill Salaman sat through it with a great deal less agitation than his retinue, almost as if he were subdued, if not entirely sedated. He grinned and nodded like a puppet, speaking only when permitted by his legal aids.

"Look Ms McCullock, if you have a case, and wish to arrest our client, then please say so! We'd like to know on what grounds, and we'd like to end this witch-hunt that dredges up the past with little bearing on anything. The statute of limitations on any criminal act or intention is long past. We ask that you show your proof of evidence, or end this nonsense..."

"Gentlemen. There is no statute of limitations on murder!" said Karen.

 She took a deep breath and dove in with her questions. Little of it useful to any case for the People of the State of New York.

Paul leaned forward, and looked her deeply in the eyes. His meaning was clear. *Keep Going.* Don't be intimidated!

"We can show that the father of Mr. Salaman was a man named Alpha who had on his possession access to assets misappropriated during the war and used for his personal gain and profit..."

"In addition, he used that misappropriated asset to defraud people of their money with the use of Bonds. The money that he gained from that scam was used to established the company which his son inherited...."

The room fairly bristled with heckling.

"Right and you can claim that case, because of a cold case...?" said someone.

"Prove it!" bellowed another.

"Further" continued Karen "In the case of Mrs. Green, we must consider that the murder of her husband was connected, especially when his body was discovered with a diamond lodged with his remains, a diamond that was of a rare batch and found only to have been stolen by Alpha..."

"There's no connection that Salmon had anything to do with that..." pushed someone in the chorus of protestation.

Karen felt like she was beginning to buckle. But she had a duty to perform, and she must disclose their position.

"We believe that Mr. Green was murdered by Alpha. We believe that Alpha was known by Mrs. Green, as evidenced in her Testament..."

"which she does not prove..." interrupted someone.

Outside the glass conference room, someone was trying to get Paul Talbot's attention. He excused himself, got up and went outside.

"We believe that Mrs. Green points the finger to Alpha, and we have evidence to show that she was in possession of a diamond from the same batch that her husband ingested at the time of death at the hands of Alpha..."

"And... you have proof, right?"

Paul Talbot reentered the room. He handed Karen a slip of paper. Karen looked up and smiled.

"We have evidence to show that Mrs. Green was sexually assaulted by Alpha... "
"So what? That was over 70 years ago!"
"We believe that Mr. Salaman used his father's money to achieve phenomenal success with his investment bank, money that was stolen:
The implications should not be lost on you Gentlemen, especially since the Firm was financially implicated in the merger case before the Judge."
They listened.
"Further, since Mr. Salaman has voluntarily agreed to a blood test, we'd like to now show the results...
"We now know that Mrs Green had a daughter. Her daughter's DNA is known...
"Mrs. Green's daughter is genetic half-match consistent with the DNA of Mr. Salaman's family. He is Alpha's son. I have in my hand a report from the Medical Examiner who completed his tests on Mr. Green's remains. "
The room fell silent. They were stunned.
Karen gathered her papers.
"Gentlemen, we are done here. Thank you. See you in Court..."
Talbot smiled at them.

* * *

The mountain ski resort was full of surprises.

The Sports Bar penetrated deep into the mountain. Unlike the upper structure deck levels of glass, open hearths and vistas of glacial wonder of the Canadian Rockies, this grotto level was tunneled in rock and granite, if occasionally lined with cedar wood and slate as décor.   Only the ski resort hearth was consistent with the upper levels, and it was alight. But not by fire-burning wood. It was lit by electric simulators.

Tray entered the place with a bevy of friends and office colleagues. He recognized the reserve of wild partying and heavy drinking - something desirable for the young singles ski guests and travelling *ingnitos* well hidden from the public. Strangely for him, the place held less the allure of adventure than of an underground chamber.

Still, he was surrounded by one happy crowd, and the music was pulsing with bodies, dancing, simulated star light-shows.   Drinks   flowed generously, and he was twice lured onto the dance floor by the girls in his party.

Pointless finding suspicion in every shadow, he decided. At least he was out with friends that he knew. Sophie, who had may have enjoyed one drink too many, pulled him up for a spin on the dance floor.

"Not again?" he feigned, exhausted.

"Yes again!" they all chanted. Clearly, they were having a good time with him.

It happened after midnight, perhaps on the fourth round of drinks, in a swirl of Rock-n-Roll moves when Tray stepped back inadvertently into another couple dancing behind him. He apologized, and the girl acknowledged him with a nod. But the man, his head shaved smooth, growled and shoved him back roughly, bringing his face to within inches of Tray and spat off a string of language.

The girl spun her partner off him, and Tray wiped clean his face.

The dance ended and he returned with Sophie to the table where a new song ripped through the air. Fresh drinks approached laden with frothy Austrian mountain foam.

Tray stood up calmly, and moved toward the Gentlemen's Restroom. Just at the door, as if waiting, he saw the shaved head man at the door. He gave Tray the finger then spun around a sharp stiletto to demonstrate that he could slit a man's throat in one motion. He froze the stiletto, mid-air, then re-inserted it into its sheath when someone walked out into the hall.

Tray walked on, unaccustomed to overt aggression, and he took a minute to catch his breath and dowse his face in cold water. When he re-emerged, the hallway was empty and he made his way back to the table. But just as he turned the corner, he felt a sharp jab down the side of his arm, and he clasped it instinctively, wondering if he had snagged himself against an unseen wall protrusion.

He looked about and saw nothing, except perhaps the leg of a man disappearing down the next hallway and into the crowd.

Tray sat down and was about the drink his beer when the pain persisted, and he brought up his free hand to press upon the injury. He felt moisture, and he knew he was bleeding.

He removed himself from crowd, avoiding the general area where he'd been and propelled himself to the entrance of the grotto, his hand now red and his face hotly perspiring. By the time he reached the entrance, his body was burning with discomfort and his shirt sodden. He staggered outside, and instead of climbing to the upper decks, he walked into the cold snow and padded the gash in his flesh with a wad of wet snow. He felt light-headed, and with his cell phone ringing against his chest, he fumbled a reply that he'd be back at the cabin.

With blood now leaking on the moonlit snow, he knew he must stem the flow of blood loss. The night was dark and cold, all decks deserted. Pressing hard on the wound, and with every effort of strength he vaulted up the deck stairs, across two overlook decks of the chalet, and over towards the court roadway that led to the area of parked ski-sleds.

Twice he paused, leaning to catch his breath. He pushed forward, inserting snow into his mouth and swallowed it cold. Whatever hydration he received was sufficient to keep him moving.

Fumbling for his cabin card, he entered and headed for the shower, tore open his own sodden Tee shirt and bound a towel tightly around a knife wound. It served as a tourniquet. He let the warm shower water revive him.

Slowly he cleaned himself off with a fresh application, and lay on his bed. He fell asleep for an hour. Twice he reached for pain killers, drank water, and inserted a mouthful of peanuts and crackers. He needed to get it stitched, he knew.

Outside, the ski lodge central courtyard were flood-lit for night-skiing events. Parties coming off the slopes milled about wearing ski gear and boots. Two ski-runs were floodlit and ski-lifts operating all night.

Tray buttoned up, headed for the Pharmacy dispensary, and had a nurse stitch up his wound. He claimed he took a rough fall on the slope and ripped himself against a sharp tree branch.

By dawn, Tray managed to brew up some coffee and called for an early breakfast in his cabin. Then he slept another three hours.

It was Sophie who came pounding on his door at noon. "Afternoon for test runs!" she announced. "...Before the big diamond slope run tomorrow!"

"Right!" he grinned.

* * *

Amanda didn't count on skiing. Yet here she was at the ski lodge shop of *Le Massif de Malderock Mountain.*

It was the strangest of coincidences, she thought. She'd left Canada, and barely arrived at her apartment in New York when she got a call from Rebecca.

"You'll never believe this, Amanda. But I got a call from Trevor in London. It was just after you had left here, and I told him that he'd just missed you..."

Rebecca was besides herself - trying to re-align the coincidence of Trevor missing Amanda by just hours!

"That's ok Rebecca. What did he say?"

Rebecca laughed happily, veiling the anxiety in her voice at the sudden loom of Trevor, while at the same time remaining calm.

 Trevor hadn't communicated in weeks. And if there was one thing that Amanda knew, it was not to question his defensive response to danger. Something was wrong.

"Err...So what did he say?" she asked again casually.

"He...he wanted to surprise you, he said."

"Oh no..." chuckled Amanda "Sounds ominous..."

"He said he wanted me to forward you from the bank in Toronto a Gift card purchase for skis & clothes for your trip to the *Le Massif de Malderock Mountain.*"

"My trip to...?"

"Amanda..." interrupted Rebecca. "Did you say you hadn't *heard* from him. Surely, I mean..."

"Yes. What a sudden call to get...Rebecca, thanks!"

"Right!"

Amanda gathered her thoughts.

"Amanda?" said Rebecca "Hello, are you still there?..."

"Umm...I wasn't expecting such a message. That's lovely to hear, if he got in touch... A surprise Gift card at a ski resort? What's that all about I wonder? Thanks for playing go-between!"

"Amanda, you said your son was going there with his friends to ski?"

"Yes. That's right. End of this week, in fact."

"Well, obviously Trevor knows about that. He perhaps supposes that you'd be there skiing too?"

Amanda laughed. "Yes. That's entirely possible. Though you know, we give Tray all the room he needs. He is very much his own man."

"Oh, I couldn't agree more! Offering respect to our children is the best way to encourage their independence and development" said Rebecca. "Wait till they land you with grandchildren!"

Twice, Rebecca called to reiterate the message and again they went over the matter with some excitement. Obviously, Trevor expected Amanda to be at the ski resort at the same time as their son. Or as close to that event as possible.

Still, the phone call left Amanda wondering what on earth Trevor was trying to signal.

For one thing, it was totally out of the blue. Sure, they had enjoyed spontaneous events together. But this was not his way.

He was always careful to make preliminary arrangements in advance, and he was considerate to keep her informed of his plans. Much like his plans to be in Miami, if interrupted...

No. Tray was in danger, and he wanted to alert her to be there.   x x x

Chapter 15

The more she thought about, the more it became clear that Trevor's call was more than a casual coincidence. It was an urgent message. Tray was in danger. This she had to tell herself a thousand times as she flung herself into preparations, and booked a flight up to Canada.

The door squealed as she entered the Gift Shop.

Here she was, she thought, in the Mountain ski shop... taking collection of the Gift card that would pay for the bundle that Trevor her husband had arranged.

He had derived a way to reach out to her, through Rebecca, and to get her up there! This he had done without disclosing his position, nor any information that might arouse suspicion. Just a gift of clothes to be ordered and picked up at the ski shop.

Since he did not mention any meeting-up with their son, nor any family plans about getting together, then clearly their son was *not* informed, and *not* expecting her...

Trevor wanted her there *without* their son knowing.
Why?

The more Amanda thought about it, the more it occurred to her that this was an alarm.

She got it. Exactly what was she supposed to there, she wasn't sure.

She picked out a Down jacket, boots and wool hat. It seemed strange though, being here, yet on her own...She moved to the counter to pay for her purchase. The purchase totally a little over the amount of the Gift Card.

She pulled out her credit card, and paid the difference. The attendant looked at her card carefully. It was the same name as the Gift Card. Amanda Wells.

"Do you ski?" asked the Norwegian, looking down at her. A smile broadened his face.

"Marginally" she said "I used to, in my younger years...It's not exactly the pass-time of the retired" she smiled.

"Oh you'd be surprised! We have gentler slopes here for all ages and skill. Those who want to take it slower..."

"Like Bunny Hills?"

"Yes!" he laughed. "I have children myself and that's a good way to start them. But actually, what I was going to say is that there are Alpine trails and slopes very beautiful here - for those wanting other activities, like viewing-stations, to stop and take in the scenery, or jet skies for two... By the way, we have coffee shacks placed everywhere on the mountain, food snacks like hot dog or something like that?"

"Really?"

"Yes!" he affirmed. "For the slopes, we have snowmobiles that run silent, or run fast - everyone's favorite ...and allow for a gentler descent down the hill slopes?"

"Thank you!" said Amanda, taking her package to go. "But err...you are...excuse me, you are not exactly the typical retired looking person?"

"Oh?"

"I mean... Most people retired are...well. But you ...a beautiful woman at *any* age!"

Amanda headed for the door. "I can see why they hired you!"

He waved with a wide tooth-gapped grin.

The Norwegian actually gave her much to think about. Especially that evening as she sipped hot chocolate from a chalet halfway up the mountain of Petite-Rivière-Saint Marie de Charlemagne.

She was less than an hour away from Quebec City, and less than a mile from where her son and his party would be skiing over the next few days. But she told no one.

Amanda was worried. She moved to the table and spread out her laptop, her notes and her phone. She put on her reading glasses and worked into the night, her tiny chalet lit up in a golden glow like a crucible. The mountain forested and covered by snow.

Much had transpired since she landed in New York, she noted.

For one thing, she had met with Barbara. For another, she had received a message from Rebecca that propelled her forward into a plan way beyond anything she had imagined for herself.

Spying on her son!

For that reason, she chose to stay at a resort nearby, and not at the same resort her son was attending with his party.

The place she picked was a simpler arrangement, less opulent and slightly smaller in its range of options, but she found it charming.

The cabins were adequate and clean. With just a few slopes for ski-runs, and a standard mountain Lodge with a restaurant, she was perfectly content. The only drawback was the lack of wireless connectivity. Sporadic, at best. And only in her room could she connect to a server. That rendered her electronic devices unreliable.

Amanda didn't venture into the main village where she might be spotted, but she did have a four-wheel rented vehicle at her disposal. She discovered sources of exercise, such as an indoor swimming pool, a dedicated ice rink, and a modest horse-trail and sled ride schedule.

Still, if appearances mattered, it was her mission she must focus on.

But for the visit to the gift shop, she kept to herself. She had time to work on her computer, time to think, and opportunities to observe a mountain from a distance...

What was it that so alarmed Trevor?

Where was Tray?

Clearly, something had happened to expose their son?

 Was he being played with, as if a hostage perhaps. If so, by whom? For what purposes? What was the secret that they had strayed into?

Tray's brush with heart failure induced by ingestion of a substance was just a warning?

Under the message that brought her to the scene, was he the intended target for harm?

An assailant? An assassin? How should she assess the situation? Who would do harm?

She postulated a possible profile: Someone so deeply hardened by his delusions that the world of beauty or humanity barely existed for him. Someone wanting to do harm? If so, where was this danger coming from?

If it was a threat, that meant that someone would come. Or, was *already* here?

Was she the cause of her son's vulnerability? And if so...why? Or, was it key to his father's financial bank accounts in London?

She paused. There was a simultaneous approach going on. First to her family business and her husband's reputation, then to her son...

It all started with the statue, and the event of donating it to the Museum. *Why?*

She spent most of the night sketching out her thoughts, finding links, searching notes, outlining motives...

Ever since the quest for the provenance of the statue began, everything started to pile up – If not before, considering the bullet that hit Trevor in Spain...

There was something behind that statue and its story, something that someone was trying to hide.

Why? Was there any connection?

Barbara had told her that Karen did not have sufficient evidence for a trial. Was that possible? Was there something else...

Why derail Trevor? Litigation against his former company on allegations of fraud based on a claim of lost cargo relating to a sinking in WWII?

Was the SEC leaning on Karen McCullock about the Green case? The Securities and Exchange

Commission dealt solely with financial fraud in modern-day stock markets and investment. Compliance?

Was there any connection to the diamonds in New York - Especially when one showed up at the Museum and implicated Barbara?

Worse. Had their son been roped into the Salaman Firm as an Intern and exposed to danger *deliberately?*

Was that the cause for Trevor's alarm?

It wasn't until the morning that she realized one consistency: All indicators pointed one party. Ever since she brought the Statue to New York...

Salaman .

x x x

Amanda drove to the Scenic Overview Promenade on the side of the mountain, a protected pavilion and parking lot for visitors. From there she could see the celebrated resort of *Le Massif Resort*.

She parked and joined a few tourists taking pictures. Amanda returned, parking her car and staying longer during the day hours. She positioned herself to view *Le Massif* from a ledge just beside the parking pavilion.

 She became familiar with the site across the ravine, its tourists, visitors and skiers who took to the slopes. She viewed through a pair of binoculars. Occasionally she brought out her camera with long telescopic lens.

"Aren't the bird species incredible..?" someone remarked, lingering.

On the fourth day, it started to snow and Amanda surrendered her post at the Overview Promenade. She wanted to download some shots to her laptop. Her camera lens was sharply focused for distance-frames, but the minute it started to snow, all bets were off.

Back at her cabin she made herself a warm cup of coffee and arranged the table for desk work on her laptop. Canadian TV offered a soft stream of background news and weather updates. Christmas lights beckoned from every news-worth city on TV.

Amanda sifted through her collection of imaged data files of various individuals on the slopes and at the Resort. They appeared periodically, and she began to recognize various teams, color-gear and activities they engaged in. It was a happy time for all of them.

She hadn't seen her son yet, but she recognized a few from his party. For some reason, they were on the practice slopes today, and he was not. She recognized Sophie.

Further, she recognized some of the other people. Two were new, and some were administrators - like the attendant at the Ski Shop at the slopes of *Marie de Charlemagne.* He appeared regularly, and just as she deduced, he was an excellent skier. Clearly, he helped with some coaching at both resorts.

Amanda was curious about one new party though. He was tall, of dark complexion. He seemed almost Latino, but his wool hat tightly suggested he had shaved his head. She couldn't be sure.

Still, she was able to put together a collage for the day with notes of observation and she was pleased with the data on her laptop. Tomorrow might be the day she'd see Tray.

She'd make a few phone calls today even...If she could get through. The weather was closing in.

Still, something nagged. It was perhaps the posture of a couple of new arrivals. Normally, she noticed, new guests to the resort were all giggles and fun, even falling over in the snow with peels of laughter. But for some reason, two of them looked serious. Less interested in having fun than in sifting through the crowd, nudging, pushing and shoving as if looking for someone, they were belligerent. For them, the place was all business.

It just seemed odd behavior for a vacation resort.

Regardless, she'd send off some email and pack a picnic of hot coffee and snacks. If the snow hadn't accumulated, she might even return to her observation post. In fact that's what she decided to do.

She bundled up and opened the rear gate of the car to load up her picnic basket, adding a warm throw-rug. She checked her gas, made a note of the miles travelled, and even found a good station on the radio in French.

She waited. Watching. The scenery was beautiful...

Two scooters popped up on the snowy road behind her. Loud and playful, they appeared in her rear view mirror. They were kids evidently, and the two wore dark visor helmets and black leather jackets. Like everyone else on these mountain roads their headlights were on, and they flew over bumps gathering snow as if taking leaps of joy through the air. Their ability to stay upright impressed Amanda, then she realized that their tires were spiked for ice traction. They could pretty much bounce off anything...or scale any vertical surface with their claw- grip.

She waved again, only to find them interfering with her visibility to negotiate the steep curves of the mountain side.

The wind picked up and clouds gathered swiftly over the peaks, plunging the temperature. Though it wasn't exactly snowing, drifting snow had turned shiny as if icy. She realized only then that she should not have ventured out: This was no Disneyland. This was Canada's Rocky mountain arctic winter.

It snowed. A weather Front was closing in.

Close to her destination, she averted a collision with the bikers in close proximity, and she skidded. They pressed, revving their engines and interchanging their position around her.

Only then did Amada realize that she was prey to capricious goading. She'd been made to drive into a bank of snow that was unstable. The car lurched to a halt. But there was no traction on the rear wheel, and she could not drive back out of her rut.

Repeatedly, she tried. She got out. It was silent on the mountain.

With whatever utensils she could find in the car tried to burrow a channel for the front wheels to find traction. The wind was picking up, and small drops of ice rain fell like sharp pellets. Weather changes at these elevations could be sudden and treacherous, she knew. Mad with herself, she knew she should have been more cautious.

She looked at her watch. The afternoon was waning fast, and she was running out of daylight.

She sat in the car momentarily, and then revved her engine with some success. She gained purchase, and moved a few inches. But now the front tires were slick with ice.

Once around the bend they stopped suddenly in unison. Facing her, with their headlights on, they paused, legs planted firmly on the road.

Her instincts told her to get back into the car. As she did so, it started to snow again, heavily. Now all she could see where headlight beams.

Worse, she had walked herself into a trap, she knew.

The bikers roared up, then charged at her car, bouncing into the rear end. They nudged her bumper, and she let out a yell...

Whatever traction she had on the side of the road was already tenuous. Her tires had no grip, and even less tolerance for maneuver. Her wheels were dangerously close to the cliff ledge, and the precipice before her was a steep drop into timber ravine.

She looked back, thinking the bikers had given up on their misguided ideas of help. But no. They turned around and together stood to watch her just as they had previously.

She thought about getting out of the car. She decided against it.

Now she felt vulnerable. She braced herself with a seat buckle, and tucked the rug tightly around her arms and neck. She turned the wheels to a slant right where she knew a thick stand of pine were rooted just off the ledge. She pulled hard on the Emergency brake.

They came with a final assault that pushed the car over the ledge.

The car was bumped forward, angling to its front steerage and veering sideways, then tumbled.

The fall was arrested by a ledge, and the car spun rather than slide. A tree snapped, and the car bounced on its tires, resting there...

Snow fell like a blanket and covered everything.

Amanda screamed, and hit the horn, anticipating in terror a steeper fall to come. But none followed. Again she hit the horn, an alarm for help.

In the snow, the sound was muted like a pup's yelp. She felt unharmed, if terrified. She sat there, her body still and unmoving lest she precipitate a motion that might plunge her to her death.

Slowly, as the minutes passed, she breathed again, and notice that the car had not slipped.

She looked about her. Remarkably, only the rear window was shattered. The car seemed normal on the interior.

She peered out her window, frost now creeping up her windshield, and she saw the darkness overtake the landscape with nothing but trees and branches.

She leaned forward and realized that the car was wedged. It was gripped between three trees and a boulder. It was going nowhere.

She pushed at her door, it was damaged and sealed. She scooted across to the passenger seat and the door opened freely.

She got out and saw that while she was out of danger, she had been lucky. What might have been a steep drop into a ravine was broken by trees on a cliff outcrop. Tall timbers had grown upon it, and snow was now falling on branches like powdery mantles.

Amanda was not visible to any roadside assistance. That is, if there was any...

She packed a light bag, pocketed a few essentials, including a small knife and started climbing. By grasping whatever branches she could, she managed to get herself up to the road.

It was dark, and she found no sign of the scooters.

 Well, so what?

Yes, she was furious. But she decided she need not panic. Though not entirely definable in the distance, she could hear hat the resort of the *Le Massif* was alive with night-time activity and flood lights.

The car rental would have to be reported as an accident. All insurance papers were in order.

It was dark. She would have to walk.

Walking up a mountain in Canada in winter was not the ideal condition for exercise, she thought, but she'd make it.

She was only two miles from her cabin.

She turned up the next bend, pausing periodically for a mouthful of snow, and approached steadily the Ski Lodge. Twice she'd spotted elk, and heard a few rabbits rush from her approach.

She was perhaps a mile away when she saw the puppy. She approached it with some wonder, its ears perched up and its head steady, eyes glowing in the dark. It sat in the middle of the road, motionless. Then she saw the pair of green eyes peering at her to her left through darkness.

She froze. Off to the right side, another appeared. Larger. To her left, a fourth creature. She was confronted by mountain wolves.

She decided to play loud. She surged forward, clapping her hands and shouting for scatter. They fled.

She walked swiftly to the Lodge. These were natural predators. She was the intruder.

By the time she reached her cabin, Amanda was exhausted.

Later that night, in the warmth and safety of her surroundings and with a cup of hot tea in her hand, she thought about it.

There had been a belligerent act. Was it perhaps purposeful, she wondered. Or was she dealing with a couple of capricious kids?

She spent the night making arrangements for her car to be found and collected by the company that leased it. She made calls to her own insurance, and though tired by morning, she had her life back on her feet. Especially when a fresh delivery of another Car Rental vehicle showed up for her use.

Whatever notions she had of a prank were dispelled the next morning when she found the two bikes parked outside a breakfast shack. On them were the two unmistakable helmets. She peered inside the restaurant and found the two riders. They were not kids.

Discretely, she took their images on her cell phone, plus images of their bike tags. These men had been bought to do her damage, she felt certain.

For now, she would remain out of sight and stay safe. But the thought gave her little solace. She felt unsteady.

The next day, she borrowed her neighbor's vehicle to return to her observation post. She would not show her own new Rental... This time, she sat on the outer rim of the Overview, concealed from the road.

Plus, she had changed her gear.

Today would be an ideal day for skiers.

The view was terrific. The sun was out, and the view was stunning. *Le Massif* had a vertical ski drop of 2,526 ft - perhaps the highest points in Eastern Canada and east of the Rockies.

For those looking for adventure, this was the place to be. The resort was filling with more visitors for skiing, and the ski lifts in full operation to the summit.

From her position at the Scenic Overview this morning, she had a full panoramic view of the Resort.

Amanda was ideally positioned adjacent to the summit for her best photographs yet. Including the deck of the Lodges, and those moving about towards the ski lifts...

By now, they'd an average snowfall of 250 inches of snow on the slopes. At the summit the snowpack easily cleared 90 inches. Below her, there was a steep trail with a pitch of 64%.

The ski-lifts were full.

Many emerged, clearly athletes with experience and training. Others were a little less resolved. If there was hesitation at the summit to launch down this trail, she could understand why.

The ski-slope trail was flanked by an escarpment with a sheer drop into the distant ravines of the Saint Lawrence River. Experience down this trail was necessarily.

One large crowd exited the ski lift platform. Yes. There was Sophie and Alex. Charlie. Mark Ruttenberg. Two girls she didn't know, and finally Tray.

Amanda grinned proudly. He looked terrific!

Unmistakable in his red head, still without a wool hat, he was wearing a yellow and black parka. He had inherited his father's height, she could tell, and he was standing the far end of the crowd, laughing.

In the end, not all of them launched from the summit: Sophie and the girls backed away and returned to the ski lift for lesser trails. Only Mark, Charlie and Tray pushed off the ledge to begin the descent.

A cloud appeared with a local fall of snow, if not filling the sky, it dodged around the sun and cast its long shadow as it passed. Then another appeared. They disappeared down the slopes, then Tray reappeared on the next ski-lift car going up.

By mid-morning, visibility was limited. Falling snow and spruce trees in shadow obscured Amanda's view.
But their jackets were clearly visible as they swayed down the jig jags of the trail with stunning smoothness and speed.
Amanda held her breath.
Tray was a good skier, she knew. Over the years, the family had frequently taken winter ski vacations to Switzerland. From childhood, the children all learned to handle themselves on skis. Thus, it was only three of the men, Tray included, who negotiated the diamond slopes of the mountain.
Charlie was in the lead, and it worried Amanda that the three were staggering apart, with Tray in the middle, Mark at the rear. Occasionally the gap closed, and they descended evenly. But the rule was that you should always have sight of your lead skier for safety...and check behind you for any oncoming skier.
It came very suddenly, the intrusion.
A fourth skier from a hidden trail at two hundred meters from the summit bounced forward.
He was tall, strong, fast and muscular with a Rod slung from his back.
He was in the pack, lining himself in a position behind Tray, and coming down the mountain fast with zig zags on a ski-run, steep and sharp, between fir trees and rock.

He skidded to a higher abutment ledge of slope escarpment, sheering off a tree limb and slicing deftly with an electronic device a second wedge for a sharp point. Aligning it into the bowstrings of a rod from his back, he knelt to take aim at the slope-run below him, military-style.

The skiers were just turned into the bend and coming down the next run. Charlie came first and sailed by.

Tray came next around the bend and was about to align to the next slope when he shifted his weight, stood upright on his skis and leaned sideways, lifting one ski from the snow.

The projectile was released directly into his path, a billow of snow sloughed off a tree, and then the archer was gone.

It had started to snow.

Tray fell, tumbling into a thick stand of pines below the escarpment in a powdery burst of snow cover.

Mark was still coming down behind him, and either due to poor visibility in the bend, or the speed of decent, he sailed right past Tray, and on downward the trail.

Tray was off his skies and tumbled against a Spruce tree thick with low branches. His purchase broke free, and he rolled like a snow ball to tangle in the next tree line.

Amanda barely saw the snap.

Wait... *Where was Tray?* Amanda could not see him.

Snow, mist, trees – her view was obscured.

What happened?

Then came more motion, and the trees against which Tray had snagged himself gave way. She saw his body toss further down the escarpment, and he fell out of sight.

She spotted the rogue skier through her binoculars. He quickly regained his stance, re-braced the rod in that was evidently a bow, and proceeded down the hill into a parallel trail, out of sight.

In just that second, Amanda recognized him. He was the Alpine Norwegian skier in the Gift Shop. .

Too shocked to draw a breath, she knew Tray was in trouble.

 She had her cell phone, her fingers frozen as she fumbled for a number, her mind numb. She dialed, once, twice...

She called for an Emergency Rescue at the *Massif,* giving his approximate position. Top slope, level turn five and on the East side of the ski run. A skier was over the ledge, and caught in the underbrush...

Tray was out of sight and over the escarpment.

It was less than 15 minutes later that a rescue team of snowmobiles and two transports arrived down the trail. Several paramedics were on hand; two mountain climbers strapped onto rigging and went over the side. Amanda spotted Tray being lifted on a stretcher.

He was alive.

He had suffered injuries, including a tree limb that pierced his left thigh. But no sign of assault, or any other person in the vicinity.

Amanda's incident, on the roadside was perhaps unanticipated. But the assault on her son was not. *Why?*

* * *

New York

Amanda was getting dressed.
She picked a black dress with a wrap white chiffon collar. She chose black patent-leather heels, and looked at herself in the mirror.
Her hand went up to her collar.
There was no joy. No color. No Amanda, she decided.
The necklace were pearls given her by Trevor from his mother's estate. She arranged them carefully, for assurance.
Tray her son was in town, and certainly, they'd had time to chat. But this weekend, he was at CUNY for a college sporting event that had been scheduled months prior. She urged him to go... He agreed, saying he'd make it back later in the night, perhaps in time for the banquet presentation.
Trevor was still in London, she supposed.
The place was quiet as she got ready to leave. Carla the housekeeper had been dismissed early since there was no reception to prepare for. Besides, Carla's husband was taking her to a family party that evening.
Amanda stood.
There were no flowers in the foyer, neither drinks or wine decentered for party guests, nor buffet in the kitchen. She felt alone, isolated, and removed from the people who gave her solace and warmth.
Of course Barbara had called. Rebecca had called, and a host of other arrangements had been made. Tonight was the dedication event of the Statue to

the Museum, and she was to give a short speech about the statue.
A blown-up photograph as museum poster was framed on the wall, displaying a stone nght-lit rendition of the statue.
Amanda looked at it periodically. Strangely, she found comfort in the calm shape of the woman kneeling, as if nobody was ever really alone...
Still, she was sitting quietly when the call came. Her ride was downstairs.
She picked up her coat, tucked her speech notes in her bag, and shut the door. But not before glancing back.
Without Trevor, she decided, her life was hollow. Their place was empty.

x x x

In England, Trevor had known the extent of the danger. He was to be shut down, pending a civil hearing. His solicitors surrounded him, but he knew he must take this challenge alone.

He knew what he must do, and he had been working to that end prior to his lawyer's council. Under the provisions of his Charter, the bulk of his Bank's assets had been moved from this soil and placed in the safekeeping of the parent company. It was the only way around the problem.

In his deposition for the case of the government, Trevor exposed the connection that was most damning.

Trevor identified Alpha. He was Kurtz who had stolen his partner's stock of diamonds and betrayed his people. The diamonds were marked by the handiwork of his partner, Klein, drawn from a particular batch known to the board of diamond certifiers.

The Bank vault of the Sterling bank showed ledgers to the Court that proved to be accurate in accounting.

Further, since the allegations of the prosecution could not be proven, the Court decided that the bank could continue operations as service bank; financial clearinghouse and fiduciary warehouse. The case was closed.

The Salamans had been relentless in their pursuit of his holdings. Now he was vindicated.

The case of "Alpha," he knew would not stop there. There was too much at stake. The legacy estate of the Alpha heirs had fingerprints all over their collateral. The assets had been misrepresented and used to invest money in large quantities: An investigation would shut them down.

Their charter would be pulled; their assets seized and their Partnerships dissolved. They could possibly be indictments for criminal knowledge and obstruction of justice, if not money laundering and fraud on the stock exchanges. It was a fraudulent investment bank up for investigation by the United States Government. Especially if there was a link made between the identity of a man named Green and the activities of Alpha at the time of the war.

Only Alpha had access to the particular brand of diamond that was found on Green's remains. The rest had been disbursed to the US Treasury in 1942 in Canada.

They were now playing with him because he was the only one who could make the connection. Their tactic was to be suing him with legal injunctions in every possible way to damage his credibility, if not ruin his bank and brand reputation.

And it come from a Ledger record, citing shipment listed by a shopkeeper in Spain where a Jeweler who had used the diamonds for his trade, had also been commissioned to make a statue at that date.

Trevor had worried. He knew there was going to be more trouble. There would be threats against his family. By staying away, he could best protect them. There wasn't a day his thoughts were not with Amanda and his son, in harm's way.

x x x

The statue of the *Kneeling Woman* was placed at the heart of the great pavilion of the Museum. Under full lights, she was set upon a glass pedestal surrounded by tall fresh blossoms. She made a stunning display as a centerpiece.

The guests to the Museum Gala of New York arrived with enthusiasm in support of their tradition of Acquisitions. The lights went on, and the event went Live.

Assembled in a profusion of perfume, glitter, colorful gowns and bow ties, all gathered in excited mirth and anticipation

The Auction of the previous night had been a great fundraiser, and the event was to celebrate those donors. Inside the grand ballroom where dining tables prepared for an array of guests.

Under bowers of long stemmed roses flown from Costa Rica, the gala fairly glowed in candlelight crystal, shimmering with silverware, glass and gold-rimmed porcelain.

A Quartet played, even as lively band began to set up for the later program of dancing. At the head table, an array of speakers told of the generous donations to the Museum.

Off to the sides, full Media coverage with cameras flashed and hummed at the glamorous array of presentations. Guests from across the globe came to patronize the Arts and the Museum Gala, many representing institutions, sovereign governments, corporate interests and even some political establishments.

Finally, it was Amanda's turn to speak, and she was called up to the head table.

x x x

Chapter 16

The applause quieted, and the room hushed for her words.
Amanda spoke calmly and directly, giving its full story, and wishing neither to lecture, nor to delay their festivities, she kept it short. She thanked them for their unerring support for such an item of value, she said.
"In conclusion, I'm not sure of the details, for this was a deeply personal possession in Roosevelt's surroundings...
None of us can possibly imagine the pressure upon his shoulders as he saw the daily consequences of a grinding war. But his faith in humanity prevailed..."
"This statue, it was said, was the item that inspired him. For when another was commissioned by him to take its place - one sculpted expressly by an American artist whose heart and mind was equally caught up in the culture of this war, it came back as a work of muscular and defiant, sculpted in granite with strong and heavy arms built for labor, an expression of control in her breath..."
She paused.

"The President had one comment. It came just before he died. "Take her away – out of my sight, he said. I wish never to see it!"

The room fell silent.

"It is not that we should pass judgement on works of art for their dynamics and meanings. Rather, it was the inspiration for a man that this particular statue represents...

"It was kept in his garden, they say, the statue of a kneeling women in a gesture of supplication for grace. For the owner of this statue, civilization only worked when God dwelt in the heart. Even if it demanded a war of incalculable cost for good to vanquish evil...

"It was this statue that was commission by the leader of a world at war in 1942. The grace of supplication to God is seen in the gesture of a *kneeling woman*"

Amanda paused, the room hushed.

One man stood up. He applauded. Others joined in. Then the room erupted in applause. Amanda smiled, her presentation concluded.

Amanda looked down at the guests, and for just a moment, she wondered if she were in fact alone. She saw her table where her friends were seated: There was Rebecca and Roger from Canada; Barbara and her Date...

Behind that table was another with a younger crowd, Tray with his arm in a sling and his leg crutches nearby, flanked by Sophia and her office crowd.

At another table was Karen McCullock and her escort. Also she recognized detective Talbot and his wife with two others from the Police Commissioner's office.

A Master of Ceremonies came to the podium. "Thank you Amanda Wells. This statue is a great addition to our museum collection. We are delighted to have been part of a wonder that you saw when you spotted her in Spain. It is an item that we accept with gratitude and pride. Thank you!"

No, decided Amanda. She was not alone.

With applause still ringing in her ears, she spotted a tall figure standing at the entrance of the ballroom. Her heart skipped a beat.

Wearing a black tie and suit, the wavy hair and lean posture of Trevor McDonnell was unmistakable. He was looking at her directly, an expression of adoration in his eyes.

Another round of applause, and Amanda said simply, "Thank you. It was my privilege. Your outpouring for the Museum is fabulous. She is a beauty, isn't she? Yes. And now, err... if you'll excuse me..." the room fell silent "Well...My husband just came home!"

They all spun round and a rise of excitement electrified the room as he came forward.

"Dad!" yelled Tray.

The evening was full of goodbyes and hellos all at once, Amanda wasn't sure which. Who was going where, why or when ... None of it mattered.

The music came up. Her feet were off the ground as Trevor asked her to the dance floor.

Only later in the elevator to their apartment, when she felt his hands gently cup her face, and his kiss warm her lips, she knew she was home.

"Yes" he murmured "you did look stellar tonight. But what I'm looking at is something closer to

sainthood. You were brave and terrific...Can you forgive me for staying way?" he asked.
"Umm..." she said, drifting "only if we pick our next vacation for somewhere in...France mebbe?"
He looked deeply into her eyes.
Somehow, she felt as if the world had survived.

* * *

THE END

www.ingramcontent.com/pod-product-compliance
Lightning Source LLC
Chambersburg PA
CBHW070759120726
47910CB00001B/237